Blue Canary

A NOVEL

Virginia St. Claire

Blue Canary
Published in the USA in 2019
by Virginia St. Claire

Copyright © Virginia St. Claire, 2019
Written by Virginia St. Claire
virginia@virginiastclaire.com

Published by Kindle Direct Publishing
ISBN 9781086470444

Cover illustration by Virginia St. Claire
Cover and book designed by Devika Khanna
devika@manifest.in

Blue Canary is a work of fiction.
Any relation to anyone is purely coincidental.

for Claire and Frances,
my Iowa companions

CHAPTER

1

The house was a 1920s bungalow with a broad covered porch and a pair of leaded glass windows flanking the oak front door. Phil's chair sat to one side of the door. On rare occasions, Catherine sat on the swing suspended by chains from rings in the porch ceiling.

Mount Pleasant was a peaceful Iowa town of nine thousand on a muggy early July day. The air was so hot you could have spread it on toast if it weren't too hot to toast the bread. Summer pedaled faster and faster, building momentum. From where Phil sat on the front porch, he could feel the grass, the bushes and the trees sighing right along with him.

"Rained last night; supposed to clear the air, but it's even thicker today," he thought.

The weight of the air pushed at him. Phil tracked storm clouds across the sultry sky. "Too high for more rain," he thought.

For a moment, the sun broke through. He squinted as a faded blue car clunked in and out of the pothole in front of the house. Automatically, he checked the license plate. Boone County, not Henry. No one he knew, then.

To his way of thinking, his mind was divided into compartments where he'd been stashing memories for sixty-seven years, filling up compartment after compartment. He figured they all must be pretty full by now.

Blue Canary

Phil parked his truck next to the garage behind the house. He didn't drive it much these days—out to the country to see his mother; back and forth to the lake to go fishing; once in a while to the Jug to play darts. Mostly, Phil sat in his blue metal chair on the porch, summer days and evenings, too.

This morning, the boy who mowed the lawn had come by and pulled the mower out of the shed behind the garage. Phil watched while the boy mowed the part of the lawn he could see from his chair. Back and forth, swath by swath. If the boy missed a bit, Phil said nothing. He had cut lawns himself—beginning with his parents' and continuing with his own—for more than fifty years, and he had missed his share.

Every week the boy came and took Phil's push mower out of the shed. Phil liked its quiet clickety-click. Catherine had tried to persuade him to buy a power mower, but each time she brought it up, he quietly said no. Finally she stopped asking. When the boy started coming a few years ago, Phil showed him how to put a drop of oil on each end of the axle after mowing. Once every few years he took the mower into the fix-it shop to have the blades sharpened. The old mower worked as well as ever.

Phil breathed the scent of fresh cut grass. Smells brought life back like a rope coiled hand over hand. He could either glance and see the whole of it in a moment, or he could examine it loop by loop, look at any one loop for as long as he liked. This was his most persistent pastime: looking back at life.

On Fourth of July when he was fourteen, about the age of the lawn boy, he and Billy Perkins had dropped a bunch of firecrackers into a hollow stump out in his Grandpa's south pasture. Nothing happened for so long that he and Bill became impatient. When they went to look, the firecrackers exploded, blackening their faces and singeing off their eyebrows.

You might not think Phil would remember that fondly, but he did. The fond thoughts, though, led inevitably to what came after. Bill was killed in Vietnam. Being raised Quaker, Phil himself had registered as a Conscientious Objector. He was a pacifist by upbringing, and his mother had been relieved when he applied for CO status.

Every Fourth of July, especially, Phil remembered Billy and the stump. That set him to thinking about the war. Bill had gone and he had died while Phil sailed in safe waters on a ship carrying supplies. The last time he had gone to the Quaker Meeting was a Sunday morning in 1969, the day he heard that Bill had been 'killed in action'.

Catherine had also been relieved that he had not gone to war. He wanted to blame his Quaker upbringing or Catherine for keeping him from going, but he couldn't. Deep down he'd been terrified of fighting and probably dying. Now, he sat with the compartments in his mind nearly full while Billy Perkins had been dead for fifty years. Phil shifted his weight in the chair. Couldn't get comfortable.

* * *

He turned his head toward the screen door. "Catherine?"

From the back of the house Catherine called back, "Yes?"

"Will you come out here?"

Catherine came to the door wiping her hands on her apron. She took a flowered handkerchief out of her pocket and wiped her face.

"What do you want?" She emphasized the word 'you'. "I'm in the middle of scrubbing the kitchen floor."

"I thought maybe you'd bring us some iced tea and sit a while."

Catherine gave him a long look, then without a word went back into the house. A few minutes later she reappeared at the screen door, a glass of lemonade in each hand. She leaned down and pushed the handle with her elbow. She handed Phil his glass and sat on the swing with her own.

Phil took a sip and said, "This is good. Just the way I like it."

"It's awfully hot," Catherine said, wiping her face again. "It's cooler in the house."

"Bit of breeze stirring the maples." Phil pointed to the top of the trees on either side of the front walk.

"Think I'll go out to Amanda's this afternoon," Catherine said. "Do you want to come along?"

"No. Think I'll go fishing. It'll be ten degrees cooler on the lake."

Catherine pushed off the floor with her foot, setting the swing in motion. She drank her lemonade and looked down the silent street. Phil looked the other way and watched the busier cross street at the end of the block where an occasional car passed.

"Amanda's helping Jessica with a project for the fair," Catherine said.

"Think I'll go out to the lake and catch some fish for supper," Phil said. "It's been a long time since we had fish for supper."

"Jessica's sewing an apron in 4-H. Almost nobody but me wears them anymore," Catherine said. "She's been baking cookies, too. Trying to make some unusual ones for the judging at the fair."

"Maybe you can bring home some cookies. They'd taste fine after the fish."

Catherine finished her lemonade and stood up. She picked up Phil's glass from the little table at his side and took the glasses back in the house. The screen door crashed behind Catherine, her hands too full with the lemonade glasses to catch it and silence its closing. Annoyed by the noise, she clanked the glasses down in the sink and turned the water on full force.

"Phil." She shook her head, rinsed the glasses and shut the water off.

For fifteen years before Phil retired from the feed business, he had sat in his chair evenings and most weekends, porch for summer, den for winter. A few hours fixing pipes, mowing the lawn, a little fishing now and then, but mostly he sat.

Catherine was not a sitter; she was a worker. As a tiny girl she would pull a kitchen chair over to the sink, climb on it to stand on tiptoe so she could scrub vegetables or wash the mountains of dishes that always seemed to appear on the sideboard. When she married Phil, from the first, she filled the hours of every day with chores. It wasn't that she enjoyed work so much that she chose to pass her time that way. She never realized she had a choice. The endless round of cleaning, laundry, cooking, and marketing took nearly all the time she had, that was all. When the children were little, she dreamed of their being grown so she would have time to spend any way she liked. But that was the problem. Except for gardening and walking in the park at Oakland Mills, she couldn't remember what she liked. She didn't like to think about it, either.

Catherine kept on as she always had. Only where there used to be muddy fingerprints to wash off the doorjambs and three times the laundry to do, she now cleaned a nearly clean house and washed nearly clean clothes. Every morning she worked the crossword puzzle in the *News*. She rarely sat down at the table where Phil read the rest of the paper over breakfast. Instead, she moved around the kitchen, pausing now and then to fill in a word. In the evenings after wiping down the counters, she would finally sit and read books from the library. Even that she did fast.

She told herself she liked "doing for Phil," but while her chores in the long days kept her hands busy, they left her mind free to think. Often thoughts that Catherine was ashamed to show herself, let alone mention to Phil or anyone else.

Often she thought of that day in American Government class Senior year. The high school secretary came from the office to tell her she had an emergency phone call. Hurrying to the office, Catherine had worried: her mom, dad, what? When she picked up the phone, it was Phil's voice at the other end of the line. He was calling from Ag school at Iowa State. He said he had heard from a friend that she had been going around with Mike Hopkins. Everyone knew his reputation with girls. Was it true?

Catherine had thought her heart would stop. What could she say? In that moment she knew what it felt like to be utterly helpless to change anything. Her mother had told her often enough, "What's done is done." There was Phil on the line: silent, waiting. The sadness of what she had to say rose up from her heart and filled her head. "Yes," she whispered, "Yes, it's true." She said it because there was nothing else she could do, said it knowing things would never be the same between them again.

* * *

While she scrubbed the kitchen floor, she thought about killing herself. She wondered if the garage was airtight enough for her to gas herself in there. The main problem with killing herself, though, was that she couldn't be certain she would be successful. She would be mortally embarrassed if she tried and failed. She thought of Phil discovering her body. Saw him only eventually find her in the garage after looking everywhere else. She could see the puzzled look on his face as he began to search, calling her name, "Catherine, Catherine," hurrying from room to room, finding her at last, dead.

Or maybe she would take an Arthur Murray dance class. There was a dance studio, she knew, upstairs from the hardware store. She had always wanted to dance. But Phil had made her promise on their wedding day never to ask him to dance. Even at their wedding reception in the church hall, everyone was dancing except them, the bride and groom. Catherine remembered endlessly examining her bridal shoes and wondering how they had made the little bows all of pearls. Now while she scrubbed the floor on her knees, she swished the brush from side to side in a wide arc and imagined it was herself, swaying in the arms of a man in the Arthur Murray class.

Then she thought of asking Alice Hudson over for coffee and cake. Catherine made a wonderful crumb cake, her mother's recipe. It was more crumb than cake, really. Since Phil retired she hadn't seen Alice much. She couldn't have Alice over with Phil on the porch.

Besides, Alice had her own Marvin sitting in his chair in the garage. Marvin liked being in the garage—always knew he'd be in the shade. Unlike Phil, Marvin had to be led to his chair and sat down. Their garage door was always open with Marvin's chair to one side and a chair for Alice next to it waiting for her. Like Catherine, she rarely did, and then only for a moment unless she was armed with her knitting.

"Whew," Catherine said, "It's hot." It was too hot to think. Too hot to walk in the park or work in the garden. Catherine sat down at the kitchen table and fanned herself with the coupon section of the paper.

* * *

After Catherine had gone back in the house, Phil resumed thinking. "Here I am. On the porch. On Monroe Street. In Mount Pleasant, Iowa. Surrounded by farm country. Surrounded by the rest of the world. Which is only a speck in a vast universe. I sleep eight hours at night. Eat meals, three hours at the most. Two hours in the evening in front of the TV. The rest of the time, I'm out here sitting. That makes eleven hours of sitting."

Phil propped his head on his hand and looked at nothing. "Maybe a day fishing on the lake would perk me up."

He had planned to do more fishing once he retired. But now he'd been retired for two years, and while he'd been out a few times the first summer, this year he hadn't gone out there once. The lake was easy, too. He belonged to the Isaak Walton League and fished the lake whenever he felt like going. He had an aluminum boat with a little outboard motor. He and the other League members kept their boats chained up at the water's edge just below the clubhouse. All he had to do was grab his rod and tackle box and his gas can and drive the three miles to the lake. Pushing the boat into the water only took a moment, and he could stay as long as he liked. He could start the motor if he felt like it. Mostly he liked to set his oars and row just for the quiet of it.

There was one spot where he especially liked to fish. He caught the most fish there, but that wasn't the only reason the spot drew him. To one side, a big old willow tree overhung a little cove. He and his boat could nestle in there, around the bend and out of sight of everyone.

No houses had been built along that shore and the trees and bushes grew right down to the water. Curtained by the willow, Phil could be alone to think. Sometimes he wondered whether he thought too much. He figured though, with all the years he had been alive, he had naturally built up a store of memories to think about. He puzzled things out and filed them in the compartments that, as far as he could see, made for an orderly mind.

All in all, Phil was satisfied with himself. As far as he went, that is. There were certain things that might come into his mind that he would carefully file without investigation, leaving those thoughts alone as much as possible.

Not that he never thought about them. Once in a while he let himself think about Catherine never seeming happy with him over the years. But what was he supposed to do? She wasn't the easiest person to live with either. He had done his best, he thought. Worked everyday for the first forty-five years of their marriage. Now that he was retired, he figured he could rest. Relax.

* * *

After lunch Catherine slipped the grocery list from under the apple magnet on the refrigerator and sat down at the table. In her strong round handwriting she added apples, oatmeal and walnuts to the list. She had a yen for apple crisp.

She leaned her head out the front door and announced to Phil. "I'm off to Amanda's now. Anything you need before I go?"

"Nope."

Catherine went back inside closing the screen door carefully. Stopping in the kitchen, she added ground beef and baking potatoes to her grocery list. The likelihood of fish for supper was remote at best. She slipped the list into her purse and gathered a bag of books from a chair by the table.

* * *

On her way out the back door she noticed movement on the other side of the hedge that separated their yard from the one next door. Pretending not to look, she looked nonetheless. Her neighbor, a woman named, of all things, Jaz, was carrying a load of what looked like heavy clay tiles out to the old shed at the back corner of her yard.

8

Jaz had moved into the house next door a couple of years before. She was a bit younger than Catherine. For some reason Catherine felt embarrassed around Jaz, so, as much as possible, she pretended Jaz didn't exist. Jaz—she explained her name was short for Jasmine—had been married and, rumor had it, they split up not because they didn't love each other any longer but because they each had new things to 'pursue' that didn't include being married.

Alice reported that one day on the street Jaz confided to her that she had always wanted to live in a quiet town in the Midwest. She'd bought the house in Mount Pleasant because she "liked the name."

When Jaz moved in, she took out walls and painted the white house lavender with deep violet trim. Jaz told Betty, her neighbor on the other side, that rather than a dining room what she needed was a music room. She filled the dining room with the piano and who knows what else. In summer with the windows open, Catherine heard Jaz playing one jazzy tune after another. Once she had glanced through the window and saw her leaning over the keyboard, weaving back and forth as she played.

All of that, however, Catherine could have overlooked without thinking about it. But the first summer after Jaz had moved into the neighborhood, in broad daylight with the windows wide open, Catherine had heard the unmistakable sounds of Jaz making love. With whom she never did find out. She knew Phil must have heard it, too, from where he sat on the front porch. They never mentioned it to each other.

Today, Jaz disappeared behind the shed, and Catherine put the bag of books on the back seat, backed the car out of the garage and turned the radio off. She didn't want to listen to oldies' radio today. Sometimes she felt there was way too much noise in life.

* * *

After Catherine left for Amanda's, Phil leaned back in his chair, and the porch wall came up to meet the back of his head.

Catherine. She was a slender girl when he married her, but here she was, sixty-five, and she had rounded out and softened up during the years.

He closed his eyes and thought of his mother. Round, too, like Catherine, but her faded blue eyes, soft and misty. Trusting he thought. Phil pictured Catherine's eyes—gray green and sharp, always trying to see into a fellow, to know his secret thoughts. Phil believed every person had a right to private thoughts. He kept a hidden reservoir he never showed anyone, especially Catherine. What bothered him was that her eyes kept asking.

Phil kept his secrets from his mother, too. When he was a kid, every time she saw him there was another chore for him to do. It took Phil a long time to see that his mother had been trying to make up for his father who worked hard on the farm when he was sober, but slacked off something fierce when he was not. He realized his mother had been afraid. With cows, they've got to be milked, or else. And corn needs to go in, needs to be cultivated, tasseled, picked, all on time. No matter who had to do it.

After his dad died he had begun driving out to the farm to visit his mother more often. That's when he began to love her. One day he surprised them both when his formal, "Mother," muttered through stiff lips softened to "Mama," and he bent to brush her fine white hair with his lips.

Day after day she sat on the front porch in the old wicker rocker, waiting. Waiting for what or whom he couldn't say. He never asked her. He would drop by the old farmhouse, two, three times a week. There she would be, waiting.

In summer, two old rockers sat side by side on the porch. She would lean her head ever so slightly in his direction indicating he should sit. Down he would sit in the chair by her side and put his hat on his knee. They would look out over the lawn to the fields across the road. Usually they were quiet, but sometimes Phil would find himself talking, saying whatever came into his head. Mama never looked his way while he talked, just sat with her hands quiet in her lap.

Catherine didn't know he had been to see his mother because he didn't tell her. He would drive out on his lunch break from work—the farm was only six miles from town. Why didn't he tell Catherine about his visits out there? He told himself it was a matter of self-preservation. He couldn't imagine why, but his mother had never liked Catherine. He figured the less said to either one about the other was the best way to have peace.

Since he retired, funnily enough, as the early months of his retirement slid by and turned into years, he found staying on the porch the easiest thing to do. The time between visits to the farm stretched out.

Phil settled deeper into his chair and squinted up through the branches of the maple trees that flanked the front walk. The sun had risen high in the summer sky. Fish would have stopped biting by now. Maybe he would go tomorrow.

* * *

Catherine's car knew the way to Amanda's. With her mind free to travel roads of its own, she found herself puzzling over her phone conversation with Amanda a few days before. It had started innocently enough.

Amanda said, "Benny reads all the time. I can't keep enough books in the house."

"Sounds like you and your brother," Catherine responded. "Remember? You'd lie on your bed and read. You had stacks of books all over the place. Jack, too. He had his nose in a book morning until night up in his tree or on the porch swing. Find Jack and you'd find a book."

"Benny's not that bad," Amanda retorted. "Just that it's summer and we live so far out of town."

Catherine wasn't surprised at Amanda's ruffled feelings. Still, she did her best to smooth them out. "I think a child loving to read is a wonderful thing. I still have all the chapter books from when you and Jack were kids. I could bring some out to Benny."

"No, that's ok. The library has plenty of books for him to choose from. Besides the house is a mess."

"You know I don't care about that. I come to see you, not your house."

"I know, but Benny has so many books already. They're all over the place."

"But hasn't he read them all?"

"I guess so."

"The books are just sitting over here gathering dust. I'll bet Jack would like Benny to have them."

"Well, all right. But don't bring too many. I'll never find room for them all."

So Catherine had sat on the floor in front of the bookshelves and chosen books she thought Benny would like. She found the story of Homer Price and the doughnut machine, *Stuart Little*, a story of King Arthur and his knights; *The Lion, the Witch and the Wardrobe, My Friend Flicka.* She pulled the entire stack of orange biographies—Abraham Lincoln, George Washington Carver, Marie Curie—from the shelf.

Catherine was a collector. She had boxes of old Christmas cards, tins of buttons, a basket of rocks, an assortment of obsidian arrowheads and a stone mortar and pestle her brother had found plowing when they were kids.

When Jack and Amanda were small, Catherine had tucked away their clothes as they outgrew them. Then when Jessica was born, Catherine found the box labeled 'Amanda's Too Small Clothes' in the attic and gave it to Amanda. Amanda had been nonplussed. Babies these days wore much brighter colors than they had when Jack and Amanda were little. Also, Amanda didn't like old things. However, she had thanked her mother, and Catherine gave her the 'Jack's Too Small Clothes' box when Benny was born.

Catherine had also kept Jack and Amanda's favorite toys, thinking that one day there would be grandchildren to play with them. As it turned out, Amanda rarely brought the children over to visit, preferring to have Catherine and, more rarely, Phil come to her house. The toys stayed in the wooden box Phil had made for them when Jack was small. The box sat in the den, the top stacked high with fishing magazines.

Catherine was happy Benny liked to read, and she liked the idea of the books cycling through another generation. As she pulled into the driveway, Tom, Amanda's husband, was climbing into his truck. He paused when he saw her.

"Hi, Catherine," he called. "Nice to see you out here."

"Hi, Tom. Good to see you, too. How do you manage to be home in the middle of the day?"

"We're surveying for the new highway south of town so it was easy to come home for lunch." He took the bag of books from her and carried them up the steps and into the kitchen. "Well, I'd better be off. See you soon?"

"I hope so," Catherine said.

Tom drove away, and Catherine took the books from the bag. While she was arranging them into piles Amanda walked in.

"Hi, Mom. I didn't know you were here yet."

"Tom was just leaving when I arrived. He helped me bring the books in. Where are the kids?"

"Jessica's over at Marcie's experimenting with some cookies for the fair. Benny's down in the basement reading. Its cooler down there. Would you like some ice cream? I have a new carton of mint chip."

"My favorite," Catherine said.

"I know. Mine, too."

Amanda dished up the ice cream, and Catherine moved the books aside to make room for the bowls.

"So here are the old books. I haven't thought about them in years." Amanda looked through the stacks Catherine had arranged on the table.

"Do you think Benny will like them?" Catherine asked, suddenly shy.

"Here's Flicka," Amanda said. "I loved that book. And Homer Price. Benny will like these."

The crack of thunder not far away startled both of them and they laughed. The wind picked up and whistled around the windows.

"We could use a good thunder shower," Catherine said.

"Let's hope it clears the air and cools things off," Amanda said.

The rain began plopping, then pelting on the roof. Amanda switched on the light, and they sat listening to the storm and looking through the rest of the books. A typical Iowa summer shower, the storm passed quickly, and Catherine closed the book she was looking at and stood up.

Amanda walked her to the door. "Thanks for coming out, Mom. The fair's next week, you know. Would you like to go with us?"

"It would be fun to go with you and the kids. You know how much I love the fair."

Driving back into town after the storm, Catherine opened the windows and breathed in the scent of wet fields and roadside wildflowers.

* * *

Catherine stopped at the market on the way home from Amanda's. As she drove down their block, she noticed that Phil was still sitting on the porch. She knew he saw her arrive because Phil saw everything. She drove the car around back and parked in the garage. It didn't occur to her to ask him to help her bring the groceries in. He went on sitting while she made several trips back and forth to the car.

Catherine put the groceries away except the makings for the apple crisp. She cored and sliced the apples into a pan, melted butter and stirred in brown sugar, cinnamon, oats and walnuts. Catherine never measured anything, and she rarely used recipes.

When she prepared a meal she always started by making the dessert. That way, she reasoned, even if she ran out of time to make everything she had planned, at least they wouldn't have to do without the best part of the meal.

She was also frugal. Her dad had taught her to make the most of everything. If she were going to bake the apple crisp she might as well bake the meatloaf and potatoes at the same time.

After the storm, the wind stayed fresh and blew right

through the house. One of Catherine's favorite things about the house was the cross-ventilation. She loved fresh air.

Once everything was in the oven, Catherine took her basket out to the garden. After the rain, the rows of green stood bright against the dark earth. Catherine picked a couple of kinds of lettuce and some parsley, pulled a handful of radishes, and picked the last of the sugar snap peas. She checked the tomatoes that were beginning to color. It would be another week or two before they would be ready. Then she picked some Swiss chard to steam.

Supper was quiet. Phil sat down at his place, the same place he had sat in for over forty years, and Catherine served him. Her own place was set but she rarely sat down for long.

"Glad to see it cooled off some," Phil ventured as he put ketchup on his meatloaf.

"Good for the garden," Catherine agreed.

After supper Phil went back to the porch and watched the day turn to dusk. He listened to the cicadas sawing in the maples that flanked the front walk. As the light waned he saw the first lightning bugs hover over the grass.

"Quiet end to a quiet day," he thought.

* * *

The cool weather held overnight, so the next morning after her chores, Catherine headed south of town to the park at Oakland Mills. As usual, she walked briskly on the trail above the river. Her mind kept pace with her feet, traveling over familiar ground. Catherine would have preferred not to think about the past, but once she started, it was not easy to stop.

At school Catherine had loved art class most of all. Her pieces were always prominently displayed in school art shows. In high school, her art teacher, Mrs. Graham, began encouraging her to pursue a career in art. Catherine loved working with paints or pastels, clay or paper. Senior year she created a mosaic of colored glass that went to the state art show in Des Moines.

She sometimes stayed after school to complete a project or to sit at one of the big tables looking through the art books stacked on shelves at the back of the room. Catherine had begun to dream. She would go to art school or even to Paris. She had heard that artists there walked down the sidewalks bumping elbows just like anyone else.

Catherine's mother had been raised a Mennonite. Although she left the community to marry Catherine's dad, it didn't mean she had left the Mennonite ways. She ran a strict household and kept her traditions. No pictures hung on the walls of their house. Art was for function, not for show. Quilting, huck toweling, fine stitchery in the garments she made for Catherine and her sisters—these were arts her mother could understand. Painting a scene of the fields and the sky? What was the use of that?

One afternoon Catherine was helping her mother make grape jelly. The memory of their talk that day left such an impression on Catherine that she had never after eaten grapes in any form.

Her mother had asked, "What do you want to do after high school?"

Catherine had responded without hesitation, "I want to go to art school and be a painter."

Even today, Catherine could see the look her mother had given her and remembered her words: "That's no profession. What you should do is be a teacher. That's a fine thing for a girl to be. No daughter of mine is going to be an artist."

Catherine's face had burned as she poured the hot jelly into glasses.

Her parents supported her going to college, urged her, even. Her dad, Catherine suspected, would have been happy for her to study art if that's what she wanted. And he would never go against her mother. She couldn't hold it against him. Her dad had often been ill and tired easily. Even then Catherine knew that her mother had to be the stronger one. Looking back, one of her most poignant "if onlies" was, "If only I had really known her, I know my life would have been different."

When Catherine married Phil shortly after high school, the quandary over her future was decided. As she was packing to move into the apartment up in Ames, she filled a box with her favorite art projects and carried them up to the attic. She left the dream of art school in the attic with the box and never visited it again.

Catherine stopped on one of the bridges on the Lazenby Trail. She gazed into the stream and remembered the last time she had done a drawing.

One afternoon when Jack was an infant she had laid him to sleep on her bed. Feeling a sudden irresistible urge to draw him, she took out a piece of stationery with her name printed at the top in blue: Mrs. Philip Lewelling. She sharpened a pencil and sat gingerly on the bed so Jack wouldn't wake and drew his picture. Catherine loved the drawing. It embodied something of Jack's spirit, which Catherine saw clearly even while he slept. She kept the drawing in the drawer under her handkerchiefs. She would take it out and look at it from time to time. It was gone now. She couldn't remember when she had thrown it away.

Catherine suddenly realized she was standing still on the bridge staring into the water. She walked to the car and drove home.

* * *

During the next few days the heat came back. Phil stretched up out of his chair and looked absently over the porch railing at the front garden to see if it needed water. Garden looked all right. He ran his hand over his clean shaven chin, finding that he'd missed, as usual, a patch of whiskers under his nose.

Retirement had caught him in good health. He still dressed the way he had in college—old soft jeans and a short-sleeved button shirt. The one today was a blue and white stripe. All year he wore his shirt open at the neck, and, no matter how hot it was, he always wore a v-neck undershirt and carried a well-pressed handkerchief in his back pocket.

He pulled his father's watch from his pocket to check the time. The silver filigree cover had broken off before it came to him, but it still kept time well. Out with it came the pocketknife with a horn handle, well sharpened. He used it to mend small things around the house. It also gave him something to play with while he thought. He ran his thumb over the handle, polished like a bit of exposed root on the path in the county park. He slipped the knife back in his pocket and then checked the time. Three o'clock. Nothing to do until the paper came at four. Phil sighed and sat down again.

He pulled the knife from his pocket again and opened the blade. He held it up and peered down the blade as he had a thousand times. He kept the blade sharp, and it was true as it had been when his grandfather gave it to him when he was twelve. Grandpa had given him the knife as a going away present when he had gone to church camp by himself for the first time.

"If you're lonely, take your knife out and think of me. I'll be thinking of you at the same time," Grandpa had said.

Phil believed him, too. Phil had admired Grandpa more than any man alive. Or dead for that matter.

When he was in high school, Phil and his dad hadn't been able to work together. They lived on a hundred acres south of town and, as with any farm, there was always plenty of work to be done. Maybe because they argued so much, it had been easier for his dad to work by himself or with a hired man than with Phil. Two or three summers in a row, he had sent Phil down the road to work with Grandpa.

Every morning Phil would grab a couple of pieces of toast and walk down the blacktop until it met the gravel. Down and around one bend was Grandpa's farm. Their two big jobs were mowing hay and cultivating corn. He and Grandpa were both persistent workers, but they liked to work at a slow pace. They respected each other. They were also both long thinkers and formed solid ideas over time. They were willing to give each other's ideas a try. No way with his dad.

When Phil thought of his dad, the phrase that came to mind was 'bull-headed'. He figured his dad had to be bull-headed, though, just to climb out of bed most days. His dad worked diligently and long. 'Sunup to sunset,' that was his motto. Sometimes he forgot to eat lunch, just worked straight through. Looking back, Phil supposed he had been a little afraid of his dad.

With Grandpa though, he felt safe. Every morning when Phil would arrive for work at Grandpa's, they would have devotions. The three of them—Grandma, Grandpa and Phil—would kneel down, each leaning on a chair. Then they would take turns and say a prayer. He remembered Grandpa praying. He was quiet and humble—mostly real quiet. Phil had never been particularly inspired by the Quaker meeting. His grandfather, though, had inspired him.

Grandpa had been the one person Phil could talk to besides Bill Perkins. And Catherine when they were young . . . . The thought startled him. He rarely thought of those seemingly endless days of quiet happiness. Nor the deep sense of rightness when he and Catherine were together. With that thought the old ache pushed back to the surface and with it, the other unbidden thought: Jack.

Maybe if Grandpa had still been alive when Jack was growing up, he could have made a difference, set him on the right path. But Grandpa died when Jack was a toddler. Phil himself had not known how to father the boy. When Phil took Jack fishing, Jack couldn't sit still in the boat. Nor had he had any interest in the farm during those years when Phil tried to keep things going for his mother. Phil had finally become so discouraged he gave up and leased the whole lot.

Much later, when Jack had been gone for a long time, Phil sold all but the ten acres surrounding his mother's house. No, as a boy Jack would rather read his books than be out exploring the countryside as Phil had as a boy. Phil had even given Jack a horse that they kept in the old barn out at his mother's. Jack, though he obviously wanted to please Phil, had not taken to the horse either.

And then the shock of Jack's pronouncement followed by all these years of separation. Phil missed Jack as much as he did Grandpa.

"Argh." Phil dropped his head into his hands.

No. He wouldn't think about it anymore. He pulled his watch out again and checked the time.

"Darn paper boy," he thought. "Late as usual." It was 4:02.

CHAPTER

2

As planned, Amanda drove in from the country to take the kids
and her mom to the Henry County Fair. Jessica was proud of
her 4-H entries—lemon drop cookies and a hand-stitched apron
—and a little nervous. She'd go right away and look to see what
color ribbons the judges had given her. Benny wanted to look at
the puppies. His mom and dad had been hinting he might be
able to have a dog and he was eager.

Catherine was ready an hour early, dressed in a well-pressed
yellow blouse and a long soft blue skirt. Now she sat at the
kitchen table waiting for Amanda to come. The radio was on,
and Catherine stared out the back window. She might have been
watching the maple leaves turn in the hot August breeze that
propped up the yellow sky. Instead, Catherine stared unseeing
and absorbed. Phil wasn't the only thinker on Monroe Street.

Phil leaned his head slightly toward the screen door from his
chair on the front porch and called, "She's here."

Catherine left the world to make its own way, turned
abruptly and stood up. After replacing the chair to its centered
position at the side of the table, she pushed it in until it sat three
inches from the edge, settled but inviting, walked through the
house and onto the front porch.

"Do you want to come along?" she asked Phil. She briefly
glanced his way; didn't wait for his standard 'no' response. She

continued down the stairs and the walk to Amanda's car. Amanda was standing half in and half out of the car, leaning on the door.

She smiled at Catherine. "Hi, Mom."

Catherine eased herself into the front seat, closed the door, then turned to the back seat where Benny was looking through an illustrated book of dog breeds, and Jessica was listening to music through earphones.

"Hi Gram." Jessica looked up and took off her headset.

"I'm going to look at the puppies," Benny said.

Amanda called to Phil, "Bye, Dad."

Phil waved. Catherine waved back. She watched him sitting there as Amanda started the car and they drove away.

* * *

The fairgrounds were on the south side of town. Catherine had only missed the fair twice in fifty years. Once when she caught the chicken pox at an end of school picnic. She was fifteen at the time. How she had missed the chicken pox until then puzzled everyone, herself included. The other time she missed the fair was the summer she sprained her ankle chasing Jack through Johnson's horse pasture when he was four.

On Walnut Street, she watched for the entrance to the fairgrounds on the right. Amanda drove through the gates and out back, behind the fair buildings, to park in the dusty rutted lot. To make their way into the fair itself, they climbed under a wire which fenced off the parking lot from the yard where the calves were groomed before being shown. Catherine looked at the boys and girls grooming their calves and wondered if she knew any of their families. That red-haired boy with the ears sticking out looked a lot like Elmer Fortnoy, a boy she had shared lunches with for a while in eighth grade.

Catherine wondered how the calves liked being groomed. The fact that they stood still for it always surprised her. Long-suffering in the face of human intervention she supposed. Growing up on the farm, Catherine had often been sent to round up the cows and bring them into the barn to be milked in the evenings. She thought she understood bovine nature.

Catherine, Amanda, and the grandchildren entered the livestock barn through the back door. Heat and the smell of warm animals and hay greeted them. At this end of the barn, calves, lambs and piglets, which were being groomed and tended by 4-H and Future Farmers of America members, stood or lay in pens. Catherine observed that the youngsters with their animals were as well-groomed as their charges—boys with hair slicked down, girls with hair pulled back in sleek ponytails.

As they moved closer to the front of the barn, the large animals gave way to pens of rabbits and fowl on one side and puppies on the other. Benny and Amanda stayed with the puppies, some of which were for sale. Jessica went ahead to the Exhibition Hall to see how her cookies and apron had fared in the judging.

Catherine walked slowly along in front of the row of cages lined up on the cement floor. She breathed in the rich but not unpleasant smell of a hot July day inside a barn. Large ceiling fans whirred constantly but soothingly and muffled the sounds of the animals shifting and moving in their pens.

She loved animals—all kinds. When the kids were small they had rabbits and, once, a dog—a stray Jack had found next to the railroad tracks and brought home. Mostly, though, Catherine liked to see animals in the wild. On her long walks at Oakland Mills she kept an ear tuned to birdcalls. She scanned the trail for tracks of deer, rabbit and raccoon.

Catherine passed by the bunnies and into the guinea fowl section, admiring the bright eyes which looked back into her own. At the front of the barn, a row of cages held the smallest birds. Catherine peered in at the birds, read a tag here and there, and felt increasingly sleepy.

After a few minutes she found herself stopping in front of one of the small cages. In it, a tiny blue bird huddled against the back wall of the cage. Catherine stooped down and looked in. What kind of bird was that? It was too small to be a bluebird and it certainly wasn't a jay. She picked up the cardboard tag which hung by a wire from the door: Blue Canary, experiment,

Joey Evans, Cloverleaf 4-H Club. Catherine couldn't believe it. A blue canary? Certainly, there was no such thing. She looked closer at the little bird. It had pulled so tightly into itself that it looked more like a bit of blue fluff than a bird.

Catherine straightened up and stood staring at nothing. All these animals in cages and now this helpless little bird. Its eyes were squeezed shut. Its feathers were so bedraggled she knew it couldn't feel like itself.

Catherine felt a pang in her heart. She pushed on her chest and spoke to the little bird, "Someone should rescue you."

She looked around. No one. What could she do? She thought, "One thing about me is that I have always been law-abiding." She remembered the day at the market when she had arrived at the cash register with two bread pans nested together and the checkout girl only charged her for one.

Immediately she had said, "Whoops, there are two pans here." She had felt good saying that. Honesty felt solid to her. She would never have stolen anything in her life, yet here was this pathetic canary. Catherine felt so sorry.

"Poor little thing," she muttered. "Why did they do this to you? What could . . . what was his name?" She peered at the tag again. " . . . Joey Evans have been thinking? If you stay here you will die before the fair ends on Sunday. That's what I think. Frightened to death. That's what you'll be."

Catherine looked at the tiny bird. It would be bad enough to be stuck in this hot and crowded barn in that cage. But to have been dyed blue. It was too much.

She thought, "I should pull myself away."

But Catherine couldn't walk away. She couldn't take her eyes off the little bird. Then almost not knowing what she was doing, not giving herself time to think about it or talk herself out of it, she unlatched the door of the cage. She reached in, gathered the little bird into her hand and slid it into the deep pocket of her full skirt. She closed the door of the cage and walked quickly out the front door of the big barn without looking back. She stood blinking in the sunlight of the main thoroughfare.

"Why did I do that?" she asked herself. She had stolen the bird, stolen something for the first time in her life. And she was surprised to find that she didn't feel bad about it either. She felt like singing. Her heart felt lighter than it had in a long time. Fluttery, it's true, but definitely lighter.

"Poor little thing," she thought again. She cupped her hand protectively over her skirt pocket from the outside, feeling the quivering bird beneath the light fabric.

* * *

She was still standing in the same spot when Benny and Amanda came out of the barn. Benny startled her.

"Gram, you should see the puppy I'm getting."

"Oh." She put her hand over her heart again hoping to stop its pounding. She could feel the bird, a soft small lump against her thigh where it huddled in the bottom of her pocket. "What color is your pup?"

"It's golden," Benny said. "I'm going to call her Goldie."

"That's a fine name. When will you be able to take her home?"

"She's too young to leave her mom," Benny said.

"The Mortensons have her. Their farm is down the road from us. I had no idea anyone was raising dogs out our way. We'll bring her home in a couple of weeks." Amanda sounded distracted. "Well, let's walk over to the exhibition hall and see Jessica's projects."

As they walked, Catherine was constantly aware of the little bird. Without bending her head, she glanced down to see if the bird lump showed from the outside. A couple of times she touched it through the cloth of her skirt, and once she reached her hand in and gently stroked the fluttery feathers.

Jessica had been around the Exhibition Hall looking at the projects from 4-H clubs all over the county to see who had won the blue ribbons. Some of the kids she knew from school, and some were in her own club. She met Catherine, Amanda and Benny near the entrance and led them to where her exhibits were displayed. Her cookies had a white third place ribbon on them, and her red plaid apron had a blue first place ribbon pinned to the pocket.

"You must be very proud," Catherine said absently to Jessica. She was conscious of the little bird in her pocket.

"I'm disappointed in my cookies," Jessica said. "They taste good, but I had to bring them out here before they were cool so they all stuck together."

Catherine said the first thing that came into her mind. "They look delicious, Jessica. Judging on taste alone, they're probably the best cookies here."

The way the bird was trembling, she was afraid it would die before she even brought it home. She tried to think soothing thoughts to it. Once or twice she caught herself quietly crooning to it. Next thing she knew, the voices she hadn't allowed to surface before opening the cage and taking the little bird shouted at her now. The first one was the worst.

"Stealing is a felony. If they catch you, you will probably end up in prison."

Then she thought, "I don't think they put old ladies in jail. There must be an age limit for that sort of thing."

Her muddle deepened. "What will Phil say? He'll think I'm crazy, that's what . . . . I am crazy. This only proves it."

One thought finally stuck. "I'm tired of wondering what Phil will think. It's time I did what I want."

* * *

She remembered the old birdcage in the garage rafters. The bay window in the kitchen was sunny most of the day. Then she found herself wondering about Joey Evans. From the handwriting on the card that hung from the cage, she would guess him to be about ten or twelve years old. Maybe he really cared about the little canary. Dying the bird blue had obviously been a mistake, but that was no reason for her to assume he wouldn't feel bad when he found his bird gone.

She looked vaguely at the exhibits of plaid skirts and vests, dream houses modeled in cardboard with the furniture placed room by room, and wooden birdhouses hanging from the branches of a sapling someone had cut down and nailed to a stand. The birdhouses brought her back to her dilemma. She would most have liked to set the little bird free, place it on the limb of a tree at Oakland Mills and quietly slip away. Of course she knew it would certainly die then.

She didn't know where canaries came from originally but the weather in southeast Iowa could be pretty extreme in the winter. No, she would have to take the bird home, Phil or no Phil, and do her best to make up for the terrible things that had happened to it so far.

While they walked back to the car she kept her hand in her pocket gently cradling the canary hoping it wouldn't feel so lonesome and would stop shivering. When she sat in the car, she carefully arranged her skirt so the little bird in her pocket rode safely. On the short ride home from the fair, the chatter of the kids and Amanda washed around Catherine like wind in the trees. By the time they turned onto her block, Catherine was imagining the little bird, yellow and handsome, swinging from its perch in the sunny kitchen window, warbling a heavenly song.

The car stopped in front of the house. Catherine, startled out of her daydream about the canary, asked Amanda, "Do you want to come in for some iced tea?"

"Thanks anyway, but it's nearly time for afternoon chores. We'd better go home."

"Thanks for taking me along." Catherine stepped carefully out of the car and waved to the children before starting up the walk.

* * *

Phil sat on the front porch where she had left him two hours earlier.

"How was the fair?" he asked as she walked up the steps.

"Jessica won a blue and a white ribbon. Benny is getting a puppy." She looked steadily at Phil for a moment, thinking. Should she take the bird out of her pocket and show it to him, tell him all about it? Maybe that would be best. No, she scarcely told him anything. Knowing Phil, he probably wouldn't have an opinion anyway.

Instead, she said more loudly than she meant to, "Will you find that old birdcage in the garage. I think it's still up in the rafters."

Phil looked at her and shrugged. "I guess so." Phil stood up, and Catherine walked into the house.

He watched her go, wondering. What could she want with that birdcage? Maybe some exhibit she saw at the fair. Like the year she needlepointed Christmas stockings and gave them to everyone including his mother.

He backed Catherine's car out of the garage, hauled the stepladder into place and, after some rummaging around, pulled the old birdcage and its stand down from the rafters. He carried it out into the yard and hosed it off while Catherine stood watching from the back porch.

Handing Phil an old towel she said, "Dry it off good, especially the inside."

Phil dried the old wire birdcage as best he could. "Anything else?" he asked.

"Bring it in the kitchen and fold some newspaper like we used to do when Jack had his parakeet."

Phil brought the newspaper and fitted a thick square into the bottom of the cage, then stood back and watched as Catherine lifted a little bit of blue fluff out of her skirt pocket. "Now what in heaven's name is that?" he wondered. She brought the fluff up in front of her face, murmured to it and placed it gently on the floor of the cage. She unfastened the plastic water dish from the side of the cage, filled it with water and set it on the floor of the cage not far from the blue fluff. Then she latched the cage door and picked her purse up from the kitchen table.

"I have to buy some birdseed. Won't be gone long." She closed the screen door quietly behind her.

Phil walked over to the birdcage and peered in at the tiny tremble in the bottom of the cage. It was a bird, after all. He had thought for a minute that Catherine had gone crazy on him while she was at the fair. But there in the cage was a tiny blue bird, not like any bird Phil had ever seen, but obviously alive. He shrugged his shoulders again, and after pouring himself a glass of water, went back to sitting on the porch.

* * *

After the bird episode, however, his mind wouldn't settle down again, so a few minutes later he walked back in the house for the truck keys purposely not looking at the little bird. However, he, too, closed the screen door quietly. He drove out in the country to visit his mother. When he came home just before supper, he found that Catherine had moved the birdcage into the bay window of the kitchen overlooking a big yellow rosebush. Early evening sunlight slanted in through the window. Catherine hummed to herself as she moved from the sink to the stove making supper.

Without turning around she said hello to him. He stopped and looked at Catherine's back, wondering what had possessed her. A mood that would have her humming was an unusual one at anytime, suppertime most of all. He went to gather the evening paper from the front walk.

At supper Phil ate the mashed potatoes, roast beef and peas Catherine served him, but he continued to wonder about her odd behavior. Catherine was barely still enough to eat. She kept turning to the cage. She hummed to the little bird through half the meal and, it seemed to him, almost didn't notice that he was even at the table. The bowl of ice cream she brought him for dessert was twice as big as usual. He looked from her to the bowl, shrugged, and ate it.

"Probably cooled off by now," he said pushing away from the table. "Think I'll go sit a while."

When she finished washing the dishes, Catherine went over to the cage and spoke to the bird. "Now, don't worry, Blue. I'll be right back." The name just popped out. "Blue," she said. "That's your name."

Earlier that week the fall bulb catalogues had arrived in the mail. Catherine had stacked them on her bedside table. Now she carried them into the kitchen and spread them out on the table. She angled her chair so she could easily see the little bird in its cage. As far as she could tell, it never moved. She spread out the order forms and selected her usual new batch of bulbs—hyacinths, her favorite, and tulips, jonquils and narcissus.

At bedtime, she found an old yellow tablecloth in the linen closet. She murmured to the canary and gently threw the yellow cloth over the cage.

* * *

The first thing she did the next morning was to uncover the cage to greet the little bird and see how it had come through the night. The canary continued to huddle in the bottom of the cage pulled into itself as tightly as it could. From the look of the little dish, she thought it had drunk some of the water and perhaps pecked at the birdseed sprinkled on the floor of the cage, but she couldn't really tell. If it had eaten or drunk anything, it wasn't much. She opened the door of the cage and stroked Blue's feathers with one finger.

"Now, Blue, it's going to be all right." Catherine looked at the little canary for a long moment before closing the cage door.

While she made breakfast, she hummed what she thought was a canary tune to Blue.

"Breakfast," she called in the general direction of the back of the house.

Phil came in. Not looking at Catherine or Blue, he sat down and began reading the paper. Absently, he ate the cereal and toast she served him and drank a cup of coffee. As usual, Catherine ate breakfast standing at the counter. She spread butter and jam on a piece of toast and munched it while puttering through as much of the daily crossword as she could figure out.

After breakfast, Catherine carefully moved the cage into her bedroom where the morning sun shone brightly through two east windows. She didn't want Blue to feel alone. After a quick trip to the laundry room, she set up the ironing board next to the cage. Although she did her best not to have to iron in the summer, by mid-morning she had emptied her basket. The whole time she ironed she hummed to Blue, and she was surprised to find how quickly she finished.

Catherine put the iron and board away and carried the cage back to the kitchen.

"I can see life's going to be easier for me with you around," she said, "but what about you, Blue?"

She opened the door of the cage and stroked the tiny blue head. "Still shivering. Now Blue, you're safe now," she reassured him, "There's nothing to be afraid of."

In the long summer days that followed, Catherine moved the cage from window to window following the light. She crooned to Blue, sang to him, talked to him. She worried as the days passed, and the bird still hadn't hopped onto the perch stretched across the middle of the cage nor did it sing. In fact, it made no sound at all. And its feathers continued to be a bedraggled blue.

Catherine wondered what went on in Blue's head. Did he try to puzzle out what had happened to him? He had no doubt started life in the same way all canaries did—curled in a shell which was growing too small, then pecking his way out into the light. Catherine supposed he must have begun life in a cage, so he wouldn't be expecting anything different. Yet the idea of being dyed blue—she shuddered to think of it. Then the tiny cage at the fair and now being with her. What must he think of it all?

* * *

Catherine herself had been thinking quite a bit since bringing Blue home. First of all, she couldn't believe she had stolen the canary. Often she had felt crazy, but she had always held herself within the bounds of what she thought was right. Not taking something that belonged to someone else had always been the easiest rule to follow.

Now she had taken something not from just any someone, but from a child. A 4-H child. Why did she do it? She didn't know why, but she did know that she had to do it. She couldn't leave that bird there in that big stifling barn in that little cage all by itself. Thinking of Blue in that cage made her feel like something big and menacing was pushing at her from all sides. And suddenly she realized why she'd stolen the canary.

She put her face by the cage and whispered to the small creature huddled inside, "I've spent my life in a cage. I've wasted the whole thing."

Catherine had never felt so disheartened. But as always, she couldn't let herself sit in misery so she did the only thing she could do next. There were always chores to do. She rummaged around under the sink in the laundry room for a bucket and squeegee so she could wash the windows.

"Blue will feel better if the windows are clean," she thought.

As she washed the windows she did start to feel lighter. Working just worked. With her hands in and out of the bucket, using the squeegee to render the glass truly invisible, Catherine felt free. She could almost feel the tall grass swishing against her bare legs. In her mind she ran again through the orchard to the row of tall old pear trees at the back edge of her parents' farm just before the woods began. She could pull herself up to the lowest branch of her favorite tree and, hidden by the leaves, easily climb higher. Sitting on a broad branch, she would pull out the notebook she had shoved through the sash at the back of her dress, take the pencil out of her pocket and lean back against the trunk. Time to draw.

Looking through each window as she finished washing it, she could still picture those early drawings. She drew what she could see from her perch in the tree—leaves, branches and pears; the slope of the far meadow and the woods beyond. She also drew what she couldn't see—fairies, horses with wings sailing through the sky, a little cottage surrounded by flower gardens.

She dreamed that as soon as she finished high school she would leave the farm and go to school, a fine college where she could draw and paint all day long. She also thought she would find someone to marry, that she would have her own children to play with, that she would have a little cottage and her paintings would hang on the walls. Even through high school, Catherine climbed the old pear tree. When she fell in love with Phil, she was positive he would be the one she would marry and share the cottage with.

* * *

As it happened she had married Phil. Their marriage began awkwardly, and their brief conversations through all the years nearly always had to do with the details of daily life—the children and what they needed, food, insurance, house repairs. Despite Catherine's urging, Phil said little. She knew he liked having his own thoughts. As far as she knew, he didn't share them with anyone.

Catherine suspected that if she were only—she didn't know what—something indefinable, different in some way, Phil would open up and talk to her. Tell her what was on his mind. Tell her he loved her for one thing. He never did that. Or at least he hadn't for a long time, since before they were married really. She was finally so embarrassed asking him if he loved her and having him say only, "Yes, of course," that she stopped asking.

She knew that she herself was the reason for Phil's silence. She felt it in her heart like a stone. He didn't open up to her because she had hurt him so terribly he stopped trusting her a long time ago. She was certain he would never trust her again. She knew this without asking him because she remembered what it had been like with her and Phil before he went to college and she had had sex with Mike.

Phil had an old pick-up truck even then. They drove all over southeast Iowa in it, sitting high on the seat looking out over the fields, not having to say anything. The talk was thick between them with no need to speak aloud. She would crank the window down and lean her arm out so the wind would push against her. She felt alive then. And Phil—a tan, smooth-skinned, strong farm boy. She loved the way his hair shot up from his forehead in a cowlick his mother could only control by barbering his hair almost to bald. She loved everything about him then and, to tell the truth, she had never stopped. Only their life together hadn't turned out anything like she dreamed.

They went to the same high school. She was two years younger than he. They didn't know each other until Phil's cousin's wedding. Catherine was the bride's cousin. Phil noticed her at the wedding. He called the very next day. Then he started visiting. Soon they were spending as much time as possible together. Often when they were together, Phil would drive the truck back into the woods at the far edge of his parents' farm down a dirt lane to a clearing. He would turn the truck around and park it. Catherine would sit with her back against the door and her feet in Phil's lap so they could talk. He would stare through the windshield and, not looking at Catherine, tell her what he thought about life and his plans. Together they planned that they would marry, that they would have two children, and that, one day, they would build a house in this clearing.

Sitting in Phil's truck, Catherine felt she had come home. The sadness of her life at home would melt off her. There was a steadiness in Phil which she knew she needed and didn't have. She didn't want him to be that steadiness for her, but she hoped to learn it from him. Sitting there in the clearing, she felt she could. And when he kissed her and held her close, she knew everything would turn out right.

He graduated and went to Ag school at Iowa State. He would live in the dorm. She didn't know what that would be like, but she was convinced he would meet other girls up there. Maybe he would fall in love with someone else. She would be alone again. She was so afraid of that happening that she suggested that they date 'other people' while he was away. Yes, they would be married as soon as he finished school. Meanwhile it would be best to date around. She had said it in a rush, hating what she was saying every moment, but not being able to stop herself. If he were going to fall in love with someone else, she didn't want to be the fool waiting at home and have no one.

As it turned out, Mike Hopkins, captain of the wrestling team, asked her out. She was flattered. Mike had a reputation of going with the prettiest girls. As far as Catherine knew he had gone out with almost all of them. She didn't consider herself pretty, though Phil had told her enough times how much he liked the way she looked. She went out with Mike. He would arrive at her house in his old '49 Ford and blow the horn. Her mother didn't like that at all, but Catherine would go out to him anyway. Before long they had kissed a little. Then he tried to touch her breasts. When she said no, he said she was naive and young, and why was he wasting his time with her anyway. She gave in. The next thing she knew, he wanted more. Without thinking about it and because she was afraid he would find another girl who would, she let him go 'all the way' with her. After the first time every date was the same. During the next few weeks Catherine felt sicker and sicker about what she was doing.

Finally she told him that yes, she wanted to continue dating him but kissing was as far as she would go. He teased and pressed her but she was firm that she wouldn't. After that night he never called her again.

A couple of months later, that terrible phone call came from Phil while she was at school. It was even more painful for her to bear when she found out that Phil hadn't dated anyone at college. He told her he hadn't wanted to.

When he called, she could hear in his voice how badly she had hurt him. His voice was so quiet and deeper than she had ever heard it, sounding like it came from a deep dark well.

During the years the children were growing up, Catherine was mostly too busy to feel the sadness. After college, Jack had moved to Baltimore. She had only seen him twice in all these years, but they often spoke on the phone and exchanged letters. Amanda stayed in Mount Pleasant, and taught school. She was busy with Jessica and Benny and her gang from high school. Most of them were still living in Mount Pleasant raising kids themselves.

Mostly, Catherine accepted her life as it was. The biggest part of her was convinced her estrangement from Phil was her own fault and she deserved it. There was, however, a small soft voice that told her it wasn't fair, and hadn't she suffered long enough, and would he ever forgive her? Sighing never helped her feel better, but she did it often enough anyway.

Often Catherine thought, "I'm alone, and that's that. I've always been alone."

* * *

Now she had Blue to keep her company. Catherine did everything she could think of to help the canary feel safe. After the first few weeks, he had stopped the terrible quivering. Still he pulled into himself when she came near. The last thing she did before bed each night was to chirp softly to Blue and cover the cage with the yellow cloth. The first thing she did in the morning was to uncover the cage so she could check on him.

She hummed to Blue as she worked about the house. She hummed tunes she remembered her mother singing during her childhood. She hummed the tunes she and Phil had fallen in love to. She hummed some of the songs Jack and Amanda had filled the house with when they were teenagers, and which she now occasionally heard on the oldies' station in the car. It seemed the canary would never relax no matter what she did. She moved him carefully, talking to him all the while, from window to window. She opened the windows so the breeze and the scents from the garden would come in.

Phil watched her and heard the unfamiliar sound of Catherine humming around the house. He wondered but said nothing. Sitting on the porch as July turned into August, seemingly against his will, his thoughts kept falling on that day when his life changed. He had been sitting on a sunny bench in the quadrangle on campus when Jake Monroe stopped to tell him that his little sister had seen Catherine going around with Mike Hopkins. Phil had shivered in the sunlight, his mind had gone numb, and he couldn't breathe.

When he finally caught his breath, he called Jake a liar and Jake's sister a little creep. Deep down he immediately knew it was true. Something wasn't right. In the past few weeks, when he had called Catherine for their usual Thursday night phone date, there was something in her voice. He couldn't tell what it was, but he felt uneasy. Like something was being pulled away from him and if he could just see what it was, he might be able to bring it back and hold it close. But he couldn't see.

One night shortly before Jake told him about Catherine and Mike, he had a dream. He was caught in a tornado and he could feel himself being sucked away. Head bent against the storm, the wind pulled him back with each step forward. He was going to be blown away and there was nothing he could do about it.

Now Jake had given a name to his uneasiness. Phil had always been direct. He grew up on a farm. His family were rural Quakers and he was raised to become quiet with God and then say what was on his mind. He called Catherine at school. Knowing the answer in advance, he still needed to ask her if it were true.

After the call, Phil sat on the bench in the quad for a long time doing the only thing he could. He shoved the pain in his gut so deep and so forcefully it found bottom and settled in there, as far as he was concerned, forever. When he rose from that bench, he assured himself it was done. He returned to the daily routine of school again, and as the days passed, he became used to feeling nothing. Not happiness or grief. He just kept going, but no matter how he tried, he couldn't forget Catherine.

That puzzled him. After a few months he called her and they began to date on weekends when he went home. The first time he drove to pick her up, his heart was pounding so loud he could barely hear the radio. When she came to the door, his chest tightened. He thought for a minute he was going to cry. Instead he took a deep breath and began playing the 'everything's ok' game. That lasted until Catherine became pregnant with Jack and they were married.

After the wedding, they moved into an apartment in Ames so Phil could continue his Ag program. Then his application for CO was accepted and he decided to do his alternate service in the Merchant Marine. Phil thought Catherine could live with his mother while he was gone, and, when he came home, they would build their house in the woods. Catherine flatly refused. In fact, she refused to live in the country at all. After all, she was the one who was pregnant. Phil moved them into a little house on Cherry Street, and went to sea. Jack was born six weeks later.

Phil had always planned to farm his family's land using the 'practical agriculture' techniques he learned at school. Instead she insisted that they live in town. Phil felt guilty for her being pregnant. By the time he came home, Jack was crawling. He settled into the house on Cherry Street and took a job at Kent Feeds. He did try to farm, but it was too much—driving to and from the farm for chores before and after work and all weekend long. Even with a hired man, he couldn't keep up with it.

If only he could have talked to Grandpa. Grandpa would have helped him make sense of what had happened. Grandpa was the holiest man in the Quaker Meeting. Phil had watched him from as early as he could remember. Grandpa would have known what to tell him, but because of the Parkinson's, Phil hadn't been able to talk to him then about Catherine nor about his despair a year later when Bill was killed in the war.

He sat on the front porch. Memories paraded by relentlessly. Suddenly the most painful memory of all showed up: Jack. The thick hot air pushed at him.

"No," he said tightly, "I will not think about Jack."

He pushed himself up from his chair and went to put the sprinklers on. At least the grass would have some relief. Back from the sprinklers, Phil settled deeper into his chair and drew his eyebrows together.

CHAPTER

3

Driving out to Amanda's, Catherine's mind wouldn't stay still either. During the few months that had passed between that awful phone call and Phil's next visit home, she did not hear from him. When Phil came home for Mother's Day, he called and asked if she would come out with him. Heart pounding, she had said yes. When he came to pick her up, he acted as if nothing had happened. Yet that sweet door between them, through which a strong clean breeze had blown, was slammed and locked. Phil continued to treat her with kindness. He continued to appear stable and strong. But he stopped telling her his dreams. When she turned to him, he wasn't really listening. Where he was she couldn't find out. All her attempts to follow him there came to nothing.

Catherine tried to win Phil's trust again. She told him how sorry she was. She pledged undying faithfulness. She said that she loved only him and always had. He received all her pleas with equanimity. He swore he didn't hold anything against her.

One day that summer they went for a walk around the lake at Geode Park outside of town. They were walking through some high grass, talking and laughing in the midday sun. Catherine had on shorts and felt scratchy and itchy from the prickly grasses. Her upper lip was perspiring and her hair felt hot as she walked along behind Phil. Suddenly, he turned around, grabbed her and started kissing her. The next thing she knew they were down in the tall grass. Their clothes were coming off, and, before she had time to see how she really felt, he was thrusting himself into her.

Thinking this was what he wanted, and perhaps now things would be all right between them again, Catherine submitted. Much later Phil told her that he assumed she wanted sex. He figured that was what she had gone after with Mike. When she had heard that, she felt sick. It was never sex she wanted. She wanted to have someone to love and be loved by, that was all.

* * *

The following May, a month before her high school graduation, Phil again came home for the Mother's Day weekend. Shortly thereafter, Catherine discovered she was pregnant. When Phil came home for the summer holiday, they were married in a small morning ceremony in the Methodist Church.

Brunch was provided by the Ladies Auxiliary in the church basement. A band played quietly while everyone ate and then shifted into dance music. Catherine wore a blue linen suit that day and the shoes with pearl bows, but Phil didn't dance, then or ever.

That fall they moved into married student housing in Ames where Phil did one more semester of Ag school. They moved home just before Phil went to sea with the Merchant Marine. After the war, Phil didn't go back to school. He still wanted to put a trailer to the side of their clearing until they could build the house. Catherine wouldn't hear of it. Without Phil's friendship she couldn't imagine living in the country. She insisted they live in town, and it was a good thing. Through all the years since, Catherine did her best not to think about their dreams of the country. She couldn't bear to.

* * *

In the weeks that followed the coming of the canary, Catherine settled into a routine. The memory of having stolen the little bird began to give way to the wonder of it. She belonged to Blue. He was an anchor to something solid. Her loving him, crooning to him, humming and singing to him created just enough space for her to finally feel the enormity of her misery. Life was too big, and Catherine didn't fit anywhere in it. Of course life continued. She cooked, cleaned, folded the laundry, talked to Phil as much as necessary, moved Blue from window to window. All the while, the vague unease which had been her companion since girlhood pressed ever more insistently.

She felt like she was flowing downstream in some great wide river, the Des Moines maybe. She didn't know where the river would take her but she was on her way. Any moment she might jump out of her skin, but still the river carried her on. There was a creeping feeling at the nape of her neck under the downy hair beneath her curls. All of her memories—the past heaped up into a mountain—shoved at her.

She turned to Blue and watched him as he sat in his cage. Maybe he could tell her something that would help. He sat silent. She thought, "I don't even know who I am or what I'm doing here. I was born, grew up, raised two kids, and still I don't know."

Catherine couldn't remember one real conversation she'd ever had with her mother. Of course, her mother had been caring for nine children, and life on the farm required constant work. She rarely spoke, only hummed or sang quietly to herself while she moved from task to task. She sang church songs Catherine knew must be from her Mennonite childhood. She liked the sound of them. Watching her mother's constant movement, Catherine sometimes imagined grabbing her arms to keep her still and demanding to be seen.

When Catherine was born, her maternal grandmother was already an old woman. Her mother had left the Mennonite community to marry Catherine's father, and from that moment, according to tradition, she was lost to her family and her past. It was as if she had never existed. Catherine's mother's eight brothers and sisters had stayed in the community. She was the only one who had left.

The only visit to Grandmother Catherine remembered, when she was nine, was prompted by the death of her mother's father.

At the funeral and later at the house, Grandmother had never once looked at Catherine's mother. To the children she had been civil but anything but warm.

Catherine mourned being cut off from her mother's family. Her grandmother and most of her aunts and uncles lived in the country outside Wayland, northwest of Mount Pleasant. Catherine imagined what it would be like to live in the Mennonite community. She thought everyone would help each other and no one would feel alone.

Once when she had driven out with her dad to see some sows he was buying for the farm, Catherine had seen a group of men building a barn. Long tables were set up under a tree nearby. Women in long dresses and white caps were setting out platters of food. Children played with a ball. When she asked, her dad told her these were Mennonites. They would build the barn in one day. He told her, too, that the women would join together in the same way and piece a patchwork quilt in one day and quilt it the next. He told her he admired the Mennonite way of life. Her mother rarely mentioned her family. Once she did say that Grandmother and her aunts made dozens of quilts. From her faraway look Catherine thought she must be sad, too.

* * *

Catherine's mother died when Amanda was in college. Catherine, as the oldest daughter, was expected to 'see to things'. In going through her mother's dresser, Catherine found a box of smooth stones, a book, and a few withered letters. The names on the letters meant nothing to her, and their wording, where she could make it out, was stiff and formal. One by one she picked up the cool stones and held them in her hand. She knew they had a story to tell but she couldn't hear it. The book, surprisingly, was a collection of poems. She felt restless in the presence of these few fragments of her mother's life. She put the letters in the trash and packed the book and the box of stones away in the bottom drawer of her own dresser.

When her mother died, Catherine's sadness became even worse. Through the years, she had kept hoping to learn something from her mother—perhaps a hint about how to live a good life, maybe even how to be happy. They rarely saw one another, and when they did, her mother only seemed interested in what Jack and Amanda were doing. If Catherine turned the conversation to her own thoughts or feelings, her mother changed the subject. When her mother died, Catherine gave up hoping for answers.

The silence of the house gathered around her and brought her back to herself. "What?" she wondered. "What am I doing?" She waited for an answer, but all she heard was quiet.

* * *

Catherine went out to the car and headed to the county park, south of town. Walking in the park had been the only thing besides her garden that gave Catherine relief through the years. With Blue's coming, she felt a new sense that her life had been passing her by without her being able to do much about it. Driving through the tree-lined lane that led into the park, she had a sudden flash that perhaps her life could change after all.

In the park, two streams crisscrossed several miles of forested trails. Catherine walked the trails all year round. Spring and autumn were her favorites, but Catherine traipsed through the snow or slogged along in the humidity of full summer, too. Today was a typical late summer day, warm enough but soft and fragrant with rich woodland scents.

Despite the gentleness of the forest trail, her kitchen thoughts surged over her, and she walked faster. She didn't notice the silence of the woods.

She had hoped that when Phil retired, they would talk; they would have time to do things together. Catherine didn't know what those things might be or what they would talk about, but she hoped that with their coming, she would feel her life had been worth living after all.

As babies and when they were growing up, she had loved Jack and Amanda with her whole heart. Raising the children had kept her sadness at the distance between her and Phil at bay, but always her deepest wish was to reclaim the joy she and

Phil had shared in their early days. Her dream had been Phil.

When the children had grown and gone, her desire for a friend in Phil grew stronger, but the years passed with no opening from him. Now he was retired, and their life had been going on as it always had.

Yet deep down, Catherine suspected that she herself was as responsible as Phil for their lack of closeness. She was crabby. Perhaps that had kept Phil away at least as much as the memory of her long-ago betrayal. Through the years, she had stayed so busy she rarely looked at Phil when he spoke to her, and sometimes cut him off when he did speak. Worst of all, she felt sorry for herself, that she had been cheated out of the happiness she felt was promised to everyone just for being born.

Catherine thought of Blue. He had no doubt started life as a small yellow bird. Somewhere Blue's life had been taken in someone else's hands, and perhaps he now felt as confused as she did. Yet even with that thought came a hint of hope. She could see that Blue was relaxing, that while he hadn't hopped up onto his perch nor had he sung, he was definitely becoming more interested in his surroundings. One day, she was confident, he would sing.

* * *

It was September. The days grew shorter, and the evenings began to cool. Catherine prepared the garden beds for autumn. She divided and reset the bulbs. Her fingers lost in the cool autumn earth, she daydreamed roots and a bed to grow in. She wanted her own peace on the earth.

The first few cold days sneaked up on Phil. Sitting on the porch one brisk day, he noticed the maples in front of the house were beginning to change color. A little red, a little peach and yellow amidst the green. Fall was his favorite time of year. Perhaps because it was his birthday month, he liked September best of all. He loved it, too, because the changing season reminded him of starting school, the smell of the new pencils and paper his dad had brought him from the store a few days before school began.

Phil had liked school because in the early years it was nearly the only time he saw kids his own age. Their farm was at the end of a dirt road. Phil and his sister were the only kids within, he didn't know, maybe five miles. His grandparents lived down the gravel on the next lane, but the nearest neighbors were half a mile further on and they were old.

On rare occasions when he was small, his mother would take him by the hand and carry a loaf of warm bread or muffins down there. When he got old enough to go by himself, he would sometimes help Mr. McNulty with the chores, but the old man was a silent sort and not much company for Phil. The highlight of his young life was when the Watkins salesman or the chicken feed salesman came to visit because it gave him somebody different to talk to.

Coaxing himself off the porch and out to the lake to go fishing was a real challenge. Sometimes he thought the seat of his pants had probably adhered to his chair, he sat so long and so many days in succession.

One morning, Phil stepped out on the porch to see if the paper had arrived. The air this particular morning had something new in it, and it sparked Phil. It was more than just the chill of early autumn. The cool air reminded him of fishing. He pictured himself in his boat, nestled into his private cove, casting and sitting. Waiting for a fish to see his fly placed expertly on the water looking as nearly like a skitterbug as was possible. Phil had tied that fly himself two or three winters ago, and it was about time he tried it out. After a quick breakfast by himself, he gathered his fishing gear from the basement.

"I'm on my way to the club. Going fishing this one last time before the water's too cold and the fish are sluggish," he called in the direction of the laundry room.

"What did you say?" Catherine called back, coming into the kitchen wiping her hands.

"Off to the lake," he repeated. "Be back later."

Over her shoulder as she turned back to the laundry, Catherine said, "Don't forget to clean the fish before you bring them in the house."

Phil grabbed some bread, a hunk of salami and a couple cans of soda, shoved them into a canvas bag along with his gear and headed for the lake. He drove his old truck fast because the fish were biting now but wouldn't be for long. He knew from long experience that once the sun rose in the sky, the fish would be through biting until it went down again at the end of the day.

* * *

After Phil left, Catherine carried the laundry basket out to the backyard. She loved the smell of laundry fresh off the line. While she was hanging the wash she saw the mailman crossing the yard on his way to the neighbor's. She dropped the towel she was about to hang up back into the basket and went to check the mail.

Catherine did her best to bring the mail in before Phil had a chance to see it. That wasn't easy with the mailbox hanging on the front porch on the other side of the door from his chair. But most days Catherine managed it. She was looking for a letter from Jack.

Jack had been Catherine's ally. As a small boy he stayed close, playing with the pots and pans on the kitchen floor and later with his trucks and cars, scooting them around her while she cooked or cleaned up. As he grew older, though he moved out into the world of friends and sports, he still hung around with Catherine in the kitchen when he came home, telling her about his day. Jack hadn't dated in high school. When Phil worried that Jack didn't seem to be going for the girls, Catherine reassured him saying Jack was a 'late bloomer.'

When Jack came home for Christmas his first year of college, they were at the dinner table that first evening. Amanda, still in high school, teased Jack about finding a girl now that he was away from home.

Catherine remembered that evening like it was set in crystal.

She herself had said, "The next thing we know you'll be telling us you're going to marry some girl from Minnesota."

Jack was in college at Northern Iowa and, despite her wishing that he come home weekends, after a couple of visits, he stayed at school, coming home only for a day and a half at Thanksgiving. Now he planned to be back at school for New Year's Eve which didn't give them much time on this visit either.

When she made the remark about his marrying, he had visibly stiffened.

Then, taking a deep breath and looking first at Amanda, then at Phil and finally, letting his eyes rest on Catherine, Jack had said, "I won't be marrying a girl from Minnesota or Iowa either. I'm gay."

Catherine wasn't certain what happened after that. Only that the room had become way too hot, and her head had expanded to fill the space. She knew that she had said something in the silence that followed Jack's pronouncement, and though the sound still echoed in her ears, she had no idea what she had said. In her confusion she had looked to Phil, hoping he would save her this once, but he sat there so still he might just as well have been made of wood.

Amanda had blushed, then hidden her face in her hands, giggling. Catherine remembered that.

Then Phil had tossed his napkin on the table, pushed his chair back so abruptly it fell backwards as he stood up. Ignoring the chair, he had fled from the room.

And, as far as Catherine knew, that was the last time Phil had communicated with his son. Jack had not stayed for Christmas but left early the next morning. Catherine, lying in bed, had heard the front door open and close, then the car door, the engine starting up, and the car driving down the street. She had lain in bed listening in the silent house until she was way past hearing the sound of the car in the winter morning.

She had wanted to go out to him; to catch him up and hold him; to say, "Don't go. It's going to be ok, I love you no matter what." But she hadn't. She often wondered, "Why did I let him go?"

It had taken years for the distance between them to diminish enough so they could communicate comfortably again, and, despite Catherine's wishing, they had never regained the closeness of Jack's childhood.

After Jack's early morning departure, Phil would not hear Jack's name mentioned. He stopped sending money for Jack's schooling. Catherine sent what she could hold back from her household budget, and with the checks, she sent letters, over time telling Jack what she knew of her life—enough that he saw how disillusioned she was. Eventually he softened toward her and began responding. Now, they still wrote regularly and often talked on the phone when Phil was out of hearing.

Jack lived in Baltimore where he worked as an editor for the *Baltimore Sun*. Catherine didn't know exactly what he did, but she knew his area was People and Events. Jack and his long-time partner, Jeff, had renovated a house in the Mount Vernon neighborhood. Catherine had been to visit a couple of times, driving herself to the airport in Cedar Rapids and leaving the car in long-term parking. She loved the stately two-story brick house set on a hill amongst towering old oaks and maples. By the time she visited, she had long since been happy that Jack had Jeff. She had been able to tell from his letters that they loved each other, and when she met Jeff, she liked him right away. Jack's being with Jeff felt as natural as anything.

Today there was no letter from Jack. Instead, she found the box of fall bulbs she had ordered. She shoved them to the back of the refrigerator to chill in preparation for going in the ground. She put the mail on the kitchen table unopened, finished hanging the wash, and walked over to the market for milk and bread before lunch.

* * *

Though it was still early when Phil arrived at the gravel lot next to the Isaak Walton Clubhouse, he saw three cars there ahead of him. Two of them he recognized. Carrying his gear down to the lake, he found Walt Jamison and Jim Lauer engrossed in conversation by the shore.

"Well, if it isn't Phil," Jim called when he saw him. "Haven't seen you in months."

"Yep." Phil set his gear down on the gravel.

"Where've you been keeping yourself?" Walt asked.

"I don't know," Phil answered. "Been keeping busy at home, I guess. How's the fishing been?"

"Better than last year," Walt said. "Can't give them away, there're so many."

"Big ones, too," Jim added.

"Good to see you," Walt said. "You always were a good one for thinning out the fish when they got too thick out there."

Phil knew they were kidding him. It had been a long time since he had hung around with these guys, and he realized now how much he missed it.

"I'll see what I can do," he said. He picked up his gear, walked over and untied his boat. He turned it over, swiped out the cobwebs with one hand, and tossed in his gear.

"Boat's surviving pretty well," he said.

"Looks like you're surviving yourself," Walt said. "How do you like taking it extra easy to make up for all those years of working?"

"Finally figured if I came and sat in my boat instead of on the porch, maybe I'd catch a few before it was too cold," Phil said.

"Sitting on the porch, is it?" Jim asked. "And how's Catherine?"

"She's fine," Phil answered. "Same as always, I guess. Well, I'd better row on out there or it'll be too late."

Phil shoved the boat out into the lake, set his oars and pulled into deep water. He could feel the muscles across his shoulders open up and stretch. It felt good, and for a few minutes he rowed without thinking of anything. When the shore looked to be far enough away, he stopped rowing and looked over his shoulder for his bearings. Back-paddling with his right oar, he turned the boat to starboard and headed to his cove.

The morning sun slanted onto his back and warmed him through the plaid flannel shirt he wore against the chill of the early autumn day. The trees along the lakeshore stood sentinel to his passing, and as Phil rowed, he touched back into himself to a place nothing else led him to. The water lapped against the bow as it cut through the water. His eye traveled the wake as it spread out from the stern at his feet. Mostly the trees still wore green but the blush of scarlet, rust and gold had begun to wash over the forested shoreline.

Phil pulled the boat into the little cove. The willow wept green turning to gold, great strands of it dipping nearly to the water's surface. Today, instead of sliding the boat back under the overhanging branches where he could look out through the curtain of leaves, he stopped the boat in the middle of the cove. He shipped his oars and gathered his fishing gear around him.

Phil was a fly fisherman of the old order. He had wrapped his rod himself and tied his flies. He carefully selected a fly from his box which he hoped would most closely approximate the bugs a fish might find to eat this very morning floating on the water.

He had a selection of wet flies, also, to fish at depth. But he always started fishing with dry flies. He figured if he were a fish —and didn't he try his darnedest to think like one—he would prefer a fresh skitterbug skating along the top of the water to a drowned fly or even a nymph. Also, though he didn't like to admit it, Phil knew that half the time his dry flies eventually sank if they didn't soon catch a fish and became drowned flies anyway.

Phil tied the fly on the line and cast back into the shallows beneath the shade of the old willow. With a fine cast the first time, Phil relaxed. Yes, a fish. Ah. Phil settled into the morning, changing flies as the brightness of the day called for, he thought, a lighter fly to bring the fish to his hook. By mid-morning Phil had caught three nice bass and settled back in the boat, his cap over his eyes, and drifted with the gentle breeze.

As he drifted, he found himself wondering about Catherine and that canary of hers—Blue, she called it. He had never asked her how she came to have it in her pocket that day she came home from the fair. He had given plenty of time to wondering about it in his long thinking hours on the porch, but it had not come to mind to ask her and have the mystery solved. No, he simply thought about it and watched Catherine.

She seemed different, he thought, since she brought the canary home. Less cranky. He didn't know what to make of it.

Thinking about Catherine brought up, as it always did, an ache which Phil would rather not have felt. Today when it rose, he did what he usually did: changed the subject in his own mind.

Rocking gently in the boat reminded him of riding Prince. When he was five, his dad had given him the old sorrel horse, and with Prince came Phil's freedom. He still marveled to think of Prince, sixteen hands tall, big for a kid. Prince had been sore-footed and slow, but when he was young, Prince was Phil's sole companion and friend.

In the beginning, Phil couldn't ride without a saddle. Since his dad would be gone all morning farming, Phil woke up early so his dad could saddle Prince. Otherwise, he would have to wait the long morning until his dad came home at noon for dinner. One morning while he was waiting, the Watkins salesman came and saddled Prince for him.

By the time he was six, he could ride bareback and put the bridle on himself. He was allowed to ride down the dirt road three quarters of a mile or half a mile the other way down the gravel road. One day his dad was helping another Quaker farmer on the Salem blacktop, and Phil had set out on Prince to visit him. When he arrived his dad wasn't there after all. When he finally came home it was late, and his mom had beaten him with a butter paddle.

"Knew I had it coming," he thought.

Mostly though, he would ride or walk under the big oaks and walnuts in the forty acres of timber pasture behind the house.

A gentle breeze stirred the water on the lake. The September sun warmed Phil through his jeans. His mind swinging back to the present, he wondered how the oaks were responding to the cooler weather and looked out from under his cap to see. Along the lake shore he spotted an occasional oak as green as ever. Holding onto summer, he supposed.

The sun was high. Probably near noon. He pulled out his salami and bread and had a quiet lunch. Life was good on the lake. Doing something, just enough to keep from fussing at himself. This was very good.

As he started rowing back to the clubhouse, he determined to come out here again soon, maybe even tomorrow before it was too cold and he had to wait until spring.

* * *

When Phil came home, Catherine's car was gone. He cleaned the fish on the back steps, hosed the steps down and put the fish in the refrigerator. Then he decided to begin the fall cleanup. He gathered his clippers and loppers and pruned branches broken in summer thunderstorms. Then he pruned the peonies. He was in the middle of cutting back the hydrangeas at the front corners of the house, when he heard a voice.

"Yoo-hoo, Phil."

Phil turned. There was his neighbor, Jaz, on the other side of the low hedge that separated their yards.

"Oh," he said. "Hello." There was an unspoken question in his voice.

Phil wasn't one to make friends with the neighbors. In fact, his only friends were the men he had worked with and the Walton Club crew. He had only one close friend, Hank, who was also a purist when it came to fly fishing.

Now here was Jaz, wanting something. Ok, he would see what.

"Yes, hello," he said again. "How are you?"

"Good. I'm turning that little shed out back into a pottery studio, and I need a good pry-bar. I have all the other tools I need, but I have some old boards I need to pry away to make space for the kiln. Do you have one I might borrow?"

"I have one in the garage. Come on over and we'll find it."

Phil had never really looked at Jaz before. Now that he had the chance, she looked pretty ordinary. She was wearing an old blue shirt, baggy khakis, and sturdy leather shoes. She had soft faded hair, curly and pulled loosely back from her face, a mess of laugh wrinkles next to her eyes. But her eyes. They were as bright as Catherine's little canary.

"She looks nice," he thought.

Jaz and Phil walked along the side of his house toward the garage.

"Pretty yard you have here," Jaz said. "I've always wanted a peony patch. Their fragrance is so heady."

"You like peonies?" Phil asked. Then, surprised at himself, he added, "They divide pretty easily. If you'd like some, we can divide them in the spring and you can start a bed."

"I'd like that," Jaz said.

Phil pulled the pry-bar out from amongst a jumble of tools in the front corner of the garage and handed it to Jaz.

An impulse took him. "Say," he said, "do you want some help with that shed?"

Jaz looked at him sideways.

"I mean," Phil continued, "it's usually easier to do that kind of project with two pairs of hands. Happy to help."

"Ok," Jaz said. "That'd be great."

Phil pried off the boards that Jaz pointed out while she carried them away and stacked them by the street for the fall pick-up. Together they laid heavy clay tiles on the old floor to make a pad for the kiln that would be delivered the next day.

"What did you say you were going to do out here?" Phil asked.

"Well, I used to be a potter and I miss it. So I thought I'd set up a studio and start throwing pots again."

"Throwing pots?" Phil asked vaguely.

"Not against the wall, you know. I shape the clay on a wheel. It's called 'throwing,'" she said.

Phil shrugged. "I see. And then will you sell them?"

"No. I know they'll find good homes. A pot usually doesn't stay with me long. I just want to play with the clay."

"I never thought of that," Phil said. "Doing it because you want to."

"I figure life's too short not to do everything I want." Jaz's laugh took Phil by surprise.

"Well, I'd best be going," he said. "See you."

"Goodbye and thank you," Jaz called after him.

When he went into the house, Phil found Catherine talking to the canary.

Turning to him, she asked, "How'd the fishing go?"

"Three nice ones in the fridge."

"How about fish and potatoes for supper?"

"Sounds good," Phil answered. "You know, that Jaz is a nice woman. Turning her shed into a pottery studio so she can make pots for the fun of it."

"Oh, really?" Catherine asked absently, busy with Blue.

Phil watched her for several moments.

"Say, there's something I've been meaning to ask you. Where'd that canary come from? I mean, how'd it end up in your pocket that day?"

Catherine turned and looked him straight in the eye. "Do you really want to know?"

"Yes." He guessed he had better be willing to hear whatever she said.

"I stole Blue from one of the 4-H children at the fair."

"You what?"

"I stole it," Catherine repeated.

"But why?"

"I saw that little bird, and, all of a sudden, I felt squished nearly to death. I couldn't breathe. Know what I mean?"

"I guess so," said Phil. That breathing thing he could relate to anyway.

"At the time, I can tell you, saving Blue was a matter of life and death. I can't explain it so don't ask me."

"I won't, don't worry," Phil said.

They stood awkwardly for a moment; then Catherine turned back to the cage and chirped to the bird. Phil watched her for a moment, then quietly walked through the house and out onto the porch.

He turned what Catherine had said over in his mind but he couldn't make sense of it. As far as he knew, Catherine had never stolen anything in her life. And the feeling of being 'squished'? That was what she said. He closed his eyes to make it easier to feel what that might be about. Bumping up against that feeling in himself—forty-seven years of being responsible for food on the table, roof overhead. Yes, he knew the feeling of 'squished'. Made him itchy in his skin. He stood up abruptly, walked back through the house and took his truck keys from the rack where they hung next to the back door. He drove down the street.

Catherine watched him go from the window and wondered.

In a few minutes, Phil was back. Catherine watched him climb out of the truck carrying a small brown bag. When he came in, he pulled a cuttlebone out of the bag.

"Bought this for your bird. Thought it might perk him up."

Catherine watched while Phil opened the cage door and clipped the cuttlebone to the cage where Blue could peck at it.

"Thank you, Phil," she said. "Thank you."

* * *

Catherine always walked the same route to the mom and pop market at the corner of Washington and Pine. How many times had she walked to the store? Hundreds, she supposed, yet she had barely noticed the big field on the corner of Monroe and Pine she walked by each time. Yet on this day in September, on her way home, she found herself gazing over this place full of scrawny weeds and wild bushes in the throes of Indian summer.

Catherine picked her way amongst the weeds, poked the toe of her sneaker into a crack looking for receptive earth, but the field was as unyielding as a stone. She set her groceries down, picked up a stick, and scraped the soil aside grain by grain.

How did she come to be here? Today, without forethought, she had stepped off the sidewalk into this field which, she realized, was the only vacant land left in the neighborhood, a shaggy growth surrounded by orderly yards and houses laid out in grids. Catherine stood and turned full round, suddenly hearing the clamoring of the blackberry bushes entwined in the hedge along one of the yards bordering the field. Then the quiet pleas of the sycamore tree back in the corner tugged at her. "Why are they shouting at me?" she wondered. Feeling confused, she retraced her steps and walked home.

In the next weeks, every time she walked by the field, she averted her eyes, perhaps whistling or humming. Yet never did she walk past without glancing into the clamorous din which she heard, yes indeed, she heard even above her whistles or humming. She tried driving, but all the time she scolded herself. "Don't be silly. Plants don't make noise. Maybe it was the wind. How can I drive four blocks for milk? I should have my head examined."

So in the end she walked. One day it occurred to her that she might step into the field and listen. What could it hurt? With her first step, the dither died away. By the time she stood in the center of the field, she was surrounded by silence. The noise of all the earth seemed to be swallowed up by the dirt beneath her feet.

Catherine listened, for sound had begun again. It began as a murmur; rose and fell always upward. She became ears alone, settled into the earth, herself a weed, why not, or at most a gnarled sapling, grown old but not tall. A breeze pushed against one side of her face. The sun warmed her forehead.

Did no one walk by and wonder at seeing her there? Catherine looked down at her hands softly resting among the folds of her old cotton dress. She looked at the plants holding onto life in the dry earth yet full of song. She turned tenderly away from the field and started home. But as she walked the uneasy feeling returned.

"Why you old fool," she said to herself. "Weeds singing. What next?"

Still feeling uneasy when she got home, she opened the front door and walked through the house. She dropped her sack of groceries on the kitchen table, but then she noticed that, though these last weeks Blue had begun to relax in the bottom of the cage, now he huddled into himself as tightly as ever.

"Poor little one. You just start to feel safe, and I come banging in. I'm sorry." Catherine cocked her head and so did the little bird. They looked at each other, and Catherine smiled.

Blue looked at her steadily.

"You're my friend, and so is that old field," she murmured.

The next time she walked to the store, she brought flower seeds and a little augur in her pocket. It was early October, not ideal, but she couldn't help it. Among the roots of the sycamore tree, she dug tiny holes and dropped in seeds, careful not to disturb the plants that survived there.

* * *

The day after Catherine planted the seeds, the weather turned chilly and it started raining.

"Goodbye, Indian summer," Phil said when she stepped out on the porch to watch the rain.

"Don't you sometimes plant grass seed in the fall and let it winter over?" Catherine asked him.

"Far's I know, that's the best time. Seed comes up in the spring. Just have to cover it with a little straw."

"Do we have any straw?"

"Out behind the garage, I think."

That afternoon when the rain stopped, it was chilly and clear. Catherine carried a sack of straw over to the field and spread it among the sycamore roots. She pictured the seeds sleeping all winter and waking up in the spring like the grass.

* * *

Later that week, Phil gave up on the porch and resumed sitting in his old chair in the den. Fishing magazines and *National Geographics* replaced the street as entertainment. His thoughts accompanied him when he moved inside.

He hadn't gone to the lake again as he had planned. In fact, other than finishing the fall clean up, he had done as near to nothing as a human being can.

CHAPTER

4

The morning after the rain, Catherine pulled the fall bulbs out of the refrigerator and planted them in the beds in the front yard. She set a few of each kind aside. Late that afternoon she carried a sack of bulbs to the field and planted them in the rain-softened earth under the sycamore tree. She dug deep, placed each bulb at the right depth, tamped the earth down, humming all the while.

Catherine continued walking in the county park, more leisurely now, musing. Hickory nuts were strewn on the path by shaggy barked trees with leaves turning gold. Sugar maple seeds spun through the air. Oblong acorns of the white oak lay in heaps. Leaves fluttered down, red, yellow, gold. One day she caught herself standing still, marveling at the carpet of leaves covering the path.

"Meandering, that's what I'm doing. Barely keeping myself moving along." She was amused with herself. That old whip which she had used for so long to keep herself moving didn't seem to be coming to hand.

"In fact," she said aloud, "I'm happy. Who would have thought?"

Finding a late patch of gooseberries, green with a red blush, she filled her jacket pockets to make a pie for Phil. Phil. Here she was, thinking of him. He liked gooseberry pie.

When she came home, Catherine made the pie and put it in

the oven. Phil smelled it baking and came into the kitchen carrying his magazine. Catherine was making lunch.

"That smells good. What is it?"

"A surprise. You'll see at lunch."

Phil went back to the den.

He was still in the den when Catherine took the pie out of the oven. She put it on the table in the screened-in back porch to cool and called Phil to lunch.

"Still smells mighty good in here," he said. "What is that?"

"After lunch." Catherine set Phil's plate down in front of him. "Tuna sandwich, dill pickles, chips." She ticked them off on her fingers like a waitress.

Catherine did her usual bustle around the kitchen. She ate her sandwich from a plate on the counter next to the sink.

As Phil finished his sandwich, Catherine slipped out to the porch. She carried the pie in and set it down in front of Phil.

"Gooseberry pie," she announced.

Phil couldn't believe it. He hadn't seen pie except at Thanksgiving for a long time. Gooseberry, no less.

He glanced at Catherine quizzically.

"I picked the gooseberries in the park . . . . I thought you'd like a pie," she finished lamely.

Catherine cut the pie and gave Phil a big piece. She served herself a piece and sat down across from him.

Phil savored each bite. When he finished, he said, "Mighty fine pie."

Catherine was mortified to feel herself blushing. She busied herself clearing the table. Phil went back to the den.

* * *

After lunch Catherine went out to admire the beds where she had planted the bulbs. She saw Jaz in the yard next door. An impulse took her, and she walked to the hedge.

"Hi," she said. "How's the shed coming along?"

"Fine, thanks. Nearly done with it." Jaz stood on her side of the hedge.

"Phil tells me you're a potter."

"Yes, I had a studio and taught ceramics in a high school outside Boston. I miss it."

"You're from Boston?" Though Jaz had been her next door neighbor for two years, Catherine didn't know where she had moved from. She had never asked.

"Yes. I grew up there. I have a few kids coming next week to work with clay. The shed's nearly ready. I'm just waiting for some tools and a few colors of my favorite glaze."

"You have kids coming over? Are you teaching classes?"

"Not really. I talked to the art teacher at the high school. They don't have much of a ceramics program, so I offered to open the studio."

"That's a really nice thing to do. Will the parents pay you or the school?"

"No pay. I'm doing it for fun. I like having a busy studio," Jaz said. "Besides I miss the kids."

While they were standing at the hedge talking, Catherine gazed over at Jaz's front garden, saw that it was neatly raked and trimmed back for fall.

"I've been planting my fall bulbs," she said. "I have some extras and if you'd like to have them . . . ."

"That would be great," Jaz answered. "I've been planting, too. I found some deep purple tulip bulbs. They're almost black, really. Would you like some?"

They went their separate ways and exchanged bulbs over the hedge.

* * *

The phone rang. Catherine answered. It was Stan, one of Phil's old friends from Kent, who had retired the same year as Phil. Catherine's stomach sank as it always did when Stan called. He would want Phil to go down to the Jug and play darts. After being with Stan, Phil seemed even more withdrawn and distant. Phil had barely seen Stan since he retired, and Catherine was happy about that.

Catherine had seen Stan at company Christmas parties, and he seemed a likable enough guy. But for some reason when he and Phil had been out together, Phil came home morose and, she was certain, angry. She only knew he was angry because she could feel it.

Only once had she said to Phil: "You're angry."

His face had reddened, and he had said in a slow quiet voice, "I am not angry."

She had never mentioned it again, for she had been suddenly afraid of this man who always appeared calm. Phil's calm had been one of the things that had attracted her in the beginning. She had wanted to be calm like Phil. And now she felt that, although he had been better at concealing his anger, he was capable of it, too.

She called Phil to the phone, and he went off to play darts. Catherine was left with her thoughts. A few months earlier she would have busied herself with one task or another. Tonight she wandered the house, circling back to where Blue sat in the bottom of his cage. She sang the old hymns to him, hummed when she didn't remember the words. In the bright kitchen she noticed that the little bird's blue color had a decidedly greenish cast to it. She guessed that one day Blue would be as yellow as any other canary.

Blue had also become more relaxed. He hopped about the bottom of the cage in search of seed, but had yet to light on the perch waiting above the cage floor. Nor, that she knew of, had he made a single sound. Catherine hoped she would hear him when he finally sang—and she was certain he would sing one day. As she went about the house, she listened for Blue, and this evening, she spoke her usual reassuring words to Blue. "It's going to be all right. Just you watch. It'll be fine."

A moment of happiness caught Catherine. Early mornings when she was a little girl, she would hear the dawn birds sing and feel the thrill of the day ahead. It had been a long time since she had felt that way. When her babies were born she was amazed how tiny, soft and sweet they were. For that time only, she had felt that deep happiness again. Now, after all this time, a hint like a promise flickered in her.

* * *

Driving to the Jug, Phil thought about Catherine. The appearance of the canary was strange enough, but then one day he had been driving downtown and passed a vacant lot where a familiar figure caught his eye. There was Catherine down on her knees digging in the weeds and looking like she had sprouted up out of the earth. He had driven past, looking straight ahead. He hadn't mentioned it either.

Phil was pleased that Stan had called him. He missed being at work where he could talk with his buddies off and on all day. When he had been elevated to quality control supervisor, responsible for testing and analyzing samples of every shipment, he found more time to talk than when he had been stuck in an office shuffling papers. The feed mill was like a big family.

He was especially glad that Stan had called today. He had been feeling restless. A night with the guys was just what he needed. It would settle him down, and he could relax for the winter which, from the look of the streets, was nearly upon them. When he climbed out of his truck, he turned his collar up against a biting wind.

Stan and Hank were waiting for him. He liked Stan, perhaps because while Phil spoke only after great deliberation, Stan was always ready with a quick remark. He thought Stan was really sure of himself, and he admired that. Stan was what Phil's dad would have called a "Hail fellow well met," always shaking your hand, slapping you on the back, greeting you so loudly that everyone in the room turned around.

Stan had opinions about everything, too. Phil listened and said little. When he went home after being with Stan, he needed to be alone for a while. Stan was about all he could take in one day.

"Hey, Phil," Stan called across the crowded room as soon as Phil opened the door. "Over here."

A couple of games were already underway at the dart wall.

Stan grabbed Phil's hand and shook it. "Great to see you, old buddy." He pounded Phil on the back.

Chair tilted against the wall, hands clasped on his belly, Hank sat, watching.

"Hi, Phil," he said.

"Hi fellas," Phil said.

"Have to wait for our game," Stan said. "Not like the old days. These guys," he poked his head in the direction of the cluster around the dart wall, "are in the middle of a tournament. Can you believe it?"

"Wonder how we'd do in a tournament," Phil said. "Bet I've lost my edge."

"Come on," Stan said. "We could beat these whipper snappers. Think of all the experience we have."

"Well, I don't know," Hank said. "My eyesight's not what it used to be, and my hands aren't that steady either."

"Mine either." Phil held out a hand and watched the slight tremble, thinking not about darts, but about tying flies for next fishing season.

He sat down and watched the dart scene.

"How's retirement?" Hank asked. Hank was still working.

"Not too bad. Spent the summer on the porch watching the world go by."

"What?" Hank looked surprised. "I distinctly remember your telling me they'd never drag you off the lake. What happened?"

Phil was thoughtful. "I don't know," he said at last. "I just don't find myself out there as much as I thought I would. How about you?"

"I wondered where you were," Hank said. "I'm out there most weekends like always. You can bet I'll be out there everyday once I retire."

"I hope you do it," Phil said. "As for me, it's a pretty peaceful life. Isn't that what retirement's for?"

"Not for me," Stan said. "I found a chatroom for stamp collectors, and we've been swapping stamps and chatting up a storm. And I play a round of golf at sunset everyday. Weather's turning now, but we should have a few more good weeks. Then, I don't know. Some of the guys in the 19th Hole play backgammon over beers, and I'm thinking of learning to play."

"Sounds good," Phil said. "Guess I'm not much for being out with a bunch of guys. I'm more of a loner, I guess."

"Hey," Stan said. "Dart game's breaking up over there. Our turn."

They moved over to the dart lane and pumped quarters into the machine.

Stan picked up a dart and practiced his technique. "The boss has arrived," he said. "I feel good tonight."

Suddenly, it became important to Phil to win the game.

"We'll see who's boss," he said to Stan. No, he didn't play golf or make friends on the Internet. He hadn't been out fishing much either. Darts came easily to him though. With his good eyes, he hoped he could still put Stan and Hank away.

Hank looked amused but said nothing.

Halfway through the first game, Phil had built a solid lead. He began to relax. Standing back with Hank watching Stan deliberate over his next throw, Phil said, "You'll retire soon, won't you? What then?"

"One more year and I'll be done," Hank said. "Then I think I'll go to Arizona for the winters. Plenty of fishing in the mountains. What about you? Why don't you and Catherine move somewhere warmer?"

"Catherine won't even move out to the country with me," he thought. Aloud he said, "Nope. Can't think about leaving here. This is home."

Stan finished his throw and came to join them. "I've been thinking of buying a little place in Florida. Really could play some golf down there. Not enough to do in the winter to keep me busy here."

"Yeah, I know what you mean," Phil said. "I've already done all the projects stacked up around the house. The first year, I replaced the gutters and painted the trim; then last spring I cleared out the attic and reorganized my workshop. That's about it."

"House chores," Stan said. "I can take them or leave them alone. Mostly I leave them alone."

They finished the first game and played another. Phil won both, but as he drove home, he felt neither lighter nor more settled as he had hoped.

* * *

When Phil came home, Catherine was asleep. Coming in the back door he tiptoed over to Blue's cage. The kitchen was dimly lit by the streetlight on the corner, and the cage, covered by the yellow tablecloth, was the brightest thing in the room. Phil lifted the edge of the cloth and peered in at the little bird who watched him sleepily.

"Hello, little fella," Phil said softly. "How are you this fine evening?"

Blue looked at him steadily but said nothing.

Phil got ready for bed. He slipped under the covers, careful not to disturb Catherine who always slept at the far edge of the bed. He lay on his back and stared at the ceiling. After several minutes, he turned on his side and fell asleep.

* * *

Early the next morning he drove his truck out to his mother's house. When Phil pulled into the dirt lane and parked in the back by the barn, he felt a nostalgia for Catherine from the early days. He hated the feeling and shook his head as if that would clear the thoughts and the feeling.

Coming in the back door he found his mother in the kitchen, still in her robe, making coffee.

"Now isn't this the best surprise," she said. "I was hoping I'd see you today."

Phil hung his jacket on the peg and hugged his mother. He marveled at how tiny she had become. Like a little bird. He thought of Blue and hugged her gently. It was good to see her.

"Now you're here we'll have a proper breakfast. None of my usual coffee and toast."

She gathered eggs, bacon and a pitcher of orange juice from the refrigerator.

"Will you bring the bread from the pantry?"

Phil sat at the enamel-topped kitchen table, the same one he had eaten breakfast on as a boy. In one side was a catch-all drawer where Phil remembered hiding his report card one time for several weeks.

The plate his mother put in front of him was full, and Phil ate happily.

"Mmmm, this is good," he said around a bite.

"Better'n you have at home, I'll warrant," his mother replied.

Phil pretended he hadn't heard. The fact that his mother had never liked Catherine had been more of an inconvenience than a source of pain for him.

For the first several years of their marriage, Catherine had done everything she could to persuade his mother to like her— baked pies, bought gifts that strained their budget, invited her to go shopping. His mother had responded to none of it, and finally Catherine gave up. After that, Phil had visited his mother alone or with Amanda and Jack in tow.

Now, Phil listened patiently as she talked about how the wind whistled through the old house. How her arthritis was so bad it was all she could do to leave the bed in the morning, let alone, dress. How Maxine's girl came to help her three days a week and did more talk than work, mostly talk about her boyfriend which Phil's mother surely did not want to hear.

Maxine was Phil's younger sister whose daughter, Lucy, had taken a course in practical nursing. Phil and Maxine hired Lucy to help her grandmother with bathing, washing her hair, some of the heavy housework, and any other thing Grandma needed. Lucy worked two other days at the convalescent hospital in Mount Pleasant.

Phil kept a pretty close eye on his mother. She was in full possession of her faculties, and sometimes he was certain she had more energy than he did. When his mother's complaints wound down, Phil pushed back his chair.

"Thanks for breakfast. I'm going out to the barn to see if I can find that old birdcage we used to have."

"What do you want with that old thing?"

Phil didn't want to say.

"I said, 'What do you want with that old thing?'" his mother repeated loudly.

"Thought I'd take it in for Catherine. She has a canary now, you know," Phil replied.

Phil's mother said nothing. She just looked at him. She didn't have to say much to make her point. Phil rummaged in the barn looking for the old bamboo cage. When he found it, he saw, with a little fixing, the old cage would house a little bird just as well as it had sixty years before.

He put it in the back of the truck and drove home. An unusual sound caught his attention. Startled, Phil realized that he himself was whistling as he drove into town.

When he came home he was relieved to find the garage empty. After quickly hosing the old cage off, he carried it down to the basement to his workshop. Some glue, a ball of jute twine and, half an hour later, the birdcage was ready. Phil carried it upstairs and set it next to the wire cage in which Blue was now hopping around the floor.

Then he went into the den and puzzled over an article about some new-fangled fly fishing method. Phil faithfully followed the trends. You never know. A better method than the one he had developed over the course of fifty years might miraculously appear.

When he heard Catherine come home a short while later, he stopped reading. He could hear her setting bags down on the kitchen table. Then he pictured her turning and seeing the bamboo cage. All sound had stopped. It was as quiet as a Quaker meeting while everyone communes with God.

When Phil heard Catherine calling him, Phil busied himself with the fishing article.

"Phil."

Catherine stood in the doorway. Phil looked up to find tears shining on her cheeks. He smiled, just a slight deepening of the lines around his eyes. No one who hadn't known him for fifty years as Catherine had would have detected it.

"Oh, Phil. The cage is beautiful. Where did you find it?"

"We used to have a bird at the Home Place when I was a boy, and I thought the old cage might still be around. I found it out in the barn. Thought you might like it for your canary."

This was a long speech for Phil. He turned back to his magazine.

Catherine stood watching him for a few moments, then went back to the kitchen and hummed as she transferred Blue to the new cage. She started by wondering why Phil had done this kind thing for her. Then she realized that why he had brought her the cage was not her business really. That he did it was enough.

While putting the groceries away, she thought this might finally be the year to have a winter garden. Perhaps Phil could build cold frames and set them up where the leaf vegetables had been. She would plant spinach, lettuce, arugula and kale—all the greens left in her seed basket.

* * *

The next morning Catherine was in the garden when her cousin Sarah arrived in her beatup truck.

Sarah had left the Mennonite community and lived in an old farmhouse west of town. She was tall and willowy, and no one had thought she would be strong enough to rebuild the old place herself, but she had worked day after day until it was done. She propped up the sagging porch roof and replaced the steps, rewired the place herself and repaired the plumbing. She sanded, caulked and painted the whole place inside and out—all white.

Sarah had also spent days on end in the old apple orchard on the land. She pruned and cultivated, thinned the young apples, and sprinkled chicken manure 'tea' in the drip line under the branches. The first year the apples had been a disappointment. They were nearly as wizened and holey as ever, but by the second year they showed distinct improvement. Every year since they were bigger and rounder, and were now nearly blemish free. At harvest time each year, Sarah brought Catherine a basket of apples.

Catherine stripped off her gardening gloves and hugged Sarah. She knew that Sarah had always loved her. Sarah had never spoken of it. In fact Catherine was puzzled by it. What had she done to win Sarah's love?

Now Sarah's slow steady smile spread over her peaceful face. Catherine smiled back.

"Chilly day," she said. "Putting the finishing touches on the garden. I'm going to ask Phil to build some cold frames so I can try a winter garden."

"I have a stack of old windows," Sarah said. "My brother, Floyd, wrote that he had a bunch so I drove out to Wayland for them. I only needed a few to replace the ones that broke in that hailstorm last spring. Phil's welcome to come and take them."

"That's great, thank you. I'll tell him to come out."

"I brought you some apples." Sarah lifted a basket of apples from the truck bed and set them on the ground. "This is the best year yet."

Catherine picked up an apple, polished it on her sleeve, and took a bite. "Mmm . . . Delicious. When the weather starts growing colder, my hands want to peel and slice apples."

"Just in time then," Sarah said. "The temperature's been dropping. I'll bet we'll see frost any night now."

"I'm almost done putting the garden to bed. I brought the rose geranium in yesterday. I'm going to make apple jelly flavored with geranium leaves. I found a recipe online."

"Sounds exotic," Sarah said.

"I'll bring you some. Do you have time for a cup of tea?"

"That would be nice. Where do you want these?" Sarah picked up the basket of apples.

"Let's put them on the back porch." Catherine held the door while Sarah brought the apples in.

Catherine and Sarah sat at the table with their tea.

"Nothing like fresh veggies in the winter," Sarah said. "I love clearing the snow off the cold frames and seeing the green under the glass."

"I can't believe it's taken me so long to do this. Even ordered seed a few times for a winter garden, but never used it," Catherine said. "How's your place?"

"I have eighteen chickens now. There were seventeen eggs this morning. Milking three nanny goats, too. I put up a sign to sell my extra eggs and milk."

"Aren't you lonely out there all by yourself? No one to talk to?" Catherine asked.

Sarah shrugged. "I love it, really. I don't know why, but I'm not lonely. Too much to do, I guess."

"I can't imagine it. I'd probably be driving into town all the time just to see if it was still there." Catherine thought of how lonely she had been even with someone to talk to.

When Sarah left, Catherine took out the canning kettle and jelly jars. She made a list for the market—sugar, pectin, new jar lids.

Then she fell to thinking again. Maybe she and Phil would have been better off in the country after all. This was not a new thought, but the idea of living so close to Phil's mother without Phil as a friend gave her the shivers. She had been adamant that Phil could work in town, and they could rent a house. After his time in the Merchant Marine, he took the job with Kent and settled into the house on Cherry Street with her and baby Jack. He never mentioned living in the country again.

***

That afternoon as Catherine was putting the last of the jars in the canning kettle, Phil came in. Jars of jelly lined the counter, catching the sunlight.

"Smells fruity in here," Phil remarked, sniffing. "Smells like flowers, too."

"Apple jelly flavored with rose geranium," Catherine said. "Want a taste?"

"Think I'll stick with grape," Phil said. "Where'd the apples come from?"

"Sarah stopped by with a bushel," Catherine said.

"Nice," Phil said vaguely. "How's Sarah doing out there?"

"Good," Catherine replied. "Say, I want to put a winter

garden in. I've been meaning to ask if you'd put together some cold frames for me. Sarah has some old windows you could use for the tops."

"I could do that," Phil said. "I'll call Sarah right now." Catherine noticed Phil's voice sounded brighter.

Catherine carried a bucket full of apple peels and cores out to the compost pile. By the time she turned to come back inside, Phil was on his way out.

"Off to Sarah's," he called. "If I go for the windows now maybe there will be time to start the frames before dark."

As he backed the truck out of the driveway, he turned to see Catherine standing on the back porch, bucket in hand, cheeks flushed from making jelly in the hot kitchen. The sun shone from behind her, lighting the soft silver hair which framed her face. He waved awkwardly. She raised her hand, he thought almost reluctantly, and waved back.

***

Catherine was peeling potatoes for supper when she heard Phil's truck. A little while later she heard hammering. Looking out the window she saw hay bales stacked next to the garden. A pile of old windows leaned against the garage. Phil was removing nails from a stack of lumber.

During supper, Phil talked. "I stopped at Johnson's Hardware for some heavy-duty hinges and handles." He put a bite of parsley buttered potatoes and London broil on his fork. "That way you'll have no trouble opening the frames for planting and picking."

Catherine's eyes shone, and Phil was busy with his food. "What are the hay bales for?" she asked.

"Sarah suggested them. I'll edge with bales to insulate the garden evenly. When you open the frames, the windows will rest on the bales."

"Sounds like you've thought of everything," Catherine said.

Phil finished eating and stood up. "I'll make the frames in the basement. Thought I'd do that tonight so I can put them together in the morning."

"Thanks, Phil. Thanks for doing this."

"Don't mention it." Phil went downstairs.

Phil spent the next morning assembling the cold frames. By lunch time, two rows of neat glass-topped frames were in place.

Catherine pulled out seed packets of lettuces, spinach, chard, kale, arugula and cress. She spent the afternoon preparing the soil and planting. When she was done, she closed the glass tops and admired the garden she and Phil had made.

CHAPTER

5

The phone rang early.

"Hi Mom," Amanda said, "I'm in a rush, but I just realized I have to take Benny up to Iowa City after school, and Jessica has a dance class."

"Busy day," Catherine said.

"Aren't they all? I know you don't like to ferry the kids around, but can you pick Jessica up at school and take her to class? She'll have all her gear in her backpack, and she can change at the studio."

"I'd be glad to," Catherine said. "And what about a snack?"

"That would be great."

That afternoon, Catherine picked Jessica up and handed her an exact replica of the lunches she had prepared for Amanda and Jack when they were kids, paper sack and all.

Jessica weighed the sack in her hand. "Gee, Gram, you'd think I hadn't eaten all day."

"Well, I know kids are hungry after school."

Jessica ate the whole lunch.

The dance studio was on the second floor above Johnson's Hardware. Catherine pulled up in front. Originally, only an Arthur Murray studio, these days ballet, tap and jazz dance were taught there, too. Jessica was taking jazz dance.

"Do you want me to come in with you?"

"Mom never does."

"Ok then." Catherine was careful to keep the disappointment out of her voice. "When should I come back?"

"About 5:15, I guess. Class is supposed to be over at five but it usually goes over."

"Don't hurry," Catherine said. "I'll just wait for you right here."

Catherine watched Jessica until she could no longer see her through the glass door as she climbed the stairs to the dance studio. She sat in the car thinking about how many years she had wanted to learn to dance.

"Now I'm much too old," she muttered. "Just too old."

She checked her watch—enough time for a walk around the shorter loop trail at the park. As she drove south through town, she noticed that the trees were beginning to take on their naked winter look.

Autumn was her favorite season, but Catherine loved winter with its big skies glimpsed through the bare arms of the trees. She liked to think of nature resting, gathering itself for the surge of spring. What she didn't like was the transitions between seasons. Now when a few scraggly leaves clung to the trees so they didn't have their pristine nakedness of winter, she felt impatient with it all. Then, as she turned the car into the park drive and remembered that the end of winter was a long way off, she thought, "Well, I might as well make the best of it."

The day was clear and the air brisk, and Catherine picked some of the tiny red hips of the wild roses along the leafy lane. They were pithy and mildly sweet. She liked finding things to eat in the wild.

The path climbed out of the woods and up into a high meadow. A white birdhouse sat on a tall pole leaning against the blue sky. The pole leaned at such an angle that Catherine wondered if birds would be too discouraged to make it home. She thought that perhaps they could build their nest in the angle.

When she picked Jessica up at dance class, Catherine gave her a small bunch of rose hips from which she had carefully removed the thorns. After taking Jessica home, Catherine drove back into town.

Blue Canary

That evening after supper the phone rang. Jessica had left a most important textbook at dance class, her mother hadn't come home from Iowa City yet, and her dad was at his lodge meeting.

All of this said in a rush.

"Would you like me to see if the place is open and find your book?" Catherine asked. "I could drive it out to you."

"Thanks, Gram. If I don't have that book, I can't do my homework."

When Catherine turned the corner onto Jefferson, the windows above the hardware were glowing. Something was going on up there. When she opened the door to the studio, she heard music floating down. She hesitated. How many times had she thought of climbing these stairs?

When she reached the top, she could see into the studio through the windows that separated it from the reception area. A ballroom dance class was in session. Several couples moved about the floor while a man in a black tuxedo, a pair of castanets clasped above his head, twirled slowly in the middle of the room, intently watching the dancers. To one side of the room Catherine saw a young boy sitting by an old record player watching the record spin.

Catherine looked around the reception area for Jessica's book. Not there. As she opened the door to the dance studio, the music stopped. Catherine stepped onto the dance floor. Chairs lined the wall on the far side of the room, and there she saw a fat book. Jessica's, no doubt. She nodded to the instructor.

"Sorry to interrupt. My granddaughter left her math book here." She pointed to the book.

"No problem at all." He held out his hand. "Dennis Moore."

Catherine took his hand. "Catherine Lewelling."

Catherine had never seen a more elegant person. His black shoes shone like a mirror. Catherine was surprised that she didn't feel awkward. What did she feel? Natural, she guessed. Natural as anything.

She recognized one of the dancers. What was her name? Marian Greenley? Yes, that sounded right.

"Hello. Marian?"

The woman looked at Catherine. "Ah, yes, Catherine. Your Jack played baseball with my Randy, didn't he?"

"Yes, that's it," Catherine said. "So you're taking dance lessons."

"Yes, I just started. You should join us."

"Oh, I don't think so. Well, I have to take this book out to my granddaughter. She has homework to do, and it's nearly bedtime already."

"Well, nice to see you again," Marian said.

"Nice to see you, too."

Driving the book out into the country, Catherine puzzled. At least half the dancers had appeared to be nearly her age, and there was Marian Greenley.

The next day Catherine looked the Arthur Murray phone number up. She underlined it in black ink. The day after that she looked the number up again and picked up the phone to call. The day after that she actually made the call and found that yes, there was a beginner's ballroom dance class on Tuesday nights and no, it was still early enough in the session to join.

"Please send a check to hold your place," the receptionist said.

Catherine sent off her check the same afternoon.

* * *

While waiting for Tuesday, Catherine had more doubts about her age. After sitting a while, she would have terrible cricks in her knees when she stood up. Walking, she sometimes noticed her feet scuffed the ground unless she made a conscious effort to pick them up. Looking at herself, Catherine had to admit her face had begun to show wear, and she was on the verge of being an old woman. She had seen old women who appeared to her beautiful, softened by the years—she could see it in their faces— gentle. She doubted she would ever be one of those.

Tuesday evening Catherine chose a soft full skirt that would swing out when she twirled in the arms of her partner.

She called in to Phil as he sat reading in the den, "I'm off to dance class. See you later."

"Dance class?"

"Yes, above Johnson's Hardware where Jessica goes."

"Well, have fun."

Here was something new. Catherine and a dance class. First, the canary. Then, Catherine on her knees digging in a vacant lot. Now, a dance class. What next? Even thinking about it was too much, and Phil dismissed Catherine from his mind as he had done regularly for most of his life. He went back to reading about what this particular author claimed was the best trout stream in America.

While Catherine was gone, Phil went to check on Blue twice. When he stood in front of the refrigerator looking for a snack, he could feel the canary watching him.

Phil liked to have something to eat to keep him company during his evening reading. Summers he read little, finding that sitting on the porch was pleasant enough to pass the time, but he was actually looking forward to having winter coming on, glad to have the time and his cozy den to read in. Of course, there had been plenty of winters that seemed way too long even for Phil, but mostly he liked the contrast between the warm house and the frigid outdoors he could see out the window.

He put together a six-layer sandwich from what appealed to him in the refrigerator, and when he turned around, he saw that Blue was, indeed, watching him. He went over to the cage and began whistling, a low melodious tune he had whistled while working on the farm as a boy. The same tune, over and over, rippling out phrase by phrase, quiet so the little bird wouldn't be frightened by it. Blue watched him but remained silent. He no longer appeared afraid. His feathers no longer looked straggly and had begun to have a slight sheen.

Since he'd retired and time stretched out, Phil read the entire newspaper and scanned every page of his fishing magazines. He liked being indoors during the winter. Any morning now he expected to see frost on the grass when he woke up.

The coming of winter also pointed ahead to fly tying in February and March. Not that he had fished much these last couple of years, but he was going to start again. This next year would be different, and he would begin by reading about new flies and fishing methods. Then, hopefully, he could make some spectacular flies that would catch more fish than ever. Phil had a reputation at the Walton Club. He was known for the ease with which fish were attracted to his flies and the great number of fish he pulled from the lake and the nearby Skunk River.

* * *

During the drive to the studio, Catherine found herself more curious than scared, more excited than shy. She arrived early and climbed the stairs. She watched the other dancers arrive and recognized a woman she had seen a couple of times recently while walking in the park. They had said hello but not stopped to talk. Now the woman came over to Catherine.

"Hello. I'm Fern Barclay."

"Catherine Lewelling. I've seen you out at the park. Nice to meet you."

"Yes. We just moved here from St. Louis. My husband, Frank," she indicated a man across the room, "and I have wanted to take dance lessons for a long time. A good way to meet people, too."

"Welcome to Mount Pleasant," Catherine said.

Most people in the class were in couples, but there were a few singles. Catherine found herself paired with a man in his forties named Whit, short for Whitney, he told her. Whit was taking lessons because he had found himself in several situations because of his job where he wished he had known how to dance. He hadn't learned to dance as a kid and hoped he would like it.

Catherine liked the feeling of moving in rhythm with the music, liked the feeling of her partner's hand at the small of her back guiding her. Whit counted the rhythm aloud in small whispers which Catherine found strangely comforting.

At the end of class Mr. Moore said someone wanted to join,

but they could only take him if another woman joined so he would have a partner. Catherine immediately thought of Alice. She knew that Alice liked to dance but no longer had the chance. Now with Marvin so frail, Catherine expected Alice to say no, she couldn't possibly. Yet Catherine felt certain Alice would join them nonetheless.

As Catherine was leaving, Fern asked if she would like to walk in the park sometime. They exchanged numbers, and Catherine drove home exhilarated.

Phil had already gone to bed. She made a cup of tea and sat talking to Blue. He cocked his head as if he were really interested in what she had to say.

"You're good company, little bird," she told him.

* * *

The next morning Catherine made a crumb cake and took half over to Alice's. Since Phil had retired, she rarely saw Alice. They used to take turns having coffee a couple of mornings a week after their husbands had gone to work.

After Marvin's stroke he couldn't be left alone for fear he might try to do something by himself. And now that Phil was home all day, Catherine didn't feel right sitting in the kitchen with Alice, talking about who knows what when Phil might hear what they said. Not that Catherine had secrets, really. Just that she and Alice were used to complaining a bit, and she would rather not have Phil hear that.

Catherine walked down the street to Alice's house. She mused about when she had last been over here. Must have been shortly after she brought Blue home from the fair.

Alice opened the door to Catherine's knock. "What a nice surprise," she said. "That smells divine. Your famous crumb cake, I hope."

The talk was different today. Alice talked about Marvin, and Catherine listened sympathetically until Alice was done.

Then she took a breath and said, "I know you'll want to say no when you hear about this, Alice, but I want you to come to dance class with me next Tuesday."

"Dance class? What about a dance class? You must be joking."

"You know I've wanted to learn to dance practically forever," Catherine said. "There's a ballroom dance class downtown above Johnson's Hardware. I went to the first class last night and it was fun. I know you'd love it."

"Marvin and I used to roll back the living room rug and dance—jitterbug mostly, sometimes a slow dance. I love to dance, but now? I can't even imagine it."

"I know you'd love it though," Catherine said again.

"What would I do with Marvin?"

"Have a babysitter."

"A babysitter? I couldn't do that to him."

"He wouldn't even notice. You told me he's off to bed by 7:30. That's when the class starts. You can have him tucked in at 7:15. Not only that, I bet Marvin would be just fine that you were going out."

"Well, maybe you're right. He does often say he wishes I didn't have to stay home all the time."

"See? So now all you need is a sitter."

"What about Ada Blanchard? She's alone now and might like to have a bit of extra cash." In a moment Alice had it worked out.

Catherine would pick Alice up at 7:20 on Tuesday. They would be just on time.

* * *

The next day Phil went down to the pet store and came back with a little birdseed bell. He hung it in the cage just above the perch. As he hung it he whistled the tune of the night before. Blue didn't back away from Phil's big hands as they reached into the cage to fasten the bell.

"There, little guy. Now you can hop up on that perch and eat some seed."

Blue looked silently at Phil.

* * *

Catherine stepped out the back door to check the weather. Chilly. She pulled her jacket on and felt in the pockets for her gloves. Then she headed to the park for her walk with Fern. Fern was leaning against her car when Catherine arrived. A small dog with silky gray fur pulled at its leash and sniffed around her. Fern waved.

"Hi. Come and meet Schnappsy," she called.

The little dog strained at the leash and wagged its tail. As she crossed the parking lot, Catherine noticed for the first time how tall and angular Fern was. She was much taller than Catherine.

Catherine squatted down to greet the dog, then stood to greet Fern. "I don't know why I always say hello to dogs and babies first. How are you?"

"Good. The air's crisp. Feels good."

"I like it, too."

They took the long loop, including the Lazenby and Willets trails. They walked briskly with Schnappsy pulling at the leash first to one side of the trail then the other. Finally Fern gave up trying to manage him and took the leash off.

She turned to Catherine. "He minds me really well. He'll come when I call."

"What breed is he?" Catherine asked.

"A Schnauzer," Fern said. "That's why we call him Schnappsy. It fits him, don't you think?"

"'Schnappsy.' Yes, it does." She noticed that the Schnauzer looked like Fern. Same silky gray hair. Thinking back on dance class, she recalled that Fern and her husband looked alike, too. Not quite as much as Fern and Schnappsy, but still a striking resemblance.

They walked silently on a thick carpet of fallen leaves. Pale late autumn sunlight poked through the nearly bare branches overhead. The woods were so beautiful there was no need to talk much. They walked along the bank above the river and crossed the four bridges.

When they returned to the trailhead Catherine said, "A nice walk. Schnappsy must have covered ten times the ground we did, though he doesn't look tired."

"No, but he'll sleep all the way home and go back to sleep as soon as he's in the house. Here, Schnappsy." Fern snapped his leash back on.

"I really enjoyed our walk," Catherine said.

"Yes, lovely. See you at class Tuesday."

* * *

That afternoon Phil went out to rake the last of the leaves. A few stragglers stayed on the maple trees, but they would have to fend for themselves when they fell. This was the last raking Phil was going to do this year. Period.

Phil liked raking leaves because it gave him time to think. The rhythmic raking pulled thoughts out of the past. He had finished one side of the front lawn and was starting on the other when he heard his name called.

"Hello, Phil." Jaz stood on the other side of the hedge.

"Hello."

"I saw you were out raking and decided I might as well finish mine, too. It's better to have company to do this kind of job, I always think."

"Yep," Phil said. "These are the last of them, thank heavens."

"I hate to see them go," Jaz replied. "I love the fall."

"So does Catherine . . . and well, actually, I do, too."

Phil returned to his raking.

When they had each finished raking the leaves into piles, they leaned on their rakes by the hedge.

"Raking leaves takes me back to the farm when I was a kid. My mom kept a lawn around the house, and since I was the oldest, I was expected to rake."

"It must have been fun living on a farm. I've always wished we'd lived in the country instead of the city when I was a kid."

"Well, I guess it was ok. There was always plenty of work though."

"But how great to be outside—working or playing."

"Working, playing, nearly always in trouble. On raking days I spent more time jumping in the piles than hauling them behind the barn. I'd rake a huge pile in under the oak tree, climb onto

the lowest limb—which was still pretty high up—and jump.
I was always climbing something I could jump off of. I don't
know why."

"See? We didn't have enough yard to rake or any trees big
enough to climb," Jaz said. "You were lucky."

"I don't know about lucky," Phil said, "but for some reason,
I always wanted to climb as high as I could and then jump.
Though I don't remember it, my mother tells me I climbed to
the top of the fridge shortly after I learned to walk, and when
she found me, so she says, I jumped from there onto the metal
cabinet where she kept the sugar and coffee. Then, as soon as I
was big enough to climb the ladder to the hayloft, I'd push a big
pile of hay out the door and jump into it. My mom was always
worried I'd break my neck and deserved to, but I never hurt
myself once. The only time I climbed higher than I could
manage was to the top of the windmill. I couldn't find a way to
come down."

"What did you do?"

"I shouted for my dad until he came and talked me down.
He couldn't climb up there himself. He was too heavy for the
thing."

"That's quite a picture," Jaz said, laughing. "How old were
you?"

"I don't know, about seven, I guess."

He noticed that Jaz was stomping her feet and swinging her
arms. The afternoon had turned chilly.

"Do you have a compost pile?" Phil asked.

"It's back behind the pottery shed."

"We could load the leaves on my big tarp and haul your pile
out there."

"Good idea, thanks."

* * *

After Phil lugged his own leaves to the compost pile behind the
garage, he went back to thinking about climbing to high places
and jumping off. Once, on a dare, he had set out to walk across
a beam under the roof in the high school gym. He shinnied up a

rope and swung himself up on the beam. He had pictured himself walking along the beam like it was a tight rope with the guys below holding their collective breath. Instead, he had walked only as far as he could reach the tie beams and hold on, then he crawled the rest of the way to the far wall, touched it and crawled back, sliding down the rope to the floor. Bill and the other guys had been silent the whole time, watching him. He would never back down on a dare. And he certainly wasn't going to tell Jaz this story.

Coming out of the garage after stowing the tarp, he saw her walking toward him carrying two steaming mugs.

"Hot cider. The perfect thing for a day like this."

"Thanks." He cradled the cup between his gloved hands.

"The leaves were pretty this year," Phil said. "What you said earlier about living in the country—the timber pasture behind our house was beautiful this time of year. I still miss it. Catherine never wanted to move out there, though."

"I guess the country's not for everybody."

"That's true. Can't say as I blame her, really. It certainly was easier to be in town so the kids could walk to school and have their friends nearby. I always hoped that we would move out to the country when they were grown. There's a clearing in the woods out at the Home Place where I thought we'd build a house. It's about half a mile down the road from my mother. Catherine would rather stay here."

"Must be disappointing for you, though."

"I've made my peace with it. It's not like we're in the city here, anyway. There's plenty to do outside with the gardens. Especially this time of year."

"That reminds me," Jaz said. "I have a runaway sapling blocking my kitchen window. It's too big for me to handle by myself. Do you think you'd be able to help me sometime?"

"It's nearly dark now. How about tomorrow morning?"

"Sure. How about ten o'clock?"

"Sounds good. Thanks again for the cider." Phil handed Jaz the mug.

"And thanks for the company."

Blue Canary

***

The next morning the grass was white with frost. By nine o'clock the frost had melted, but Phil and Catherine each took it as a sign. Winter was coming.

Phil collected his loppers and a small tree saw from the garage so he could help Jaz trim her sapling. Catherine bundled into a warm jacket and scarf and headed out for a walk to wish the field a good winter.

When she arrived at the field she heard a low hum, louder than before and lower in pitch. The field seemed to be keening to itself, perhaps a lullaby as it settled in for winter. Catherine pictured the seeds and bulbs she had planted waiting through the winter. As she took her usual route between bushes on what had nearly become a path, she felt, rather than heard, a subtle change in the tone of the field's song. It rose to greet her and she found herself, as before, humming along. After a few minutes she retraced her steps to the sidewalk.

"Well, goodbye then." She felt awkward. "I don't walk this way much in winter, but I'll see you."

Catherine walked home.

CHAPTER

6

Catherine looked forward to dance class all week. On the evening of the last class before the holiday break, Catherine picked Alice up as usual. Alice came down the walk carrying a pie and a small package tied with a silver bow. Catherine reached across to open the car door for her. Alice slid in carefully, balancing the pie, and handed the package to Catherine.

"What's this?" Catherine asked.

"Something little," Alice assured her. "I'm grateful you invited me to go to this class with you. I'm happier than I've been in a long time."

"It's more fun for me, too. I like going together."

"Even Marvin seems happier. He told me he likes to see me having fun again."

Catherine looked down at the package in her lap.

"Go ahead," Alice said. "Open it."

Catherine untied the ribbon and took the paper off the box. Inside was a silver angel on a stand. She turned the angel, and it twirled to the tune of "Hark! The Herald Angels Sing." She touched the angel's delicate wings and held it up so the light from the street lamp shone off the silver.

She turned to Alice. "I don't think I've ever had a nicer present."

They hugged in their big winter coats across the front seat of Catherine's car.

When they parked the car, Catherine pointed up to the dance studio. A candle shone in every window.

As they crossed the street their breath frosted in the air. The week before, Mr. Moore said he would bring a wassail bowl to the next class. Catherine assumed it must be a drink of some kind. Everyone else would bring something for the party after class.

Walking up the stairs they could smell pine. Mr. Moore and Mark, who minded the record player, had decorated the studio with pine boughs, red bows and candles. The bright overhead lights were off. Catherine felt festive.

Class began. The dancing felt dreamy to Catherine. Her cheek brushed the navy wool of Whit's blazer. She found herself thinking about Phil. "I wish he were here." Then she thought, "This is good the way it is."

After dropping Alice off at her house, Catherine drove by her field. It sat silent. She whispered, "Hello," and drove home.

* * *

The week before Christmas began with a huge snowfall and the weather turned frigid. A week of below zero temperatures, and the farm ponds froze solid. Phil, content to be indoors, meandered from the den to the kitchen and back. Catherine looked out the window and wished for a break in the weather. Unable to go out for a walk, she felt restless.

The cold spell broke on Christmas, and the day dawned sunny and clear. Catherine made her chestnut dressing, stuffed the turkey and had the bird in the oven by eight o'clock. She set out for a morning walk before coming home to prepare the rest of Christmas dinner. Amanda, Tom, Jessica and Benny were coming to eat about two. Traditionally, they had Thanksgiving at Amanda's and Christmas dinner at Phil and Catherine's.

Catherine guessed most Christmas dinners around town would revolve around a ham, but when she was growing up on the farm, she loved the piglets best. Since childhood she had never been able to eat ham or any other meat that came from a pig. Besides, in her opinion, you could never have turkey, stuffing, mashed potatoes and gravy too often anyway.

Catherine made pecan pie because it was Tom's favorite. His parents had been killed in an automobile accident the year after he and Amanda were married. Amanda gave Catherine his mother's recipe for the pie, and, though she almost never used recipes, Catherine always followed it exactly. Catherine liked Tom. He was easy to have around, hugging her when he arrived and asking if he could help with anything.

Dinner and the exchange of gifts went smoothly. When they left, Catherine gathered the wrapping paper from the gifts and clipped the Christmas cuttlebone Phil had bought for Blue on the side of the cage. She gave Blue fresh water and covered the cage for the night.

* * *

The day after Christmas was even warmer with temperatures rising above freezing. Catherine drove out to the park and took a long leisurely walk. The trail was muddy, and she was glad she had worn her boots. Even though the week before had been bitterly cold, there was still color enough to capture her. Small clumps of snow dotted the forest floor under silent evergreens. The trail led out of the woods into bright sun shining through a field of yellow grasses. A red cardinal flashed through the trees above her, and then she spotted the female, not as bright as the male but lovely in her muted brown shot through with red.

She drove home feeling dreamy and at peace. She heard the phone ringing as she opened the back door. Catherine usually found the ring a friendly sound. This time it sounded sharp and strident. Catherine rushed to answer without taking her coat off.

"Mom?" Amanda's voice was barely recognizable on the other end of the line.

"What happened?" Catherine heart skipped a beat and a kaleidoscope of possibilities swirled before her.

"Benny fell through the ice. I'm at the hospital." Amanda broke down completely.

"I'll be right there," Catherine said and hung up.

"Phil?" She rushed to the den. "Come on quick. Benny fell

through the ice. Amanda called from the hospital."

Without a word, Phil grabbed his jacket and followed Catherine through the door. He backed the car out of the garage and reached across to open the door for her.

"My God," she said. "I haven't prayed in years but I'm starting now. I've never heard Amanda sound like that."

"I'm praying, too," Phil said. He drove unseeing to the Henry County Health Center on the other side of town. They found Amanda in the waiting area of the emergency room, wrapped in a hospital blanket and pacing. When she saw them come in the door, she rushed to them and they held her while she sobbed.

"I'm so scared."

Catherine stroked her back and her hair. "It'll be all right, you'll see." She didn't know if that was true. She felt totally helpless in Amanda's distress.

"Tom's out in the field somewhere. They're trying to track him down. I want him here . . . ."

Phil, too, felt overwhelmed by the pain in his daughter.

"Come on, sweetheart," he said gruffly. "Let's go sit down, and you can tell us what happened." He gently took her arm and led her to a row of chairs along the wall.

The story poured out of Amanda in a rush. "Jessica spent the night at Melinda's, and Joey Blake came over to play with Benny this morning. They wanted to take Goldie and play out and, since it had warmed up, I let them. A little while later I heard Goldie barking and Joey came pounding on the back door. He was so hysterical all he could do was point toward the river. I knew immediately what must have happened. I closed the puppy in the house, grabbed a shovel that was leaning against the barn and ran through the pasture into the woods. Joey couldn't keep up, but I just ran as fast as I could to the river. Ice stood about ten feet out from the bank on each side. I looked down the river both ways but there was no sign of Benny. Joey caught up to me and screamed at me, pointing . . . .

"He ran along the bank and I followed to a place where an animal trail goes down to the water. The ice had broken through in that spot but I couldn't see Benny. Then, as I looked, I saw a bit of red under the ice. It was Benny's scarf."

Amanda began sobbing again.

"You don't have to tell it," Catherine said.

"No, I want to," Amanda said, then burst into tears again.

She calmed down enough to continue the story. "The next part is a blur. I must have slid down the bank somehow, broken the ice with the shovel, and dragged Benny out and up onto the bank. I don't remember. I laid him down on the bank. He was blue. When I touched him he was cold. His eyes were open and staring. I knew he didn't see me. I thought he was dead. I wanted to shake him and tell him to wake up, but I didn't. I put my cheek to his mouth and nose. He wasn't breathing. I put my ear to his chest. No heartbeat. Panic would have had me in another second but I said 'No! This is my baby and I will save him.' Thank God I had to take CPR training for school.

"I screamed at Joey. Poor kid, he was nearly as blue as Benny. I told him to go call 911, then bring me the box of garbage bags from under the kitchen sink and the blanket off Benny's bed. He took off running. I didn't have a jacket on but I was wearing a sweater. I stripped it off and laid it over Benny. I'd had him in my lap but I had to do CPR so I laid him on the ground with my sweater under him and over as far as it would stretch. I kept saying, 'Come on Benny, you can make it.'"

Amanda paused as if seeing it all over again, then continued, "I went into automatic. First, check to see that his airway is clear. Second, start CPR. He must have held his breath when he fell in. There was no water in his lungs."

Amanda was telling her story on automatic, too. All at once, Catherine realized Amanda was probably in shock. She was shivering under the blanket, but she kept talking. She didn't seem to notice when Catherine draped her own jacket around her shoulders on top of the blanket.

"By the time Joey came back, I was in the CPR rhythm. Joey doubled the blanket and together we moved Benny onto it. I covered him with plastic bags from the neck down and wrapped one around his head. I put my back to the wind and huddled over him to protect him. I sent Joey back up to the house to lead the paramedics down to us as soon as they arrived. Thank God they could drive in almost all the way.

"There I was with Benny. I thought he was dead." Amanda swallowed a sob and continued. "In CPR they told us about cold water near drowning and hypothermia. I prayed and cried and breathed for him and pumped on his chest. I willed him to survive.

"I heard the ambulance long before it arrived. When the paramedics arrived, they took over CPR. I was in their way but I was afraid if I moved, Benny would die. Finally he started to breathe on his own, and one of the paramedics said he could detect a pulse, slow, but steady. They lifted Benny onto a stretcher and carried him to the ambulance. I rode in back with Benny, and Joey rode up front to the hospital. I called Mary, and she came to pick Joey up.

"I don't know what those kids were doing down there. Benny's been told a hundred times to stay away from the river. And he always has until now."

Amanda stopped talking abruptly and looked vaguely around. "Oh God, when will they come?"

"What did they tell you?" Phil asked.

"They said because he is young and the water was so cold he has a better chance," Amanda said. "And they figure he was only in the water about twenty minutes, so that helps some, too. They said they have to stabilize him, but it's been hours and I want to see Benny now." Her voice ended on a high, nearly hysterical note.

"I know, honey, but right now I think we ought to help you out of those wet clothes and give you something hot to drink. You're freezing." Catherine had been holding Amanda's hands while she told the story and they were finally warming up.

"I'll go ask at the nurse's station to see if they know anything," Phil offered.

He walked over to a glassed-in enclosure on the far side of the waiting room and talked to the nurse behind the desk.

Phil came back and sat down next to Amanda. "They say it'll be a little while yet. They're bringing his core body temperature up. It was 86 degrees when they took his temperature in the ambulance. They have to bring it back up slowly, so they're using warmed oxygen and a warm saline IV. They say he's doing pretty well with it. So we just have to be patient. He's in good hands."

"Phil, would you mind running home and bringing Amanda some dry clothes?" Catherine asked. "I can't leave her."

"I'll be right back."

* * *

While Phil was gone, Tom arrived from the site he was surveying. Amanda collapsed in his arms, and Catherine told Tom briefly what had happened. As she finished, Phil walked in carrying Catherine's blue overnight case with dry clothes for Amanda. Catherine asked the nurse for a room where she could help Amanda change out of her wet things.

Tom took off his heavy jacket and dropped it on a chair. He ran his hand through his hair and started pacing.

Phil took Tom by the arm and led him to a chair. "Waiting's the most difficult part."

"I guess you're right," Tom replied. "I wish there were something I could do."

"I know," Phil said. "Maybe you could bring Amanda something hot to drink."

"Good idea. She's freezing," Tom agreed.

He went down to the cafeteria for some hot tea.

When he came back he found Amanda, Catherine and Phil sitting in a row. He joined them and they sat quietly, Tom holding Amanda's hand while she sipped her tea. The hand holding the cup trembled. Phil and Catherine sat side by side.

Catherine was thinking about Jack, about the time when he was two and started running down a steep hill at the playground. She had chased him, calling him to come back, but he ran on, his little legs barely keeping up with themselves until he ran right into the street. A car was driving past, and a passerby on the other side of the street reached into the street and, grabbing Jack by the wrist, swung him up in the air and out of danger. The whole incident had taken only a few seconds. When Catherine had seen Jack in the path of the car and knew she didn't have time to reach him, she pictured her baby being hit by the car. For years afterwards she flashed on that scene in dreams and waking. That had been merely a moment of fear. A near miss but over in a moment, too.

She thought of Amanda, whose moment of fear was being stretched over hours of waiting. Amanda had had the presence to break the ice and pull Benny out of the river. She had thought to cover him with the plastic bags to keep him from losing any more heat. She had done CPR until the paramedics arrived. Catherine recognized the feeling in her chest. She was in awe of her daughter. She looked over at Amanda and wished the doctor would come. Amanda hunched in the chair, pale and tense.

Phil was thinking, too. He was surprised to realize that his daughter was a strong and brave woman. He realized how little he knew her, and yet how proud he was of her. She had faced a test that Phil was almost certain he himself would not have been equal to. She had kept her wits and done, he intuitively felt, the right things for Benny. And what if Benny died? Phil remembered Benny as a newborn cradled in Amanda's arms. He glanced at Amanda and his chest tightened.

He pictured Benny as a baby, all pink and gold. Benny had the rosiest cheeks and the deepest dark eyes Phil had ever seen. Round and rosy, that was Benny. Phil felt dazed and looked for a long moment around the room, at the rows of chairs against the wall, the health-related posters on the walls, the four of them huddled in their chairs, waiting.

Then the thought of Jack rose in his mind. Something could happen to Jack even now. He remembered Jack as a small boy. Phil used to put the children to bed after supper. He would read them each a story in their beds and tuck them in. Jack had been his little boy, and Phil had felt an unspeakable tenderness toward him.

The separation of these past years, how many was it now? Twenty-five? No. Twenty-eight. The tenderness twisted inside him and he felt deeply ashamed. Ashamed of Jack and ashamed of himself for fathering such a son. Phil felt responsible for Jack's being gay. He knew he hadn't been much of a father. He and Jack hadn't seemed to have much in common, and he had been busy working and having some time to himself. He knew those were lame excuses. His deepest shame was in not accepting and loving Jack no matter what.

* * *

Finally the doctor came in.

Tom squeezed Amanda's hand and they rose to meet him. Catherine and Phil followed them.

"I'm Dr. Wade." The doctor shook hands with Tom and Amanda, and continued, "We have good news. Your boy's stable and semi-conscious. You can go in to see him for a few minutes, but we need to keep him quiet. We're going to airlift him to the trauma center in Iowa City. The helicopter's standing by."

"Thank God," Tom said.

"And he's going to be all right?" Amanda asked.

"As long as he continues the way he's going. There's some risk of heart arrhythmia or other complications, so we're going to keep monitoring him closely and fly him up to Iowa City as smoothly and quickly as possible."

"Can we ride up with him in the helicopter?" Amanda asked.

"No, I'm sorry. But if you drive up there you'll be there soon after the helicopter arrives." The doctor turned to Amanda. "I want you to know, Amanda, that you saved your boy's life."

Amanda started crying again. Tom hugged her.

Dr. Wade put his hand on Amanda's shoulder. "Come on," he said. "Let's go and see Benny."

"Can Mom and Dad come too?" Amanda asked.

"Just parents," the doctor said.

Amanda turned to Catherine. "Mom, would you call Mary and tell her Benny's going to be all right so Joey won't worry?

And call Jessica at Melinda's. Tom, do you remember Melinda's last name?"

"Peters, I think it is," Tom said.

"Thanks, Mom," Amanda said.

Amanda and Tom followed the doctor through the swinging doors which led to Benny. Catherine went to make the calls in the hall. When she was done, she joined Phil in the waiting room.

"Jessica wants to come up to Iowa City with us," Catherine said. "She's scared and needs to be close."

"I'll go pick her up now and come right back for you."

Catherine sat back and rubbed her eyes. She was feeling the strain. After a few minutes Amanda and Tom came back into the waiting room. Catherine stood up.

"He's not blue anymore," Amanda said. "And he looked at me. Oh, Mom . . . ."

She buried her face in Catherine's shoulder. Catherine held her tight for a few moments. Amanda pulled a handkerchief out of her pocket. "What a baby I am. I can't stop crying."

"Well, we'd better start up there," Tom said. "I want to be there as soon as we can."

Catherine said, "Your dad's gone to pick Jessica up. She wanted to come along. We'll follow you up there as soon as he comes back."

"Thanks, Mom." Amanda hugged Catherine.

"It's good that Jessica's coming," Tom said. "I want her with us."

"Take it easy on the way, Tom," Catherine said. "At least it's a straight road."

"Don't worry," Tom said. "We'll be careful."

* * *

When Phil returned with Jessica, they found Catherine watching for them from inside the big glass doors of the Emergency Room lobby. She walked quickly to the car. The sky had clouded over again and the temperature was dropping. It was early afternoon but it seemed much later. Catherine sat in the back seat with

Jessica who was worried and upset. Phil drove up Route 218, a road he had taken so many times he didn't have to think about driving.

Instead he thought about Benny. How close he had come to losing this grandson whom he barely knew except to ruffle his hair and shadow box with him when they saw each other. He had never considered Benny's life seriously at all. How quickly it could be taken away. Then there would be no chance to spend time with Benny, to really know him and love him. The question he asked himself was, "What am I going to do about it?"

Following the printed directions they had been given by the nurse in Mount Pleasant, Phil easily found the trauma center in Iowa City. Amanda and Tom were in the waiting room. Jessica met her mom halfway across the room and started crying. Amanda held her.

"Mommy, is Benny going to be all right?"

"Yes, he's going to be all right."

"Really?"

Doubt flickered on Amanda's face. Then she stood a little taller and said firmly, "He's going to be fine."

"Have you seen him yet?" Catherine asked.

"Yes, they let us see him as soon as we arrived. He was already settled in a room. He has tubes everywhere," Amanda said.

Tom hugged Jessica to him. "He smiled a little when he saw us. What a relief."

"How long do they think he'll have to stay?" Phil asked.

"They don't know, but they think about ten days. Apparently complications can still occur and they want to keep a close eye on him," Amanda said.

"Can we see him, do you think?" Phil asked.

"Maybe in a little while, they said," Amanda replied. "They're still rewarming him. His temperature's rising but it's not back to normal yet, and they have him on oxygen and a heart monitor."

"He has his own nurse who's watching him all the time," Tom said. "Why don't we go down to the cafeteria for a bite to eat? Maybe we'll be able to slip in to see him for a few minutes after that."

"Let's check with the nursing station before we go," Amanda said.

She and Tom crossed the big room to the desk. When they came back Amanda looked more like herself. "The doctor has just been in to see him and is pleased with his progress. They'll call us in the cafeteria if there's any change."

⁕⁕⁕

At supper, Amanda asked Catherine and Phil if they would take Jessica home with them. She and Tom would stay the night in Benny's room. The hospital would wheel two cots in for them.

"Of course," Catherine said. "We'd love to have Jessica with us."

"I hope they let us in to see Benny before we leave," Phil said. "I need to see him with my own eyes before I'll believe he'll be all right."

When they came back up to the trauma center, the nurse had good news.

"If he continues to improve, we'll be moving him to pediatrics in the morning."

"Can we go in to see him now?" Amanda asked.

"Two at a time," the nurse said. "And stay only a couple of minutes."

"Can I go in first, Mom?" Jessica asked.

Amanda looked questioningly at Tom. He nodded. Amanda led Jessica through the big doors into the corridor where Benny's room was.

When they came back a few minutes later, Jessica was crying quietly again. "He looks so small with all those tubes coming out of him . . . . But he squeezed my fingers when I held his hand."

Phil and Catherine went in to see him next. It was all Catherine could do to smile at little Benny. To her he looked as helpless as Blue had done when she found him at the fair. As she smoothed the hair back from his brow, she glimpsed the infant,

Benny, as she had seen him for the first time, new and full of promise. She turned away to keep him from worrying at the tears which rose in her eyes.

Phil stepped next to the bed and took her place. "Hi little buddy," he said so low and deep it might have been a thought and not spoken at all.

But Benny heard it, and his eyes sought Phil's. "Grandpa," he whispered.

"It's going to be all right, Benny," Phil said, the tears starting in his own eyes. But he didn't turn away. He let Benny see. "I'm going to visit you as often as I can while you're here. Yessir, everything's going to be all right."

He reached down and kissed Benny's forehead. He stood looking down at his grandson, then reached out one more time and held Benny's head in both his big hands. "I love you, Benny boy."

Catherine, standing near the door, watched. She felt moved by the tenderness she saw between Phil and Benny. Suddenly she felt like an intruder and looked away.

* * *

By the time they left the hospital, it was dark. On the way home all three of them were quiet. Jessica lay down on the back seat with Catherine's wool scarf rolled up under her head and fell asleep. Catherine watched the road with Phil, a gentle silence between them as he drove them home.

On the drive, Phil thought of how close they had come to losing Benny. Something Jaz had said to him once came back to him. "This is the only time we have. We'd better make the most of it." The weight of the years fell around him like heavy snow. Pain fell against itself. First, the pain of nearly losing Benny; then, the pain of being separated from Jack. Then, in a moment, the pain of closing Catherine out of his heart became nearly unbearable. He didn't know if he could keep the car on the road.

Then, out of the corner of his eye, he saw that Catherine herself was watching the road. He knew she was doing it for him, to keep him company on the drive. Suddenly he felt very small. In a flash he realized that his not forgiving her had been hurting him more than had her betrayal and her not being willing to live in the country after all. And that was so many years ago. Now if he didn't do something soon he might lose her—or he might die himself—before he had a chance to make up to her for all the lost years. Phil reached over and patted Catherine awkwardly on the knee. She looked at him, but he was busy driving. She looked to the road again.

At home, Catherine took out her softest flannel nightgown for Jessica.

When she was ready, Catherine asked, "Would you like me to brush your hair?"

"Nobody's done that since I was tiny." She handed Catherine the brush from her backpack, and Catherine sat behind her on the side of the bed and, counting a hundred slow strokes, brushed Jessica's long hair.

* * *

Early the next morning, Phil stepped out on the porch. Fresh snow had fallen in the night. Round white caps sat on the bushes in front of the house. He could hear the snowplow the next street over.

Amanda called while they were having breakfast. Benny had slept well. The doctor continued to be pleased with his progress.

Right after breakfast Phil put on his coat and boots and went out to shovel the walks and driveway. He liked shoveling snow. His mood this morning was lighter than it had been in a long time. For no reason he could think of, Phil felt foolishly happy. He found himself looking ahead to a bright future for the first time in years. What the future would require of him for its brightness he didn't know and didn't right now wish to investigate. But somehow, just as he had known Benny would be all right, he knew that, without any doubt, he, Phil Lewelling, would be all right, too. And that his life would have a happy ending.

So it was with particular pleasure that he shoveled the walks this morning. When he was done, he stood on the porch and admired his work. He heard the storm door slam at Jaz's house, and there she was, bundled up and pulling on her gloves.

"Good morning, neighbor," he called. "Lovely day."

"Yes, it is. Time to clear the walk."

"It's cold so the snow's light. I'll help you and we'll finish in no time."

"You don't have to do that. I don't mind shoveling, really."

"No, I'd like to do it," Phil insisted. "Come on."

A few minutes later they were done shoveling and both walks were clear.

"I haven't seen you for a while. How was your Christmas?" Jaz asked.

"Christmas was fine, but yesterday we had a terrible scare," Phil said. "Benny, our ten-year old grandson, fell through the ice into the river and nearly drowned. Our daughter, Amanda, saved his life. They airlifted him to Iowa City and we drove up."

"That's awful. You must have been terrified," Jaz said. "How is he doing?"

"The doctor says he's doing pretty well. There's a chance he may have complications yet, so he'll be staying in the hospital for at least a week. They want to keep an eye on him. I expect we'll be spending quite a bit of time driving back and forth."

"Is there anything I can do?"

"Not that I can think of, thanks, but we'll let you know."

"How's Catherine taking it?".

"We have Benny's older sister, Jessica, with us, so that helps. Well, I'd better go in."

"Thanks for helping me with the walk."

"You're welcome. See you."

* * *

Just before they left, Amanda called from the hospital again. Catherine answered the phone.

"Mom, Benny hasn't said anything yet. I'm really worried."

"But he spoke to your dad last night," Catherine said. "All he said was 'Grandpa,' but that's something. Don't worry, honey. Benny's going to be fine. You'll see."

"Do you really think so?"

Amanda sounded like a little girl, and Catherine suddenly felt fierce in wanting to protect her.

"Don't worry. It's going to be all right," Catherine said. "We thought we'd come up now and bring Jessica with us. What do you think?"

"I want you to come as often as you can. Dr. Barnes says Benny will have to be here for at least a week, probably longer. I want to stay here, but Tom will go back and forth. He has a couple of sick days he can take off from work, but that's all."

"Jessica can stay with us, if you want."

"That would be a relief. I woke up in the night worrying about her. If she's with you, I won't worry half as much."

"We'd like to have her. It's been quiet in the house for a long time. We'll see you a little later, honey. Do you want anything from the house?"

"Could you could bring my toothbrush? It's the blue one— and maybe some undies and Benny's old bear?" Amanda paused, and then said, "I love you, Mom."

When Catherine hung up the phone, she felt like singing. She crossed the room to Blue's cage and sang a wordless little tune to him. Then she told him they were going to Iowa City and he would be alone for the day.

"Not as long as yesterday, though, when we rushed off without telling you. This time we'll be back early." She checked his water dish and sprinkled some fresh seed on the floor of his cage. "Bye bye, Blue."

Blue cocked his head and looked at her.

* * *

When they arrived at the hospital, they found that Benny had been moved to the pediatrics ward. Amanda and Tom were with him, and, since he could still only have two visitors at a time, they sat down to wait.

"I'll tell them you're here," the nurse offered.

When Amanda and Tom came out to the waiting room, they looked tired. The doctor's report that morning had been a relief.

Benny's heart was steady and strong, his lungs were clear, and his body was maintaining a normal temperature.

"Benny's talking," Amanda said. "Right after I called you, he told me he loves me."

Phil and Jessica went to visit with Benny, and Tom went to call his office. Catherine and Amanda hugged each other.

"Would you like to go for a little walk?" Catherine asked. "You could probably use some fresh air."

"Well . . . , just a short one. I don't want to be gone long."

The hospital was set among huge old trees. Sunlight sparkled off the new snow. The two women linked arms and walked along in silence into a quiet residential neighborhood.

"How are you doing, Amanda?"

"I am really tired, but I'm so relieved. Thank God Benny's going to be all right. Dr. Barnes says there's every reason to think he will recover completely. I've been so scared."

"I know, honey. But you've been brave. I can't imagine what I would have done in your place yesterday. I'd probably have lost my mind. You kept your head and saved Benny's life." After a few moments she continued, "I love you, and I'm proud to be your mother."

"Thanks, Mom. I love you, too."

"When I think about you're pulling Benny from the river and giving him CPR . . . ."

"To tell the truth, I don't know how I did it either," Amanda said. "Now all I want is to take him home."

"With him doing so well, I bet it won't be long."

"I am worried about Jessica, though," Amanda said. "I'll be up here all week, and I'm missing her vacation."

"We'll try to keep her entertained."

"I'm so busy with teaching, and Benny being younger seems to take up any extra time I have. Jessica doesn't tell me about her day when she comes home from school any more. We planned to do some things together this week, and I hoped we'd talk about what's going on with her. Now we won't be able to." Amanda stopped and looked down at her feet. "I'm worried about how she'll feel about my spending the whole week with Benny."

"Of course she understands that Benny needs you now," Catherine said. "She won't mind."

"That's probably true, but this is a crucial time for her," Amanda said. "She's fourteen, and I'm afraid if we don't connect now, I'll have lost her."

"There's always time." After thinking about it a moment, Catherine added, "At least I think so."

"You really do?" Amanda asked. "She seems like she's spinning out there somewhere in space, and I can't reach her."

"Right now you have your hands full with Benny. Maybe Jessica and I can do some of the things you'd planned."

"But I wanted to do them with her." Amanda sounded discouraged. "She wanted to make a skirt to wear on the first day back to school, and she wanted to try some new cookie recipes. I guess its better for her to go ahead and do them with you than not at all." Amanda pulled away from Catherine and kicked at the snow on the sidewalk. "We've walked a long way. Let's go back."

They crossed the street and walked back to the hospital in silence. As they waited for the elevator to take them to Benny's floor Catherine said gently, "Those projects were especially for you and Jessica. Maybe it would be better to save them."

"No, she'll be disappointed if she has to wait," Amanda said. "Besides, I'm relieved she'll be with you. We'll think of other projects for spring break."

The elevator came and they pushed the button to Benny's floor.

CHAPTER

7

The next week was busy. Every day Phil drove to Iowa City to spend the day with Amanda and Benny.

Catherine stayed at home so Jessica could work on the sewing project. The first morning they went shopping and found a pattern for an easy skirt that Jessica liked. She picked a small flowered print fabric with a navy background, and when they came home, Catherine helped Jessica lay the pattern out and cut the fabric.

That evening Phil offered to take Jessica to the movie in town. Catherine was content to stay home. She was in the kitchen putting the last of the supper dishes away when the doorbell rang. There by the porch light she saw Jaz holding a casserole dish between two potholders.

"Well, hello," she said. "Come on in." She held the door open and Jaz carried the casserole into the house.

"Phil told me about your grandson," Jaz said. "I thought you might not have time to cook, so I made some chicken cacciatore. I didn't finish it in time for supper tonight, but I think it always tastes better the second day anyway."

"Thank you so much. Come on out to the kitchen and we'll put it on the stove to cool. Would you like a cup of tea?" Catherine asked. "I was just about to have some myself."

"Thanks, that would be nice."

Jaz looked into Blue's cage. "This can't be a little canary, can it? I've never seen a green one before."

Catherine laughed. "Actually, he used to be bright blue. Green is an improvement."

"Blue? Is he sick?"

"No. Somebody's idea of a 4-H project. He's still not himself."

"I'm surprised he's not sitting up on his perch."

"He's not quite up to that yet, but hopefully, soon. Next thing we know he'll be singing."

"I think he's watching me," Jaz said. "Look at that."

"I hum to him so he'll be used to singing. Someday he'll surprise himself and out will come a song. We just have to wait and see."

Catherine brought two mugs of tea and a plate of cookies to the table.

"How's your grandson coming along?" Jaz asked.

"Better each day. Phil was up their today, and Benny was sitting up in bed. He still has tubes stuck everywhere, but he's well on the way to becoming his old self."

"You didn't go up today?"

"Benny's older sister, Jessica, is staying with us. She wanted to make a skirt to wear the first day back to school. Tomorrow I'll pull out the sewing machine and help her sew it."

"I admire people who can sew. I'm not much with a needle myself."

"I grew up sewing. How's your pottery studio coming along?"

"Thankfully I finished it before it was too cold. I've thrown my first pots and have a few young friends working with the clay."

"The high school kids you told me about?"

"They're on vacation, but they want to come anyway."

"Isn't it freezing out there?"

"I put in a wood stove. It's a small place and stays plenty warm with the fire."

"It's lucky you can do it."

"By the time I moved here I had done everything I needed to do—had one career as a potter and another as a teacher. Now I can do what I want."

"I wish I could do that." Catherine gazed at Blue. "I'm always busy but I don't accomplish much."

"I like to feel needed," Jaz said. "That's why I built the studio. Did you have a career?"

"Not really. I raised the kids. After they left home, I kept on cooking and cleaning house. Same old thing."

"I guess it is a little late for a career," Jaz said, "but what do you like to do?"

"That's just it. I don't really know."

"What about your dreams through the years . . . or when you were a kid."

"My mom was a Mennonite, and when she married my dad, her family acted like she died. They never spoke to her again. Being a kid in my house wasn't easy."

"How many kids?"

"Nine, a pretty big tribe."

"I thought the Mennonites were a cloistered community," Jaz said. "How did she meet your dad?"

"Mother was the oldest daughter—just like me—and as part of her chores, she had to take the eggs to the market and check at the post office for letters from the cousins in Pennsylvania. My dad worked at the market, and one day Mother came in with the eggs and saw him. Later that day, she saw him again at the post office. They started talking and that was it—they couldn't stay apart. They would meet secretly while my mother was out doing chores."

"Did your mom tell you that story?"

"Actually, it was my dad. My mom and I never talked much. My dad was always recuperating from one ailment or another. The rest of the kids would feel they had better be quiet and not disturb him. As for me, I'd always end up in his lap. I just loved being close to him, and one day, I asked him how he and Mother met and fell in love."

"What happened when her family found out?"

"I don't know much about them, and I think she kept the worst of it even from Daddy. We only went over there once. Grandfather died, and Mother found out and insisted we go. We drove up to the house, and Grandmother came out to meet us. We stood on the edge of the lawn. Grandmother stood in the doorway and didn't even look at Mother. I could feel my mother's shame in my own body. It was a waking nightmare."

"How old were you?"

"About nine, I think. Grandmother didn't invite us into the house. We just stood there. After a few minutes of dead silence, she called across the lawn to us kids, making it clear that if any of us wanted to come back into the fold, so to speak, she would welcome us. You can imagine, none of us did. I, for one, hated her."

Jaz had been leaning forward following Catherine's every word. Now she leaned back and sighed. Catherine sat back, too. They were silent for a long moment.

Jaz spoke softly. "Well, my family was about as mixed up as yours. We didn't really have roots, no Mennonites, you know. But there were strong pulls just the same. I was born with a congenital heart defect. At that time nobody knew what to do about it, and babies born with it struggled for a few days and died."

"But you didn't die," Catherine said.

"No, I didn't. My dad was a family doctor on the West side of Boston. He was on the board of Mass General and knew a doctor who was willing to take a risk on me. Dr. Jasper operated on me, and here I am."

"It sounds like a miracle," Catherine said.

"That operation is routine now, and babies generally thrive. The problem was that I was the first. My mother watched my every move. She'd wrap me up and sit me in a big stuffed chair by the window. I'd watch the other kids play, but I wasn't allowed to go outdoors."

"That sounds awful. I was outdoors most of the time, but there were chores from first light to bedtime. Laundry, the kitchen garden, the chickens . . . . Plus indoors there was always the housework. My dad was the one wrapped up and sitting in a chair at our house. Work wore my mom down, probably more than if she'd stayed with the Mennonites. We all learned what you could call 'the value of work.'"

"At our house it was only me. I didn't have any brothers and sisters. I think my mom was afraid another baby would be born with something wrong, too."

"I don't think you missed much being an only child. I almost never see my family, and they all live within forty miles of here, every one."

"Why not?"

"I don't know. We were all busy, and the farm never did bring in enough money, so my mom went out to work. We were all pretty much on our own—my brothers in the field, me in the house minding babies, cleaning and cooking."

Catherine pushed her chair back and stood up. "More tea?"

Jaz was busy with memories of her own. "Tea?" she asked vaguely.

Catherine brought the tea and set a basket of fruit on the table.

"For me, growing up was a constant struggle to convince my parents I was strong enough to do everything the other kids did," Jaz said. "For you, it sounds like they assumed you were strong enough for anything."

Catherine laughed. "Sometimes when I was sick of trying to keep the house and the kids together, I'd wonder why life was so difficult. Maybe my mom was trying to prove she was good enough, never mind that her family had disowned her."

"Good enough? With all she had to take care of? I should think she was good enough, all right." Catherine could hear a note of anger in Jaz's voice.

"Well, I think she felt that God wasn't pleased with her either."

"Where did that idea come from?" Now Jaz was really mad.

"Once when I was visiting her after my dad died, she talked

to me about it. She wasn't that old, but she'd worked so constantly, there wasn't much left to her. She said she'd always wondered if, in breaking from the Mennonites, she had created an irretrievable breech between God and herself."

"What a burden to carry," Jaz said.

"That's what I thought, and what haunted her even more was, if so, what effect that must have on us children. Were we cut off from God, too? She had struggled with that question all her life."

"How did you feel when you heard that?"

"I felt sad and helpless. Can you imagine having your parents disown you and feeling cut off from God, too? I hated that she had to go through that."

Jaz sat back in her chair. "I don't know why that made me so mad . . . . Well, yes I do, actually. There I was staring out the window. My mom wouldn't let me walk the three blocks to school. She drove me everyday, and when I pushed open the big door after school there she'd be, in the car at the curb. She'd take me home and tuck me up in the chair to watch for my dad. When I learned to read I'd sit surrounded by books and sometimes my dad's medical journals. One day when he came home I was deep into one of his journals. From that moment on he was obsessed with the idea of my becoming a doctor."

"That's a pretty big jump. How old were you?"

"Seven or eight. He told me I owed it to the world since I'd been saved by a miracle. He wanted me to be a great researcher and discover the cure for cancer."

"What did you think? Did you want to be a doctor?"

"Not in the least. It was worse because I was really good at math and science. My dad was convinced that I had a gift and that made him all the more eager."

"What about your mom? Wasn't she worried that you weren't strong enough?" Catherine asked.

"She idolized my father. As long as I stayed in the chair I could study all I liked. I started to rebel. My legs ached to be outside. I started defying her and leaving the house."

"Where did you go?"

"Out behind the house under a tangle of bushes there was a space I could crawl into. I'd disappear in there. It was actually as quiet as the chair but at least I was outside. When I was older I rambled further afield, going down to the junkyard and looking for buried treasure."

"Jaz, the Great Adventurer," Catherine said. "What would your mother say when you came home?"

"She never said a word. She'd just look at me. Looks that could bore a hole through lead. At first I'd cringe but I soon learned to sweep off to my room like a queen."

"What did you want to do when you grew up?"

"When I was in high school I discovered ceramics."

"Did your parents give way?"

"Not really. My dad paid for college somewhat reluctantly. I spent as much time in the art department as possible. After that he gave up on me entirely. He has barely spoken to me in thirty-five years."

"That must hurt." Catherine found herself thinking of Phil and Jack.

"I understand him better now. After I started teaching, my mom told me he had wanted to do research, to find the cure for some horrible disease. His patients loved him, but he was never satisfied. He hoped I would take up his quest, and he would feel like his life had been worthwhile."

"What about your mom?" Catherine asked.

"Well, I wanted her to be my ally. I think she could have been, except that she was so—what's the word?—diminished by my father that she couldn't stand up for herself, let alone, me."

"You think if your dad hadn't objected she would have accepted your art?" Catherine asked.

"I do think so. She filled the house with beautiful things, but she was always a mystery to me. I guess she married my dad and gave up having her own opinions. His were good enough for her. She's been dead nearly ten years, and I still don't understand it," Jaz admitted.

"Our mothers were different but the same. It wasn't easy being with my mother," Catherine said. "I wish I'd been able to see how tired she was. It would have helped me if I understood."

"What was she like?"

"I really don't know how to answer that. She wasn't consistent. I never knew how she would be. Most often if I asked her advice she would tell me to 'examine my conscience.' Apparently, that's the Mennonite way."

"Sounds confusing."

"It was. I'm still not quite sure what a conscience is . . . much less how to examine it." Catherine laughed, and continued, "My cousin, Sarah, on my mother's side, is my age. Sarah left the Mennonites after her parents died."

"Was it easier for her to leave than it was for your mom?"

"I think so. Some of the Mennonites are less conservative, and her family had become part of that. She does go to visit once in a while," Catherine said. "Sarah and I talk, and I understand my mother better now. Even though Mom's gone, and I can't tell her in person, I really love her. I was never able to tell her that."

"Somehow I think our moms know. At least I hope so," Jaz said. "I love my mom, too, and I talk to her more now than I did when she was alive. My mom couldn't have been happy living in my dad's shadow, but she kept up a good front."

"I wonder if my mom was trying to make peace with God by working to make everything perfect. She tried to make us perfect, too. With me, at least, there was no hope of that."

Jaz laughed. "That's a relief."

Jaz had been listening intently, but Catherine suddenly wondered if she were just being polite so she said, "I don't want to bore you."

"I'm not bored. Far from it. I like to talk about life. It's one of my favorite things."

Catherine looked intently into her mug. "My mother never had time for us. I vowed that I'd devote my life to my children, and I wasn't going to have nine of them either."

"Nine does seem like an impossible number. I'd be afraid I'd forget their names."

"Two was enough for me. Do you have kids?"

"No, I was busy with my career. Mostly I haven't regretted it. I've had a full life, much of it with other people's kids around. Having kids can be a full-time job."

"True. When they were little, they were all consuming. Later I stayed just as busy keeping the house picked up and all of our lives running smoothly. The time went by and here I am . . . ."

Catherine looked at the clock on the kitchen wall. Quarter to ten. Phil and Jessica would be home any minute. She carried their mugs and the cookie plate to the sink.

Jaz pulled her jacket on. "Let's have our next visit at my house."

Catherine walked Jaz to the front door and looked up the street for Phil's truck.

* * *

The next morning Phil rummaged around in the bookshelves in the den looking for one particular book he wanted to read to Benny. Benny was becoming restless, but he needed to be monitored for several more days. The danger of heart or lung complications was too great to let him go home.

Other than a short walk now and then, Amanda spent her days in the hospital. When Phil arrived, she went into the lounge to work on lesson plans for the coming semester. Phil would pull a chair next to Benny's bed.

On the way home from the hospital the day before, Phil wondered what he could do to entertain Benny. A particular book came to mind, one he had read to Jack when he was nine or ten, an adventure story called *The Phoenix and the Carpet*. Phil had read it as a child and loved reading it to Jack. Here was an excuse to read it again.

Memories of Jack and Amanda's childhood streamed from the rows of tattered old books. His favorite part of fatherhood had been reading to the children at bedtime. It ended when they began having so much homework that he shifted to helping with math and science instead of having the quiet time to read. And now to think that he had nearly missed knowing Benny as more than just one of the grandchildren.

"I'm lucky to have a second chance," he thought. "Not many people have that."

He didn't visit with Amanda much at the hospital. They took turns having lunch so Benny wouldn't be left alone, but there was a feeling of camaraderie between them. He had always liked Amanda, but he hadn't spent any time just talking with her in a long time. When he left in the evening, she hugged him and the years fell away. She was his girl again.

* * *

After Phil left for the hospital, Catherine pulled the sewing machine out while Jessica gathered the pattern and fabric for her skirt. This skirt was her first attempt at sewing on the machine. On a scrap of fabric, Catherine showed her how to set the needle, drop the pressure foot and guide the fabric. Catherine was relieved to find that Jessica had a knack for the machine.

"Wow, Gram, this is easy. I can't believe I sewed that apron by hand. It would've taken about five minutes with the machine."

"Well, maybe not quite that fast. It's good to know how to sew by hand, too. If you keep sewing, you'll use everything you learned on your apron again and again."

* * *

The skirt was an A-line, so the fit was easy. Jessica was nearly finished when the doorbell rang. She went to the door.

"Hi, I'm Jaz. I live next door." Jaz held out her hand to Jessica.

Jessica shook hands. "I'm Jessica."

"I brought you and your grandma some paints and brushes and paper. I thought you might like to paint something." She handed a bulky canvas sack to Jessica. The ends of brushes stuck out the top.

"That's great. Thank you."

Catherine came out of the kitchen.

"I was cleaning out cupboards this morning and I found these." Jaz pointed to the sack Jessica was holding. "I haven't painted in so long, I forgot I had them."

Catherine didn't know what to say. Finally, she managed 'thank you'.

After Jaz left, Jessica said, "She's nice. Is she a friend of yours?"

"Yes, she is," Catherine said, surprised to find that it was true. "I like her."

Jessica set the sack on the kitchen table, and they pulled out half a dozen brushes, watercolor paper, and a tin box filled with tubes of paint. The sight of the tin tubes filled with color stirred Catherine. One thing she hadn't mentioned to Jaz the night before was that art had also been the secret love of her childhood.

When Phil arrived home from the hospital, he found Catherine and Jessica at the kitchen table surrounded by paintings. They had each painted one of Blue and one of each other. Some apples and a wedge of cheese on a checked napkin sat on the table in front of them.

"What's this?" he asked? "Painting virtuosos right under my roof?"

Catherine looked up. "Hi. How was your day? How's Benny?"

"Better and better. Today I read him the first five chapters of *The Phoenix and the Carpet*."

"Didn't you read that book to Jack?" Catherine asked, then wished she hadn't. She had established a habit of never mentioning Jack to Phil.

Phil, however, merely said, "Yes, I did." He walked over to Blue's cage, whistled a few bars and went off to the den.

A little later Jessica put her new skirt on and went to call Phil for supper.

"See my new skirt, Grandpa. I made it myself."

"All those paintings and now a skirt! It's beautiful, Jessica.

How about that?"

* * *

The new year dawned with Benny in the hospital. Amanda had to be back at school on the second and Dr. Barnes wanted to keep Benny a few days longer. Amanda decided to talk to Benny about it.

On Sunday morning after his breakfast, she said, "You know I have to be back at school tomorrow, and Dr. Barnes wants you to stay a little longer. I wonder what you think we could do?"

"Grandpa could stay with me," Benny said. "I want Grandpa to stay."

Phil slept on the cot the nurses wheeled into Benny's room each night. Except when she had gone to visit Jack a couple of times, it was the first time he and Catherine had been apart overnight in forty-seven years. He was surprised to find he missed her. But he needed to be with Benny. He brought an overnight bag and a sack of board games that had been stashed in the den. He and Benny started with Clue and ended up in a long game of Monopoly. Benny had always appeared self-confident and willing to take risks. Now while they played, Phil had a definite sense of Benny holding back, of being uncertain.

That first night lying in the unfamiliar semi-gloom of the hospital, faint noises all around him, Phil thought he would never sleep. He thought of one or two summers when it had rained nearly every weekend, and he had played endless games with the kids. He remembered laughing and hollering and wrestling matches. Had Catherine played with them? No, he thought not. She was in the background, making sandwiches or cleaning up.

There was no doubt that Catherine had worked longer hours than he had. He went to work everyday, and when he came home, he spent the evenings reading or puttering in his shop in the basement. He didn't think Catherine even sat down except for a few minutes at mealtime between bringing more food to the table and clearing it for dessert. Since he retired, she had kept on doing everything, same as always.

Phil rolled onto his side, hoping he would be comfortable enough to sleep. He had heard on a radio talk show that seventy percent of the thoughts he had each day he had also had the day before. But now a new thought struck him: He could help Catherine. The picture of himself washing dishes or sweeping the floor was almost too much for this late at night. Maybe he would end up wearing an apron.

Catherine probably wouldn't let him help her anyway, but he knew that he would offer. Now that he had thought of it there was no turning back. At last, Phil fell asleep.

* * *

Monday morning Jessica put on her new skirt and went back to school. Catherine wandered around the house, returning several times to the kitchen to look through the stack of paintings she and Jessica had completed. At three o'clock, Catherine was waiting in the car for Jessica outside the school and drove back to the house on Monroe Street.

After a snack, they sat at the kitchen table and painted in easy silence until the fading light of late afternoon. Jessica switched on the overhead light, and Catherine put the paints away while Jessica washed brushes.

They heard Tom's truck pull up in front of the house, and a moment later he walked in.

Catherine called from the kitchen. "Hi, Tom, come on in."

"Hi, you two," Tom said. "What masterpieces have you cooked up this time?"

"Look at this." Catherine held up a painting Jessica had done of a winged horse flying through a rainbow.

"That's beautiful," Tom said. "Really beautiful."

"It's not so good," Jessica said. "The mane smeared."

"Well, I like it," Tom said.

* * *

After they left, Catherine didn't know what to do with herself. She talked to Blue, and finally sat down in the living room with a gardening magazine. It was well into the evening before she realized she would be alone for several days. She felt dazed. The

week with Jessica had been her busiest in years, and now she
was by herself.

She took herself into the den and looked through the
bookshelf. An old favorite walked off the shelf into her hand.
She carried *The Professor's House* by Willa Cather into the
living room. The light was soft and golden. She curled up in the
corner of the sofa, pulled an afghan over her knees, and opened
the book. The silent house wrapped itself around her until,
much later, deep in the book, she looked up.

Aloud she said, "Nobody here but me. I can stay up as late
as I want."

She went out to the kitchen to make herself a cup of tea.
When she turned the light on, a sleepy Blue looked at her.

"I forgot all about you, didn't I?" She covered the cage so the
light wouldn't hurt Blue's eyes.

She carried her mug back into the living room where she
continued to read until the words began to blur on the page.
Finally she made herself go to bed.

* * *

The next morning Catherine lounged in bed. Soft light pouring
into her room finally pried her out. After a leisurely breakfast
for which Catherine actually sat down, she brought the painting
materials to the table. She sat in front of the white paper
wondering what to paint. She decided to paint what she saw
in front of her—the oak cabinets and counter with the cookie
jar on it. She squeezed color out of the little silver tubes onto
a white plate and mixed them with water. Catherine began to
paint.

* * *

Phil woke up when a tall imperious nurse swept into the room.

"How are we today?" she asked.

Benny rolled over in bed and opened sleepy eyes.

Not waiting for an answer, she stuck an automatic
thermometer in Benny's ear.

"Feeling fine, I suppose." She typed something into the tablet
she carried in her pocket.

Then she rolled up the sleeve of Benny's pajama top and wrapped a blood pressure cuff around his arm. Phil winced at the whiteness of the little arm and the nurse's coolness. He said nothing. Benny looked small and tense in the hospital bed. After taking Benny's blood pressure, the nurse again typed on her tablet and left the room without saying goodbye.

Phil had been at the hospital quite a bit during the week Benny had been there. He had seen several nurses come and go in Benny's room. All of them had been friendly and taken time with Benny to help him feel comfortable. Apparently, not this one. Phil went to Benny.

"Is she one of your regular nurses?"

"She comes every morning," Benny said in a small voice. "I don't like her."

"Me neither."

A young orderly with a crew cut came into the room bringing Benny's breakfast.

"How are you today, sport?" He winked at Benny.

"Pretty good." Benny answered so quietly Phil could barely hear him.

The orderly nodded to Phil. "Would you like some coffee? I could bring some in a few minutes."

"That would be nice, but don't go to any trouble."

"No trouble at all. I'll be right back."

When he left, Phil looked at Benny quizzically.

Benny nodded. "He's nice. I like him."

"I do, too," Phil said. "Let's see about this breakfast."

On the tray were a bowl of fruit, two poached eggs, toast, cream of wheat and milk—plenty for both Benny and Phil. The orderly brought the coffee, a *Ranger Rick* magazine, and a cherry popsicle for Benny.

He laid the magazine on the bed. "Shh . . . . Don't tell." He handed the popsicle to Benny.

"I won't," Benny said. Phil noticed that Benny didn't smile.

After breakfast Phil suggested they take turns reading the magazine aloud to each other. Benny was reluctant, so Phil read the stories. Together they worked the nature puzzle on the back page and played games through the long morning until lunch.

In the afternoon Phil and Benny walked down to the pediatrics' playroom. They sat at a low table on chairs so small that Phil's knees were up under his chin. They made imaginary animals out of clay and put together a jigsaw puzzle of a mountain scene. They were fitting together pieces of sky when a woman came in carrying a little girl about four years old.

The woman set the child down and sank into a chair. "I'm exhausted," she confessed. The child leaned against her.

"Been here long?" Phil asked.

"Three days. Anya had an ear infection which turned into encephalitis. How about you?"

"We've been here a little over a week." Phil didn't feel like saying why Benny was in the hospital.

"Anya's nearly well enough to go home. What a relief."

Benny brightened. "I'm going home soon, too."

"That's good," the woman said.

Walking back to Benny's room, they passed Dr. Barnes in the hall.

"Why, hello, Benny. I wondered where you were." He shook Phil's hand. "Good to see you, Mr. Lewelling."

"Same here."

Dr. Barnes smiled at Benny. "I'll check back in with you when I finish my rounds, young man."

Phil had just finished a chapter of *The Phoenix and the Carpet* when Amanda arrived. A few minutes later, Dr. Barnes walked into the room.

After reading the chart and checking Benny over, he said, "You're doing well, Benny. Barring any unforeseen complications I see no reason why you can't go home in a couple of days."

Amanda followed the doctor into the hall.

"You know," he said, "this is the first time I've seen a situation like this turn out well."

Amanda blinked back tears. "Thank you," she said.

* * *

The next morning, Phil watched Benny and worried. Benny had always been confident and out-going. This last week in the hospital though, that had changed. Benny was nearly silent with the nurses and orderlies and even with his mom. Phil was quiet anyway, so it hadn't seemed unnatural that Benny was quiet. When one of the nurses was in the room, Benny would lie perfectly still but his eyes followed her every movement. He looked scared, Phil thought.

Certainly, Amanda was still scared. Scared that something terrible would still happen. She knew it was possible, even expected. Otherwise, why was Dr. Barnes keeping Benny so long? Apparently, danger still lurked beneath the surface somewhere.

That evening, Tom brought Amanda up to visit after work. While Tom was in with Benny, Amanda and Phil sat in the lounge. Amanda told Phil that since it happened, the day of Benny's accident had been playing again and again in her mind like a movie. How she had run full on to the river, how she had followed Joey to the place where, through the ice, she had glimpsed the red of Benny's muffler. How she had stepped out on the ice, not knowing if it would hold her but having no choice, how she had broken the ice and turned Benny's body so she could pull him out. How she had pulled him as gently as she could to the shore and up the little trail to the top of the bank where she fell back rocking him. But only for an instant. Benny was dead. She could see that.

But it could not be. She knew CPR and she had laid her baby on the ground and begun. CPR put her on automatic: check his airway, start rescue breathing and chest compression. Two breaths, fifteen compressions, two breaths. The rhythm had taken her and she had settled. When the paramedics came they took over. She had remained calm, as though she were watching from a long way off.

All this she told Phil like a litany. No emotion showed in her voice. He sat and held her hand and listened. It was obvious she needed to tell the story again. How many times she would need to do that he didn't know. But he was there to listen, there to hold her hand.

"It keeps coming back." She shivered.

"I guess that's natural. You've been through something most people only have nightmares about. And look, now, Benny's all right." Phil squeezed her hand.

Amanda started crying. "I know, that's what scares me. He nearly died. I never thought about what it would be to lose one of the kids, and I can't believe I still have him. I never want to take his or anybody else's life for granted again."

"Oh, Amanda." The pain in his child brought tears to Phil's eyes.

"I go to work and then rush around the house the rest of the time. Some days I barely have time to notice Tom and the kids. That's what I have to change. I don't want to ever forget what a miracle each of them is, and you, too, Dad. You're a miracle. I love you, Daddy."

She put her head on Phil's shoulder and he hugged her. "I love you, too, Amanda," he murmured.

When Amanda left that night with Tom, Phil had time to think. Amanda had put Benny to bed, and he was asleep. Phil sat in the big armchair in the corner and watched the covers rise and fall with Benny's breath in the twilight that passed for darkness in the hospital. Amanda was right. Benny was a miracle. If Benny was a miracle, so were Amanda and Catherine and him, too, he supposed. He had never thought of himself as a miracle before and the thought struck him as funny.

He lounged back in the chair and put the tips of his fingers together to help him think better. Phil went from thinking he was a miracle to how disappointed he was with himself. Why had he been so obstinate toward Catherine all these years? She had made a mistake, it's true, and he had kept blocking all the tender feelings because . . . why? He was afraid; that was it. Afraid of what? Of being hurt again. Which he never wanted to be.

Had Catherine hurt him more over the years? No. He could see her frustration with trying to win him back. Now he admitted to himself that he had figured her unhappiness was what she deserved. But was it really? What he did know was that Catherine had been his one and only true love, and he had steeled his heart against her and against the love in himself.

The chair had become increasingly uncomfortable. This was about all the thinking Phil could stand for one night. How had he started thinking of himself as a miracle and ended up here? He went to bed and let the turmoil skim the surface of his mind until, with that stubbornness which had been his constant companion through the years, he fell asleep.

He awoke groggy and with a pall of sadness he couldn't shake. This was the day Benny would go home from the hospital. Amanda was coming straight from school to Iowa City. Phil supposed he would return to the routine of long days spent between the den and the porch. Having Benny to focus on had given him some freedom from himself. It had been a relief.

Even Benny, who had been eager to leave the hospital, seemed more and more reluctant as the day wore on.

He asked Phil about going home. "Do you think I'll have to go back to school tomorrow? Maybe I should stay home for a while. I probably have to be real quiet for a long time."

Phil didn't know and said so. By the time Amanda arrived, met with Dr. Barnes and, with Phil's help, packed up Benny's things, Phil could see that Benny was as jumpy as a fish on a line.

"Now, what do you suppose is going on with the boy?" he asked himself.

When it was time to go with his mom, Benny grabbed Phil and hugged him. "I'm going to miss you, Grandpa. Come and see me, ok?"

"I will, buddy, I will."

CHAPTER

8

The whole time Phil was at the hospital with Benny, Catherine left the painting materials set up on the kitchen table. She painted everything she could think of. One afternoon she set up the card table in front of the window in the living room and painted winter maples with the street in between. Then she painted as much of her bedroom as she could see from the living room. She especially liked painting the dim hallway between the two rooms.

Looking in the mirror she sketched two self-portraits. One she drew of herself with no hair. Then she painted from her sketches. Although it was nearly impossible to mix the right skin color, she enjoyed painting herself. She also found herself painting flowers. It was the dead of winter so Catherine painted from the photographs in her gardening magazines. She painted a green wreath covered with flowers of all colors—roses, marguerites, lavender and coreopsis.

When she finished each painting, she set it on the mantel and stood back to look at it from the far side of the room. She was surprised to find she liked them all. During those quiet days, Catherine also discovered that she liked being alone.

The third morning, Amanda called before she left for work. Benny was coming home. That meant Phil would be home, too. Catherine's stomach shivered. She had mixed feelings. She interrupted her morning painting session to call Jaz.

"Do you want to come over and have some lunch with me?"

"Remember, you were going to come over here this time."

"That's ok. I'll come over next time."

"I have some potato soup on the stove. Why don't I bring it over?"

"That sounds good. I made tapioca this morning and some oatmeal cookies. As usual I think about dessert first."

Jaz laughed. "I like your style. I'm working on a piano piece. I'll be ready for a break by noon."

After making tuna salad with plenty of onion and dill pickle, Catherine carried the stack of paintings into her bedroom and carefully laid them in the bottom drawer of her dresser under the sweaters. Back in the kitchen, she stood looking out the window. There was Jaz coming through the gap in the hedge carrying the soup pot. She opened the back door.

They sat over bowls of soup and tuna sandwiches.

"Thanks again for bringing those paints over last week," Catherine began.

"You and Jessica had fun with them?"

"Not only that." Catherine felt suddenly shy.

Jaz looked at her quizzically.

"You know the other night when we were talking about being children," Catherine began. "Well, I didn't tell you then, but I always wanted to be a painter."

"A painter?"

"Impossible to believe, isn't it? But it's true. When Jack won awards for his art at school, it was like it was happening to me."

"Now I see. You had a dream all along," Jaz teased.

"Yes, but I never painted. Every quarter they'd send out the bulletin for adult classes at the high school, and I'd circle the classes I wanted to take. I'd think, 'Why don't I take a painting class?' I never signed up."

"We never know what's going to happen. I keep a card on my desk: 'Just begin. The rest is easy.'"

Catherine felt shy again. "Well, actually I have been painting a little. Since you brought over the paints . . . ."

"That was a stroke of genius. What have you been painting?"

"Everything I can think of." The urge to show Jaz her paintings grew stronger by the moment. "Would you like to see?"

"I'd be honored."

"I'll be right back."

Catherine went into the other room and came back holding her paintings close to her chest. At first, she avoided Jaz's eyes, but then she looked into Jaz's bright curious gaze.

"Here they are." She laid the paintings on the table. The top one showed the light coming through the kitchen window shining on Blue in his cage. In the painting Blue sat on the little perch.

"Why Catherine, it's beautiful," Jaz said.

"Do you really like it?"

"Of course I do. It's beautiful. Anyone could see that."

"Thank you." Catherine set the first painting aside so Jaz could see the next. Again a window, but this time looking out to the street and the winter trees.

Jaz was quiet this time, looking. Finally she said, "The way you use light . . . I'm amazed. This is fine, Catherine. Really fine."

"You think so?"

"I wouldn't say it if I didn't. Really, these are lovely."

One by one they went through the stack of paintings, Jaz admiring Catherine's sense of color and composition, but most of all, her handling of light. "This is what makes watercolor magical. Your paintings are truly transparent."

By this time Catherine believed Jaz meant what she said, but she felt unsettled. Silently she gathered the paintings back into a stack and set them aside.

Jaz, sensing her discomfort, changed the subject. "Phil said Amanda is a teacher. What does she teach?"

"Third grade." Catherine still felt awkward. She got up and brought a plate of cookies to the table and sat down again.

Jaz took a spoonful of the tapioca Catherine had put in front of her. "Mmm, delicious." Taking a cookie from the plate she took a bite. "These are good, too. How's it going for Amanda now that Benny's coming home from the hospital?"

"Honestly, with what happened to Benny and with Jessica in high school, she's overwhelmed. It was difficult for her to go back to school after vacation."

"Can she quit and stay home?"

"She'd like to, but they depend on her income. She planned for her and Jessica to have time together during Christmas vacation, but Amanda spent her whole vacation at the hospital. She's worried about losing touch with Jessica."

"I think teenagers do best when they have something to do outside of their friends and school," Jaz said.

"I think so, too. Jessica and Benny are both in 4-H."

"That's a country thing, isn't it? We didn't have 4-H in Boston."

"My brothers and I were all in 4-H. They entered their calves every year at the county fair."

"How about you?"

Catherine ticked them off on her fingers: "My chickens and their eggs, vegetables from the garden, embroidered huck towels, tatting . . . and yes, cookies, of course."

"That's quite a list," Jaz said.

"I like working with my hands. It seems Jessica is taking after me. She's been trying different cookie recipes, and her 4-H club has done some hand sewing. The skirt was her first on the sewing machine."

"How did it go?"

"I was afraid I'd have to sit on my hands to keep from taking it away from her and doing it myself, but she learned fast. She made her skirt almost as fast as I could have."

"I know what you mean about sitting on your hands," Jaz said. "When I started teaching ceramics, I'd be explaining something to a kid and the next thing I knew their clay would be in my hands and I'd be working it."

"I tried teaching Amanda to sew, but it was a disaster. By the time she finished her outfit, she'd grown, and it was too small for her," Catherine said.

"Mothers and daughters . . . . Why is it so hard?" Jaz wondered. "Right up until the end there was a rift between my mother and me. She wanted me to have what she called a 'normal life.' Get married, have kids, settle down. Instead I had a career I loved, married late to a much older and very eccentric man, had no kids, and traveled all over the world. For me it was a perfect life."

"It sounds perfect to me, too," Catherine said, "and here you are now living your dream life in Mount Pleasant. I've been here all this time, and it certainly hasn't felt like living a dream."

"I don't know. You have Phil and a peaceful life. My husband and I don't agree on how we want to spend our so-called 'golden years'. I pictured small town life, a rocking chair on the front porch, you know. He wanted to retire to Hawaii and walk the beach everyday. So we went our separate ways, and it's great. No hurt feelings. We both have the lives we want."

"I can barely imagine it." Catherine looked into her empty mug.

"Life is full of surprises. I expect there will be some for both of us before we're through."

"I hope you're right." Catherine took another cookie. "When I was a kid I felt something great coming my way. But then, all the years . . . just waiting. Lately, though, some mornings I wake up with that feeling. Morning light dawning in the sky, the silence of winter all around. The feeling of something wonderful about to happen. A new day, perhaps that's all."

"I love morning, too," Jaz said. "I wake up, and there's a whole day ahead. The thought of it springs on me like a puppy jumping on the bed."

Catherine got up and put some more water in the kettle. Silence sat comfortably between them. Neither of them wanted the afternoon to end. Catherine chirped to Blue and sat back down.

"He's a cute little guy," Jaz said. "Has he started to sing?"

"Not yet, but he will," Catherine said. "He's still finding his way."

"Isn't that what life is about? Finding our way?"

"Maybe so." Catherine refilled their mugs and the cookie plate.

Jaz nodded toward the stack of paintings on the end of the table. "And now?" she teased.

"Ever since Blue came I've been having ideas. The paintings, of course, and there's also a vacant lot I planted bulbs and flower seeds in. I'm thinking it would make a fine butterfly garden. I'm taking dance classes, too. Me. I've never done anything."

"Dance classes? I love to dance."

"Maybe you'd like to join us for the next series. It starts the end of January."

"Thanks, but probably not. I'm a homebody these days. Especially in the evenings. What is a butterfly garden?"

"All the flowers in the garden attract butterflies."

"Sounds nice. I love flowers. Butterflies, too."

* * *

Phil drove home through the dusky evening feeling empty, but as he drove up to the house, a sense of peace settled in. The house welcomed him like an old friend.

He found Catherine in the kitchen making supper. He was surprised to find he had been looking forward to seeing her. And instead of greeting him over her shoulder as she usually did, she wiped her hands on a towel and came to help him take off his heavy winter jacket.

"How'd it go?"

"Fine, I suppose." Phil suddenly felt gruff. Like an old bear who just wants to go back into his den. Then he remembered sitting at the hospital the night before.

He tried again. "Supper smells good. I'm hungry as a bear." There, that was what he had wanted to say.

Catherine brightened. "Meat loaf, mashed potatoes and broccoli."

"My favorite."

"I know."

As they ate, Catherine noticed that he was talking to her instead of eating silently as he usually did. He told Catherine what the doctor had said about Benny.

"He told Amanda that Benny should probably stay home from school for a couple more days as a precautionary measure, but that it looked like he was going to be just fine."

"I'm relieved to hear that."

"But I have to say that I'm worried about Benny."

"Worried?"

"I watched him up there and he seems different. He's become awfully quiet and skittish."

"After what he's been through, I'm not surprised. He'll come through it."

"I hope so. I'm going out their tomorrow while Amanda's in school to keep him company. Want to come along?"

"Maybe I'll bring some lunch out and stay a while. I have some apples set aside for a pie. I'll make it in the morning, and it'll still be warm."

"That would be nice. I'd appreciate it if you would talk to Benny and see what you think."

"You would?"

Phil went off to the den to catch up on his reading while Catherine cleaned up the kitchen. Phil had thought about offering to wash the dishes but somehow this didn't seem like the night. After he left the room, Catherine settled into the familiar routine. She did some of her best thinking with her hands in warm soapy water.

* * *

Several good snows kept southeast Iowa white most of January. There were sunny days when Catherine pulled on her snow boots and drove out to the park for a walk. A couple of times she met Fern and Schnappsy, but mostly she walked alone. These days she noticed more of her surroundings than ever before as she walked the paths. The old wooden fence posts along the park boundary looked like a row of little gnomes capped with snow. The woods were quiet in a deeper way than they were in summer. Only the soft plop of snow falling from laden branches onto the forest floor broke the silence. She discovered that the pair of cardinals she had seen in the fall were wintering in a grove of pines that lined the path and watched for them each time she came.

The wooded trail provided Catherine the perfect backdrop for her thoughts. She was worried about Amanda. Benny was having a terrible time adjusting to school and being with other children since his accident, and Amanda didn't know what to do. Amanda had always known the answers to everything. Her life was orderly and planned whereas Catherine had let life happen to her rather than the other way around. Now, since Benny's accident, Amanda seemed confused and often called asking Catherine what she should do.

What Phil observed in the hospital became more apparent. Benny balked at going to school every morning. Amanda told Catherine that he started each day with a stomachache and begged to stay home. Since Amanda had to be at work early, she usually dropped the children at their schools early, too. She would drop Benny at Lincoln on the way to the high school with Jessica. Then she would drive across town to work at Saunders. Because there was so much to do before they left the house, Amanda found herself scrambling at the last minute with lunches, papers, and the kids' backpacks to get them all out the door on time.

These days, Benny crawled in bed with her and Tom well before dawn, shivering and tense. Each morning it took all Amanda's cajoling to ease him out the door. His teacher was worried, too.

That wasn't all. She had been giving Benny extra time in the evenings, and, as a result, her own lesson preparation suffered. Her class of eight-year-olds had less direction and were more unruly than usual. Amanda had also been having trouble with Jessica who rarely arrived home on the bus. She would come home later in one or another car Amanda didn't recognize. She felt that Jessica at fourteen was too young to be driving around with kids old enough to have cars. When Amanda tried to talk to her, Jessica's "try and make me" attitude had Amanda in tears on the phone to Catherine.

Jessica's attitude was familiar to Catherine. It had been her own when she was a teenager. What amazed her was Amanda's confiding in her. Amanda had always been much more independent than Jack. Even as a small child, if she fell and skinned her knee, she would rub it herself and not cry. Now that Amanda was asking for help, Catherine didn't know what to say.

She walked in the woods and pondered. She and Jessica had gotten along during the week after Christmas when Benny was in the hospital. Maybe they could do some things together this winter to take some of the pressure off Amanda. Phil had been worried about Benny, too, and drove out there several afternoons a week after school. Maybe Benny could be Phil's special project, and Jessica could be hers. But what would they do together? Jessica enjoyed painting with Catherine so maybe they could do more of that. And Jessica liked Jaz. Maybe she would like to play with the clay in Jaz's shed. Catherine was relieved she had thought of something. She walked the trail above the river listening to the fresh dry snow crunch under her boots and watching for the flash of the male cardinal through the tree limbs.

* * *

Phil liked his new routine. About three afternoons a week, he would arrive at Amanda's just before she and Benny came home from school. Some days he would bring something Catherine had baked. He would find the key under the mat while calling to Goldie whose volume increased until he opened the door.

"All right girl, I'm coming."

Goldie could nearly turn herself inside out wagging. He let her out and put the kettle on for Amanda's tea. For himself he would reheat the morning's coffee. Then he would pour milk in a saucepan and start it heating for Benny's hot chocolate. By that time Goldie was barking again, running to greet Amanda and Benny.

Benny was as happy to see him as Goldie had been, but he seemed somber still. Phil had heard somewhere that as long as a person ate well, there was no real worry. Benny always drank his hot chocolate and ate whatever Catherine sent. Phil told himself, "This is a passing thing."

Amanda took her tea to her workspace in the dining room to prepare for the next day's classes. Sometimes Benny and Phil went down to the basement to play Ping-Pong. Benny had a decided advantage over Phil and liked winning. Phil liked it, too. Benny seemed almost himself when his competitive spirit kicked in.

Sometimes they went into Benny's room, flopped back on Benny's bed to read. Phil brought a new book over nearly every week. He and Benny took turns reading to each other. Benny was a good reader, and the stories unfolded smoothly no matter who was reading. He seemed less shy than he had in the hospital which seemed a good sign to Phil. Sometimes they brought a board game to the dining room table so they could be near Amanda.

One afternoon they were playing Clue. At the end of the first game it turned out that Professor Plum was the murderer. There was no doubt when Benny disclosed him.

"I always wanted it to be Professor Plum," Amanda said from her desk. "I don't know why."

"I remember that," Phil said. "And you wanted the murder to be done with the candlestick, didn't you?"

"That's right," Amanda came over to watch. "And it made sense that the murder be done in the dining room. It all fits, don't you think?"

"I don't know about that," Phil laughed. "Benny, you should have been there. We'd start the game and on her first turn your mom would want to guess."

"Now Dad, you know that's not fair," Amanda protested. "How old was I anyway? Five or six, probably."

"Yes, that's true," Phil said. "You caught on pretty quick, but . . . ."

"I know. Secretly I always wanted it to be Professor Plum. At least I thought it was secret."

"Mom, did they really have Clue when you were a kid?" Benny asked. "That was a long time ago."

"Not so long, really. Sometimes I still feel like a kid," Amanda admitted.

"Same here," Phil said.

He and Amanda looked at each other over Benny's head and smiled.

"Difficult for Benny to understand, but there you have it," Phil thought. "We may look like grown-ups, but like the T-shirt said, 'We're all the same age inside.'" He firmly believed it.

Apparently, so did Amanda.

* * *

Toward the end of January, Catherine began to wish for spring. Winter had settled in. She liked the inward trend of her days but had been looking forward to dance classes starting up again. When they resumed, both she and Whit were more relaxed with each other, and, with repetition, the dance steps—fox trot, jitterbug, rumba—were easier and more fun.

Her winter garden was another bright spot. There was enough moisture in the ground that she didn't have to water, and weeds weren't a problem. Nearly every night they had something from the garden—lettuce in the salad, steamed or sautéed spinach or kale which she discovered she liked after all. Morning had always been her gardening time, but since she was only harvesting she waited until afternoon to go out.

Most afternoons Phil was out of the house visiting with Benny or, she supposed, sometimes at his mother's. Most days Catherine sat at the kitchen table playing with the paints and paper. Before Phil came home for supper, she slipped the newest watercolor under her sweaters in the bottom drawer of the dresser and put away the painting materials.

Although Phil had seemed interested when he found

Catherine and Jessica painting, she was reluctant to show him her paintings. She couldn't say why she kept them to herself or why she had been willing to show them to Jaz and not to Phil. One day she would show Phil. Just, not now.

**

As winter strengthened its hold, Catherine dreamed of gardens. Toward the end of January she looked for the seed catalogues in the mailbox. When they arrived, she sat at the kitchen table reading descriptions of old favorites and seeing what was new. Heirloom vegetables, berries and flowers intrigued her.

When the first catalogues arrived, she thought of Jaz. On a warm day the last week in January, Catherine walked next door, catalogues in hand. As she walked up on the front porch she heard jungle music. She thought about creeping away but rang the bell instead. She would follow through.

Jaz was breathless when she opened the door. "Perfect timing," she said when she saw the catalogues. "I've begun to question my sanity living in the corn belt in winter. Come on in."

Jaz wore an aqua leotard and a long filmy flowered skirt. Her feet were bare. She turned the music down. "I've been dancing. I love tribal music."

The only furniture in the room was a huge overstuffed chair with an ottoman and a table on each side overflowing with books. The hardwood floor was bare, and the walls were lined with shelves full of books. Catherine had never seen so many books before outside of the library. One wall held the sound system and probably a thousand CDs.

Catherine was a bit dazed by the room and the energy Jaz exuded. She half expected her to start that wild jungle dancing. Catherine's old timidity around Jaz and the feeling that Jaz was outrageous came back, making her wish she had never started talking to her in the first place. What was she doing here? And could she escape?

Then a picture of herself stealing Blue and another one of her, Catherine Lewelling, taking ballroom dance lessons flashed through her mind. Jaz was not the only outrageous one. She laughed at herself and tried to catch what Jaz had been saying.

Jaz led the way through the living room and what would be the dining room if it weren't filled with musical instruments. Again, no rugs. A grand piano stood in the bay window. Music books spilled onto the floor. Behind the piano Catherine glimpsed what she assumed were musical instruments although none of them were familiar except some drums.

Jaz's casual wave of her hand took in the room. "My music room. I actually call it my playroom."

Jaz's kitchen was bigger than Catherine's. A round oak table in a sunny alcove was nearly covered with plants in earthen pots.

Along with the catalogues Catherine had brought her garden journal in which she kept her garden plans, lists of varieties of plants she grew each year, plus any she might like to try.

"Whew, that's a load to carry." Catherine slid the stack onto the table.

"Here." Jaz pulled out a chair. "Sit down."

The chair was draped with an old hooked rug. It was especially comfortable, and suddenly, Catherine felt at home.

Jaz made tea and cinnamon toast, a treat Catherine hadn't even thought of since the kids had grown and gone.

Jaz sat down and picked up Catherine's journal. "May I look at this?"

"I thought it would give us some ideas." Catherine picked up a triangle of cinnamon toast and took a bite. "Just the way I like it. Plenty of butter."

Page by page, Jaz leafed through the journal. "This dates back to the late eighties. You've been drawing all along." She turned the book so Catherine could see the little drawings of plants in the garden plots she had drawn.

"I do that to have a better idea of how the garden will fill out as the plants grow. I've always done that."

"I like them," Jaz said. "How is you're painting coming along?"

"I'm doing it," Catherine said. "Not as much as when Phil was at the hospital with Benny, but I find a few hours here and there when he's out . . . ."

"You haven't shown him your paintings yet?"

"No. Not yet. Maybe soon."

"I've been thinking about your paintings, especially about the light in them. I wonder . . . have you thought of having a show?"

"A show?" Catherine felt suddenly muddled. She was finally painting. Something she had wanted to do all her life. She loved it and that was enough. Now here was Jaz wondering about a show.

"There's a group show at the library in March put on by the Mount Pleasant Art Association. I went to the opening last year. There were quite a few nice pieces."

Catherine felt even more flustered. "I don't know. I never thought about showing my paintings to anybody, even you. And you're still the only one who has seen them. I just want to go on painting, that's all. No, I definitely don't want to put them in a show." Catherine was surprised at how strong her feelings were. She had 'shown' her flowers and vegetables at the fair year after year. And there was school, of course, but that didn't count. Now, her paintings were personal. She painted for herself, not to show.

"Ok." Jaz nodded and turned back to the garden journal. "This year I want to plant a much bigger garden. My garden was too small last year. I can see from your journal that your garden keeps growing, too."

"That's true. I go through the catalogues and make my list. There are always favorites and the new varieties look so good I can't resist those either."

"I want to plant a berry patch. I love berries and cream."

"Raspberries are my favorite. We have a big patch which I thin every spring. I can give you all the plants you want."

"Raspberries are my favorite, too. I want to plant blueberries, too. Do you have any of those?"

"No, but I've always wanted to. Let's order a bunch of plants and share them."

"That'd be great. If we go together, we can order more things. I'd better give myself a budget before we order anything though."

"A budget would be good for me, too, since I'm going to present the idea for a butterfly garden to the garden club."

"How do you plan a butterfly garden?"

"I think it'll be pretty easy. I just need to find out what plants will attract butterflies. I've also been dreaming of planting a native wildflower garden."

"A butterfly garden and a wildflower garden both? That's ambitious."

"I guess this is my year for dreams. This is definitely the year for the wild-flowers. I read an article in *The Iowan* that said most indigenous plants have been squeezed out of the landscape. Many of them are endangered and grow only in small pockets."

"Maybe some of the wildflowers will attract butterflies."

"Maybe they will. I want to find seed for as many native plants as I can and plant them everywhere."

Jaz picked up another of the catalogues and turned to the flower section. "Look at this." She read it out: "Flowering herbs, flowers with delicate scents, heady scents, wildflowers, ornamentals . . . everything you could want."

"Wildflowers, too?"

"A whole section." Jaz spread the catalogue in front of Catherine.

"I'll go to the library to find a book of native Iowa plants," Catherine said. "I have to be careful though. You know how much it takes to actually keep up with a garden here."

"A big job, huh?"

"You must have seen how healthy our Iowa weeds are as summer heats up. I have a spot picked out for the wildflowers, but I hesitate to turn grass into garden space because I know it's a commitment I can't go back on so easily."

"Do you do all the gardening yourself?"

"Phil does all the heavy digging. And he put my cold frames

together this year. He leaves the actual garden to me."

"What about your granddaughter? Does she like to garden?"

"Jessica? I hadn't thought of that. You know, that's a great idea. I've been trying to think of things we could do together. She's been worrying Amanda lately, and I figured maybe we could spend more time together."

"I never knew either of my grandmothers. My parents were older when I was born, and both my grandmothers had died by then."

"I wonder if Jessica would like to have the wildflower garden all to herself."

"I bet she'd love it. I know I would have."

When they parted that afternoon, Catherine left the catalogues with Jaz and went home full of ideas—butterflies, wildflowers, expanding the berry patch to include blueberries, and some old-fashioned vegetable varieties she wanted to try.

***

When she woke the next morning, Catherine looked out on a crystal world. There had been an ice storm in the night, and the temperature was continuing to drop. Amanda called to say the schools were closed, and she and the kids were going to spend the day playing games and watching an old movie on TV. Phil came into the kitchen and peered through the frosty window at the thermometer mounted on the wall outside.

"Minus ten." He sat down at the table. "I was hoping yesterday was the beginning of a warm spell."

"I know. I've been thinking about gardens." Catherine joined him at the table.

"Have you? And I've been thinking about fishing. Typical winter dreams, I guess."

"I have some new ideas for the garden. Jaz and I are going to buy some plants in bulk. It'll save money that way."

"Good idea. What do you have in mind?"

Catherine glanced at Phil. They were having an actual conversation.

"Well, I've been wanting to plant a wildflower garden for

years. All Iowa wildflowers, native plants only. Quite a few of them are endangered, you know."

"No, I didn't know that, but I'm not surprised. Can you find the seeds?"

"One of the catalogues has a whole section on wildflowers. I don't know how many of them are native to Iowa, but I'm going to the library for a book."

"It sounds like a good idea. Where are you planning to put it?"

"I think just under the kitchen windows next to the rose bush," Catherine said, pointing. "That way Blue will have flowers right outside the window. I think he'll like that."

"Maybe he will."

"I'm going to ask Jessica if she wants to plant the garden and have it for her own. Amanda's been worried about her lately, and I thought some projects around here would be good. What do you think?"

"Sounds like a good thing to try. Does she like gardening?"

"I don't know. I hope she'll love it. And maybe some more painting."

"She seemed to enjoy painting that day. She was really proud of what she did."

"Well, I like having her around. She's good company. How's Benny doing?"

"Still pretty skittish. Can't say as I blame him, but I know Amanda's concerned about him, too. She has more than usual to deal with right now."

"What do you and Benny do when you're out there?"

"We read or play board games, mostly. Some cards. He likes to beat me—like all kids."

"And you let him?"

"No, never. But he does often enough anyway. He's a smart little guy."

"He'll come around. Some things take more time than others. You're a patient one. He'll be fine, you'll see."

"I think so, too. To tell the truth, I'm more worried about

Amanda than Benny. Kids are resilient. He'll settle in sometime soon, I expect. Meanwhile I like going out there. Keeps me from thinking too much."

Catherine laughed and began to clear the table. Phil carried his dishes to the sink and set them down. Catherine's mouth fell open before she knew it.

"What next?" she asked herself as Phil went off to the den.

* * *

As the day progressed, it was colder and colder. At dusk it was minus twenty-eight degrees. Catherine moved smoothly about the kitchen making supper. On a night this cold all she wanted was soup and biscuits, so that's what she made. The house was snug and felt like a little island in a frigid world. Phil came up from the basement when she called him.

"Need quite a few things before I can tie my flies this year," Phil offered as he washed his hands at the kitchen sink before sitting down to supper.

"Oh? That so?" Catherine asked, keeping her end of the conversation open.

"Been thinking about teaching Benny to fish. Like my grandfather did me."

"Now there's an idea. I bet he'd like that."

"I think so."

Near the end of supper they were both startled by strange sounds coming from Blue's cage. Blue sat on his perch squawking. Then the squawks turned to song, the most melodious and beautiful song that Phil and Catherine had ever heard. A song from Blue who was finally sitting on his perch. After singing a few moments, Blue left off and started pecking at the seed bell Phil had hung from the roof of the cage months before hoping to lure Blue up from the floor to the perch.

Phil started laughing first. "If that doesn't beat all. Coldest day of the winter and he finally decides to sing."

"And what a song," Catherine said proudly. "Sounds like the happiest canary this side of the Mississippi."

Blue Canary

* * *

Tuesday came around and Catherine was ready to leave for dance class early. It was still extremely cold, and neither Phil nor Catherine had gone outdoors since the cold settled in. "Bye, Phil," she called. "I'm off to dance class."

Phil came out of the den, magazine in hand. "Now watch the roads. They'll be extra slick in this cold."

"I will," she said. "See you in a little while."

During the evening Catherine found herself thinking of Phil while she danced with Whit. She moved gracefully around the dance floor with a softer, easier feeling than she had had in a very long time.

CHAPTER

9

The first of February dawned bright and cold. Catherine had faith in the groundhog and hoped clouds would roll in so it wouldn't see its shadow the next day. She was ready for an early spring.

On Groundhog Day, however, the sky was blue, and there were shadows everywhere as Catherine slipped through the hedge into Jaz's yard. They sat again in Jaz's kitchen to plan their seed order. Vegetables and berries were easy. Fern had told Catherine that she believed it was kale, rather than bread, that was the staff of life. People could live on kale alone and be healthy. Since Catherine had unexpectedly found herself liking the kale she grew in her winter garden, she marked the order form for regular green kale, curly kale and oak leaf kale. She had been feeling bold, almost reckless, lately, so why not kale and more kale? She and Jaz would start flats indoors long before the ground would be warm enough to plant. They ordered empty flats along with the seeds.

"How are the plans for the wildflower garden coming along?" Jaz asked.

"Good. I went to the library and found a book with pictures and descriptions of Iowa wildflowers from the earliest to bloom right through the summer. In the back, it lists sources for seed. I ordered the catalogues. They should be here any day."

"What about Jessica?"

"She's coming over tomorrow after school, and we'll talk about it then. Says she's looking forward to painting again, so that's a start."

"Sounds good."

"I have you to thank. If you hadn't brought over those painting supplies, I never would have thought of it."

"They were sitting in a cupboard not doing much good. You know, I've been wondering if you and Jessica would like to come over and mess around in the pottery shed some afternoon. I'd love to have you, if you think that would be fun."

"Fun?" Catherine replied. "I'd love to have clay in my hands."

Now began the most compelling part of their seed order—perennial and annual flower seeds. Catherine loved her flower garden best. Because every year she found new flowers she couldn't resist, it was always a wild tangle by the middle of July.

"I can always find a spot to tuck something new into," she assured Jaz. "At least there's no room for weeds, there are so many flowers."

"I'm picturing a big flower bed all along the walk between the house and the pottery studio." Jaz leafed through the catalogue. "Look at these irises. I want some of those in every color, especially that purply black."

"You ought to see Laura Percy's irises. She took first prize three years running in the annual Iris Show. Did you know Mount Pleasant is called The Iris City?"

"No, I didn't. I still don't know the town like I thought I would by now. First, making order in my house and then the pottery studio. I've done barely anything else."

"There's plenty of time. You'll find everything out. It's a nice little town."

"I know. I love living here."

* * *

The next day it was still frigid. Catherine arranged to pick Jessica up at school rather than having her walk the five blocks in the snow.

"Next time I'll have her walk," she thought. "Do her good, but I'll pick her up this once."

Jessica was waiting outside the school and talking with a couple of friends. Catherine could see the frosty breath of their laughter. When she saw Jessica with her friends, Catherine realized that she loved Jessica. Another surprise. Hadn't she always loved Jessica? No, she supposed not. She had been one of the grandchildren. Now she was a person Catherine loved. Watching her, Catherine realized she had missed her after the week they spent together while Benny was in the hospital. Today another chapter was beginning. Jessica was coming over after school.

Catherine had taken the last tray of spice cookies out of the oven before going to pick her up. When they came in the door Jessica said, "Yum. What's that smell?"

"Spice cookies. I guessed you'd like a snack while we paint."

Catherine filled a plate with cookies, and Jessica brought milk from the refrigerator.

Catherine brought the sack of painting supplies to the table, and Jessica stood the brushes in a tin can, bristles up. Catherine filled two big jars with water. They sat opposite each other, each with a white sheet of watercolor paper. They brushed colors on the paper—alizarin crimson, hooker's green, winsor yellow, ultramarine blue. They didn't talk much. Painting was enough.

Catherine finished first. She carried her watercolor into the living room, leaned it against the mirror over the mantle, and stood across the room gazing at it. Jessica came in carrying her still wet painting and stood next to Catherine.

"That's amazing, Gram. I didn't know you could paint like that."

"Why, thank you, Jessica," Catherine said, pleased. "When I was a girl I thought I'd grow up and be a painter, you know."

"I never knew that. You should have. You're good."

Jessica put her painting on the mantle and rejoined Catherine so they could admire their work.

"I like your painting, Jessica. Especially the wispy green of the trees in that valley. I think we're both making progress."

"I like painting."

Catherine glanced into the kitchen to check the time.

"Your dad will be here to pick you up soon. Let's clean up, and then I have something I want to show you."

Catherine put the paints away while Jessica washed brushes and rinsed the water jars. Then they sat at the table with the wildflower book between them. Catherine opened the book and turned several pages while Jessica looked on.

"Would you like to plant a garden of your own in the spring?" Catherine asked.

"I don't know anything about plants. I'd probably kill everything."

Catherine laughed. "I don't think you would. Flowers grow themselves in Iowa. I thought you might plant under the kitchen windows where Blue can enjoy them."

"I don't know," Jessica said, shrugging her shoulders. "I guess so."

Blue had been quiet since that evening at supper when he had sung for Phil and Catherine. Now he again hopped onto his perch and started singing. Jessica spun around in her chair.

"Listen to that! I can't believe that big sound can come out of that little bird."

Blue stopped singing and looked at her.

Jessica walked over to the cage. "Pretty song, Blue. Pretty bird."

"That's the second time he's done that," Catherine said. "The first time was on that really cold night last week. Seems like he's finally becoming himself."

"About that garden," Jessica said. "I think I would like to try it, Gram, if you'll help me."

"We can do it together."

They heard the truck pull up out front.

"Sounds like your dad's here. I'm waiting for some catalogues to come in the mail. Then we can decide what to order. Would you like to take this book home so you can look through it?"

"Maybe I should look at it the next time I come over. I'm afraid I'd lose it in the house."

"I'll keep it here then." Catherine opened the door for Tom while Jessica put her coat on and gathered her backpack and her painting.

"Look, Dad." She held out her painting.

"Beautiful, Jessica. Just wonderful. I like it."

"You do? You can have it if you want."

Tom looked at Catherine. A muscle twitched in his cheek. Kids could do that to a parent.

* * *

One evening toward the middle of February, Phil went over to Hank's house to borrow some materials he needed to tie his spring flies. Besides Phil, Hank was the most serious fisherman in the local Walton League. Phil had spent several evenings out in Hank's shop through the years solving the world's problems while they tied a few flies. Phil had been puzzling over how to present the fishing idea to Benny. He was eager to pass on what he knew—and also what he believed—about the fine art of angling.

"Honestly, Hank, I'm afraid I'll scare him away. You know me. There's no stopping me when I start talking about fishing."

"And what's wrong with that? Some of the greatest folks of all time have been fishermen. How better could a fellow spend his time than fishing?"

"I know. My grandfather made fly fishing an art, and though he was as dignified as any man I ever saw, when he talked about fishing I swear he grew bigger right before my eyes."

"See? You know what I mean. And how did your grandfather hook you on fishing?"

"That's a good way to put it. When I was about eight, Grandpa invited me to come along on a fishing excursion. We fought our way through brush and over downed trees to a deep fishing hole. He cautioned me to be very quiet for this was his secret fishing hole where the biggest fish in the river lay, and, smart as they were, they might hear us and go someplace else."

"He was a cagey codger, wasn't he? The secret fishing hole. The dream of every one of us."

"When we were at the river, Grandpa pointed silently to a fallen log where I was supposed to sit. I sat and watched while Grandpa fished. His concentration was so complete, it was as if I didn't exist. I found myself more and more silent. No fidgeting. I was a pair of eyes, watching. He tied a fly on the line and cast, then again and again."

"Don't tell me. The fish were being elusive that morning?"

"Indeed," Phil agreed. "But he kept on changing flies, casting perfectly, dropping his fly in the center of the pool. When we arrived the pool had been deep in shadow, but the sun had found its way onto the water when he turned to me and said, 'There's a trout in that pool. I can't catch him. Here, you try.' And he handed me his rod."

"The pressure was on. What did you do?"

"I took the rod, stood where he had been standing and cast. And darned if I didn't catch that trout. That was it for me. I was hooked."

"You and the fish both."

"Yep, and it's been about the best thing in my life," Phil said. "Without fishing I would've gone nuts long before this."

"Me, too, buddy," Hank said. "Me, too. Maybe you should try your grandfather's method with Benny since it worked so well with you."

"That might work, but I need to bring him aboard now before the season starts. He's had a real tough time, you know, and I'm trying to help him settle back down. Thought we could wrap a rod for him, tie some flies together, that sort of thing."

"I bet he'd like that. What do you need to start?"

"My feathers are all too old. They're brittle and they've lost their luster. I could also use some silver and gold mylar tinsel if you have extra."

Hank opened the metal cabinet where he kept his fly tying materials separated so he could find what he needed with one hand while holding a half-made fly with the other. While Hank pulled materials out of one small drawer after another, Phil fell back to thinking about Benny and how he hoped fishing would help give Benny back to himself. He wanted fishing to be as important to Benny as it had been to him.

"Just as I wanted it for Jack," he thought.

Phil caught the breath that suddenly had run away from him. But Jack hadn't wanted to fish. He was much more likely to climb a tree and sit up there drawing a bird's nest or the way the yard looked from above. Phil knew that Jack tried to like fishing because Phil wanted him to, but it never caught hold of him the way it had Phil. He wondered if maybe that was why Jack had . . . . No, Phil would not think it. Benny. Think about Benny. Phil didn't know about Benny. He would have to wait and see if Benny was a fisherman. He could offer it. He wouldn't push. But he could hope.

Hank had made several small piles on the workbench. "How's that? A half ounce packet of hackle feathers, a bunch of fancy feathers—wood duck, pheasant, and guinea fowl—a few quills. That'll give you a good start."

"I'll say. Thanks, Hank." Phil turned away. Why he was so emotional, he didn't know.

Hank put the feathers in little plastic bags. He dropped the whole batch into a paper sack along with a spool of medium mylar tinsel and another of fine.

"How about a beer?" Hank asked.

"Thanks, but I'd better go home. You seen Stan lately?"

"Speaking of beer, huh? No, I think he's been pretty busy with that 19th Hole out at the golf club. How about you?"

"I haven't seen him either. I've been busy with Benny since Christmas. I think I'm done with darts anyway."

"Really?"

"Yeah. The Jug's not the same anymore. Pretty rowdy crowd."

"I don't know. I think it's always been rowdy, but I know what you mean. I don't find myself over there much anymore either. Times change, I guess."

"Yeah. Well, thanks again."
"Let me know if you need anything else."
"I will, thanks. Goodnight."

* * *

By the next time Jessica came over after school, the catalogues had arrived. Cross-referencing the wildflower book and the catalogues, Catherine helped Jessica plan an order for native Iowa wildflower seed from two companies.

When they finished, Catherine said, "You remember our neighbor, Jaz? Do you want to go over and see her studio?"

"The lady who shook my hand when we met?" Jessica asked. "What kind of studio?"

"She makes pots in the old shed in her backyard. She invited us to come over and make something if we want to."

"You, too?"

"I think it would be fun."

"Ok, I guess so."

"I'll call our seed order in so they can process it right away, and then we'll go over. Jaz told me she'd be out in the studio all afternoon."

Jessica took the dishes to the sink while Catherine called the seed companies.

Catherine took two aprons out of the drawer and handed one to Jessica. "We'd better take these. Your mother wouldn't like it if you had clay all over your school clothes when you came home."

Catherine and Jessica squeezed through the gap in the hedge between the backyards and walked up the winding path to the studio. Before they could knock, Jaz opened the door.

"I saw you coming. Come on in where it's warm."

Catherine hadn't been in the little studio before. The building had spent most of its long life as a garden shed and still had an uneven earthen floor and rough wooden walls. Jaz had tacked foam insulation between the studs and on the peaked ceiling. A cast iron stove tucked into a corner put off plenty of heat for the small space. Windows in all four walls added weak winter light to the bright lights strung overhead. Tables lining two walls met in the corner, and shelves above the tables held pottery and other ceramic pieces in various stages of drying. A big kiln squatted next to the stove and a potter's wheel and bench stood in the middle of the floor.

"What a cozy place," Catherine said. "Jaz, you remember Jessica?"

"Of course. How are you, Jessica?"

"Good." Jessica warmed her hands over the stove. "Brr, it's cold outside."

"This place will warm you up." Jaz hung their jackets on pegs by the stove. "Good, I see you brought aprons."

Catherine and Jessica put their aprons on while Jaz used a wire to cut a hunk of red clay from a barrel in the corner. She carried the hunk over to the table and cut it again into three pieces.

"Here you go. We can start by kneading the clay so there aren't any air bubbles left in it."

Jessica and Catherine watched Jaz push the clay, then turn it and push again. They started kneading their own clay.

"I remember this from high school," Catherine said. "It's just like kneading bread dough."

"How do you know when all the bubbles are out?" Jessica asked.

"I usually count while I knead," Jaz said. "About thirty times usually does it."

Jessica quietly counted out loud to thirty and stopped kneading. "That's done."

"Now you can form your clay into a ball and make whatever you want. The only thing to know, really, is not to make it too thick."

"How thick is too thick?" Jessica asked.

"Half an inch at the most. Otherwise it may blow up in the kiln. One more thing. If you want to stick pieces together, score both pieces first and use some water. Here, I'll show you."

Jaz pulled a tray of tools and a container of water over to

where they were working. She took a sharp stylus and made several deep lines in two pieces of clay, dipped her fingers in the water and then on the score lines, pushed the pieces together, and then smoothed the joint between them. "There you are."

Jessica worked quickly, making a creature about eight inches tall with a fat belly and horns. She added curls to its head, shoe laces dangling from its shoes, and a little jacket with buttons.

"I love my little guy. Isn't he cute?"

Catherine worked slowly, smoothing the clay until she had made a sweeping wave.

Jaz had begun by dropping her clay from a couple of feet above the table to flatten it. Then she had pressed a piece of screening on the clay to form a pattern, pinched and pushed the clay until a large lumpy fish appeared.

"Phil would like that. He's a fisherman before anything," Catherine said.

"Next time you and Jessica come over you can make him a fish. I have a bin of things you can use to texturize the clay or you can bring something from home. I've made quite a few fish." Jaz pointed to the wall behind the stove where a whole school of colorful fish hung.

"Would he be surprised if I brought something like that home for him," Catherine said.

"Now we wrap our pieces in plastic so they don't dry too quickly and crack," Jaz said. "We'll put them up on this shelf, and we can fire them next week."

"Do I have to fire mine?" Jessica asked. "What if it breaks in the kiln?"

"I don't think it will," Jaz answered. "It's not too thick and your joints are smooth."

"Well, ok, if you think it'll be all right."

"Don't we paint them before they're fired?" Catherine asked.

"We fire them twice. The first time they're called greenware. Then we'll glaze them and fire them again. Glazing is fun."

Catherine looked out the window and saw that it was dark. "It's later than I thought. We'd better clean up and head home.

Your dad will be along soon, Jessica."

They scraped the table and washed it down, rinsed the clay tools at the sink in the corner. Jaz turned on the outside light so Catherine and Jessica could see their way back through the hedge.

* * *

The afternoon Benny came over to begin learning how to tie flies was cold and gray. A few snowflakes drifted in the air as Phil drove to pick him up at school. Benny would stay the afternoon and have an early supper with them. Catherine was home making a cherry pie from the last of the cherries she had picked from their tree and frozen in May. Benny was particularly fond of cherry pie, but then, Phil thought, who wasn't?

He arrived at the school and went in to collect Benny from his classroom. As he walked down the long corridor, the dismissal bell rang. Children poured into the hall. Phil side-stepped the throng and walked into Benny's classroom. A few children were still putting their leftover lunches and schoolbooks into backpacks. Phil spied Benny, his backpack on, standing to one side watching the activity around him. Phil waved; Benny looked startled, then flew to Phil's side and buried himself in Phil's soft jacket.

"Hey, Grandpa. I forgot you were coming today."

"Hi, buddy." Phil ruffled Benny's hair. "Today's our day all right. You ready to go?"

* * *

Catherine took the pie out of the oven and put it in a high cupboard to cool so it would be a surprise after supper. She left a snack for Phil and Benny to eat down in the shop and drove out for a walk in the park. There was a thaw the week before, and the trails had been too muddy to walk. Today the low gray sky looked like snow. It was plenty cold for the ground to be frozen again. Catherine and Fern had plans to meet now that the weather shifted.

Phil and Benny found the snack and a note from Catherine on the table.

"Let's take this downstairs." Phil gathered apples, cheese and a bag of corn chips into one arm.

He led Benny down to his shop, turning on lights along the way. It was rare anybody except Phil came into his shop, and this was Benny's first visit. Phil kept the shop straight but only swept it out a couple of times a year. Catherine had offered to clean it, but Phil reminded her, "It's a shop, after all." Thin light filtered in from two windows set high in the walls. Phil turned on the bright overhead light. You could never have too much light to tie a decent fly.

Benny lagged behind on the bottom stair.

"Come on in, Benny boy." Phil dumped the snack on the long workbench and held out a hand to Benny.

The workbench ran the length of the window wall. Phil used one end for carpentry projects and the other for fishing. Above the bench on the carpentry end, Phil had hammered up some pegboard so he could find his favorite tools in an instant.

"Do we use those to make the flies?" Benny pointed to the screwdrivers, chisels, hammers and wrenches that hung there.

"No, they're way too big. Would you like to learn to use them sometime?"

"What could we make with them?"

"Anything you want. We have all the tools you'd need to build anything out of wood."

"Like a tree house?"

"Yes, we can build a tree house. We can build one in the spring if you'd like."

"Do you have the wood, too?"

"I have a big stack out in the garage. We can use as much as we need."

"Can we build it out at my house? Joey and I want a treehouse down in the woods. We were talking about it that day . . . ." Benny broke off.

Phil put his arm around Benny's shoulders and hugged him. "We can build it anywhere you say. Joey can help us."

"Really, Grandpa? Can my dad help, too?"

"If he wants to." Phil said.

Phil could picture them building the treehouse together with the boys. He knew that Tom usually hired out any sizable projects around the farm, but Phil was confident that he would be more than willing to work with the boys.

"Now, over here's where we keep the fishing gear."

Phil helped Benny climb up on the high stool in front of the workbench. "Looks like we need another stool. I'll go borrow one from the kitchen."

When Phil came back, Benny was leaning across the workbench looking at the fly tying gear. The bench was constructed of heavy boards glue-laminated together, planed smooth, oiled and rubbed. It had taken on a deep reddish brown glow from Phil's many peaceful hours here tying flies and wrapping rods. He wanted to introduce Benny to this part of his life in just the right way, and he noticed his palms were sweating. Phil was relieved by Benny's interest in his carpentry tools. It had given him a few minutes to become accustomed to having Benny in his shop. Until now it had been his private place.

At the back of the bench were a couple of cabinets in which Phil kept his materials and supplies. One cabinet had slots and the other drawers. On one side sat a box with a snap lid where Phil could seal the wool, feathers and fur he used in his flies and keep them from the moths.

Phil sat up on the stool he brought from the kitchen.

"Well, Benny, let's see. Where shall we begin? I started fishing when I was your age or a bit younger, even. My grandpa was a fisherman, and I couldn't stay away from it. I don't know whether you'll like it or not. I hope you will. It would be nice to have a fishing buddy."

Benny shrugged, looking self-conscious. "I've never been fishing yet, so I don't know."

"That's right." Phil warned himself, "Moving way too fast." To Benny he said, "We have to be ready for fishing months before it's warm enough to be out on the lake."

"Do we have to make everything we need?"

"Some guys buy ready-made, but for me, the biggest thrill of fishing is taking a fish on a fly I made myself with a rod I wrapped at home."

"Can we make me a rod, too?"

"Of course. I've already ordered a blank for you from St. Croix. I made my favorite rod from a St. Croix blank, so I called them and, wouldn't you know it, they're just now beginning to make a great 7'6" starter rod. They're sending a blank and all the gear we'll need to assemble it. It should be here next week. For today, why don't we look at some of the flies I've thought up myself, and then you can make one."

Phil pulled his battered old tackle box from under the workbench and opened it. Benny clambered onto his knees and leaned over the workbench to look into the box.

"That's a lot of stuff in there."

Phil carefully lifted out a small tray fitted with tiny compartments. It was filled with colorful flies. He picked out several and laid them in a row on the bench in front of Benny. Benny hesitated.

"Go ahead, pick one up. Just be careful of the barb on the hook."

Benny gingerly held the most colorful fly up so the light caught the purple and green sheen of peacock herl. The tiny fly shimmered as Benny moved it this way and that.

"It's pretty. Can we make one like that?"

"Yes, easy." Pulling together the materials they would need took only a moment. Phil knew where everything was. He suspected he could have tied this fly and a number of others in his sleep, if need be.

"This is what we'll need." Phil listed the items as he placed them on the bench: "A couple of Number eight hooks, a spool of black nylon tying thread, some poly-yarn for dubbing, a pile of peacock herl for you to choose from, some mylar tinsel. That should do it."

"I can tell this is going to be fun," Benny said. "I can always tell."

From a tray on the bench Phil took out some hackle pliers, a pair of small sharp scissors and a stiletto.

"That looks just like the thing the dentist pokes my teeth with."

"That's exactly what it is. Dr. Blake gave it to me himself. Best thing I've ever found to separate fibers and hold bits of feather in place. Works great. Now, this vise," he said, indicating a small vise with tapered jaws mounted on the workbench, "these pliers, scissors and this stiletto are all we need to make hundreds of successful flies."

"Hundreds?" Phil heard dismay in Benny's voice.

"I can use several hundred flies in a solid week of fishing. Don't worry, they don't take long to make, and I have a bunch left over from last year. Didn't fish much last season."

"Oh," Benny said. "How do we start?"

"I'll make one to show you and then you can make the next one."

Benny watched Phil tie the tiny fly with his big fingers like it was the simplest thing in the world. Phil put a hook in the tying vise and ran a length of thread over a lump of beeswax.

"Here's how to tie in the tip." He wrapped the thread on the hook and tied in some tinsel. "Next we tie in the tail." He trimmed a wisp of fibers, twisted them and tied them in.

"How will I remember all that?"

"Don't worry, I'll help you. Next we tie in a bit of floss for the body, then we tie in the herl body in a clump." Phil held his fingers aside so Benny could see. "Now, whip finish and we're done."

Then Phil showed Benny, step by step, how to tie his own dry fly. When they were finished they compared the three flies—the one Benny had picked from Phil's tackle box, the one Phil had made, and Benny's own.

"You know what I think?" Phil asked.

"What?"

"That any one of these would catch the slyest fish."

"You think so?"

"I really do."

Just then they heard Catherine come in the back door.

"Let's take these up and show Grandma," Phil said. "Then we can go to the den and look at fishing magazines until supper's ready. What do you say?"

"Ok," Benny agreed. "But, Grandpa, when can I come back and tie some more flies?"

"Soon, buddy, real soon."

* * *

During supper Catherine showered attention on Benny. She had rarely seen him since his accident—a couple of visits to the hospital and a few brief glimpses since he came home. She had spent most of her energy on Jessica while Phil had been with Benny. She was relieved to see Benny more relaxed and talkative than he had been when she saw him last.

His first hand-tied fly sat in the place of honor on a white mat in the center of the table. Next to it, a vase of forsythia branches was beginning to blossom. Every winter when tiny buds formed along the forsythia branches, Catherine cut an armful. When the buds opened, spring felt close. Benny kept looking from his fly to Phil and Catherine, eyes sparkling. He liked the cherry pie as much as Catherine had hoped, too.

Phil felt satisfied with the afternoon with Benny. It had gone better than he had imagined, and none of his fears of Benny's being bored or clumsy had materialized. Benny had good hands and a good eye. Phil could see that. What remained to be seen was if he would love fishing. He would have to wait and see.

And Catherine. During supper he watched Catherine with Benny, how she served his cherry pie and gave him a quick warm hug after setting the plate down. Seeing her with Benny, he remembered her with Jack and found himself having to look away.

When Tom came to pick Benny up, Catherine stood in the front doorway waving goodbye. The porch light shone on her and Phil, waving from the window, looked over and saw her.

Catherine was beautiful.

After Tom and Benny drove away, Phil went back down to his shop, quietly closing the basement door behind him. The shop was one more place where he could think. He sat on his stool and arranged and rearranged the bits of fur, feather and wool Hank had given him. He twirled the gold and silver mylar tinsel and thought about Catherine. He had become used to the life they had together. He didn't particularly like the idea of it changing either. Yet the vision of Catherine in the doorway as lovely as when he had first seen her . . . . The loveliness of all those months of going everywhere together, loving each other with a joy that he was certain would never stop . . . .

Phil started automatically tying flies and before long had a row before him on the bench. Catherine. A fierceness rose up in him.

"As she is tonight, she is beautiful," he thought. "Never mind what happened. Never mind this whole long mess."

Something Jaz had said to him the first time they talked . . . . Now, what was it? One of those memories coming back like coils of a rope. Coil by coil he pulled it back to himself. Ah, yes.

"I'd rather be happy than right any day," she had said. Now he remembered. She had also said, "I'd rather want what I have than have what I want." He couldn't exactly make sense of that, but he hadn't forgotten it either.

Catherine was waiting upstairs right now, he thought. She was there everyday and, he knew without doubt, she would continue to be there no matter what he chose to do about it. She was beautiful and largely because of his bull-headedness he had missed out on her life. He could no longer deny that.

It was true: the pain was great. It was the great fact of his life. He had been lonely all this time. For the first time he realized how lonely Catherine must be, too. Maybe that was something he could do something about.

The thought of Catherine's little canary came to him. Anyone could see that Blue had suffered before he found his way into Catherine's pocket that day at the fair. Even after she brought him home, he had been sad and frightened for a long time despite the best care and loving Catherine and, later, Phil himself, could give.

Yet one day, Blue had begun to sing. All he had done, Phil could see, was what canaries do, but it seemed to Phil that Blue had courage. He came back to doing what canaries do in spite of the fact that he had been so badly hurt.

What did men do? Phil wondered. What was the natural and right thing for a man to do? A man who had been hurt as he had, a man who had been betrayed by the most important person in his life. What did a man do? Maybe the most natural thing was to love the people who were in his life. As Phil had lately been loving Benny. As Catherine had been loving him the whole long time.

He could see the change in her. It nagged at him. That she could change. In spite of his continuing to shut her out, she was beginning to be the Catherine who sang to canaries, who went off for long walks in the woods and came home with a flower behind her ear, the Catherine who went off to dance class without him because she had always wanted to dance. Tonight he had seen her. She had appeared in the doorway. She was his own private vision.

Phil tidied up his workspace, shut off the light and went upstairs. The light was on over the stove, and Blue's cage was draped in the yellow tablecloth, signs that Catherine had gone to bed.

When he was ready for bed, Phil climbed in beside Catherine. He lay there listening to her breath and his own. From her breathing and from a certain way she held herself in the darkness, he knew she was still awake. He reached out in the dark and laid his hand on her shoulder.

Catherine felt herself gasp in her spirit, but she didn't pull away. She lay, willing her heart to be still, ordering her breathing to return to quiet even breaths so Phil wouldn't know how his touch stirred her. Tears silently crept from her eyes, slid down her cheeks and fell into her ears. Smiling in the night, she reached up and covered Phil's hand with her own.

They were quiet. After a time their hands drifted apart.
Softly, Phil said, "Good night, Catherine."
"Good night, Phil."
Phil sighed deeply. Relieved of a great burden, he slept.

CHAPTER

10

The first of March howled through southeast Iowa.

"Nothing early about this spring," Catherine thought.

She harvested the last of the winter vegetables from under the cold frames. With her fingers in the dirt, Catherine looked back on the winter and declared it good. More had happened in the past five months than in the past five years.

Blue was finally canary yellow. He sang at the oddest times but more and more often. Anybody seeing him for the first time would think he was just another canary in a cage. Catherine always stopped to greet him when she came in. She sang and talked to Blue and to herself about life. She watched Phil doing the same and whistling as he moved about the house, not just to Blue, but anytime. There were the three of them filling the house with humming, singing and whistling. Maybe they would end up in a band or something.

Catherine carried her basket of vegetables into the house and set it down next to the box of seeds that had arrived the week before. She had enough beets and greens to give some to Jaz. This was the day they had planned to start the tomato and pepper seeds in flats. Catherine's back porch was glassed in and heated so there would be plenty of natural light as well as the warmth the seeds needed to germinate.

* * *

Phil and Benny settled into a routine. Tuesdays, Phil met Benny out at his house. Thursdays, Phil picked Benny up at school and they spent the afternoon in Phil's shop tying flies and wrapping Benny's first fly rod.

Benny's confidence grew visibly as he practiced until he could tie a fly nearly as deftly as Phil himself. From listening to Phil, Benny formed opinions on the validity of the dry fly versus the wet, the light fly versus the dark. Benny became a firm believer in the fly which would float and thereby give the impression of life rather than the sunken fly which would, at best, imitate an aquatic grub. At worst he knew that his dry fly might sink and look like a dead fly, but that was a chance, even at age ten, Benny was philosophical enough to realize he would have to take.

Phil loved listening to Benny expound on the different theories and methods of fly fishing. Although Phil assured him that any theory, no matter how well thought out or how much experimentation the angler did, only worked half the time, Benny's opinions were set.

Phil cautioned Benny. "I've seen a fly tied to a particular pattern take fish after fish one day. The next day the fish totally ignored it."

"How do you know which flies to tie then?"

"My best fish thinking still only works half the time. I'm used to it, but that doesn't keep me from trying new flies and new strategies. I keep hoping one day I'll find the magic formula which will draw the fish to my flies like bees to honey."

Benny also loved listening to Phil.

"I heard about a fisherman who took fish on a bare hook tied with a few threads and a bit of berry," Phil said. "Then there was Dame Juliana Berners who wrote about angling four hundred years ago."

"What's angling?"

"Fishing. She wrote about a fly made of cow dung."

"Ewww." Benny screwed up his face. "I'm going to make up flies that will catch all the fish."

"I bet you will. One famous fly is called the 'Professor'. The story is that a college professor arrived at his favorite fishing spot and discovered he had forgotten his fly box. He pulled threads from his socks to tie buttercup petals to his hooks. They were so successful that a standard fly was fashioned and named for him."

"The 'Benny'. That's a good name for a fly."

"Bet you will come up with something good. You have the touch."

"But do you think I'll catch fish?"

"You have as good a start as any boy I know."

While they worked, Phil thought of the only other boy he had known well—besides himself. Jack drifted into Phil's mind. Once, while he and Benny were working closely, heads together, Phil found himself remembering how it felt to be close to Jack when he was a little boy, and he felt an unexpected longing for his son.

Another time, being uncertain about how to tie the herl into his fly, Benny looked trustingly to Phil for encouragement. Phil felt a twinge in his heart, and before he knew it, he called Benny "Jack."

"Jack—Benny—I mean . . . ."

Benny paid no attention to the mistake.

* * *

Phil thought more and more often of Jack, his own boy who was now a man, older than Phil had been when he first introduced Jack to fishing. Jack, a man and a stranger. Phil didn't know what Jack was doing. He had not wanted to know. Until now. Now, he was happy Catherine had kept in touch with Jack. He had seen the letters. He had heard the quiet phone conversations. He had sometimes even then wanted to listen in, to read Jack's letters, to ask, "Is he all right?" But he had taken a stand, and he would stand there until he died, Jack be damned.

He was in the midst of a vast universe. The stars moved at a dizzying rate. He himself sitting on planet Earth was hurtling through space. Worst of all, Catherine was changing, and he could no longer stand fast where he had planted himself. He himself was moving now. He could feel it. Jack was, somehow, a part of that. He was no longer numb. Jack was his son, and he had been out of touch for too long.

At least he wouldn't let Benny's childhood go by without their becoming friends. Phil liked Benny and found him interesting. One day while they were taking a break from wrapping Benny's new rod, Benny came up with an idea for a 4-H project he could enter in the county fair.

"I'll make a book with the flies I use and which fish I catch with them."

"Can you use that kind of project for the fair?"

"I think I can. I'll have to ask Mr. Sanders. He'll know."

"So you'd write everything down in a fishing journal. And then what?"

"I'd have the journal and my tackle box and a display of flies and my new rod." The idea excited Benny as he talked about it. "It'll be great."

"It sounds good. That reminds me—we have to find you a tackle box."

"I want one just like yours."

"Mine's old and beat up."

"I know. That's why I like it."

"Well, there are a couple of auctions this weekend. Bet we could find some sort of box that would work just fine. Would you like to go?"

"What kind of auction? Like auctioning hogs?"

"People auction all kinds of stuff. There are two estate auctions coming up in the country north of town."

"What's an estate?"

"An estate auction is where somebody dies and their family sells the stuff they don't want. It's fun. I think you'll like it."

* * *

Catherine and Jessica settled into a routine, too. Every Wednesday Jessica walked from school to Catherine's house.

Some afternoons they painted, and others they went over to Jaz's studio. When the wildflower seeds arrived, Catherine found a small graph paper notebook so Jessica could keep plans for her first garden. She also bought her a pair of gardening gloves, a trowel and spading fork, and a basket to keep it all in. That Wednesday, when Jessica came from school, the basket sat on the kitchen table. Catherine had filled it with the packets of seed and the things she had bought.

"Oh, Gram, look what you did!" Jessica hugged Catherine and started crying. "Why are you so nice to me?"

"What kind of a question is that? Because I love you, of course."

"Thanks, Gram. I love you, too."

* * *

Tuesday nights, Catherine picked Alice up and drove to the dance studio. Mr. Moore led them through the waltz, the fox-trot, the cha-cha and the polka. Whit counted through the waltz and fox-trot. The polka was fast enough to take his breath away. He gave up counting. As for Catherine, as soon as she began dancing the polka, she started laughing and never stopped until she fell exhausted into a chair at the side of the room. Catherine loved the polka.

Fern and her husband, Frank, stayed with the class also. Although Alice didn't have a consistent partner, she loved dancing and didn't mind. As the group became more proficient, Mr. Moore introduced them to the samba, the tango, and, to Catherine's delight, the Charleston.

There was talk of their participating in dance competitions. Catherine hadn't known that there was a 'dance community,' as Mr. Moore called it, in southeastern Iowa. She couldn't see herself competing, but she was having so much fun she figured she would see how she felt when the time arrived.

Mr. Moore complimented Catherine and Whit on the smoothness of their footwork and their timing. Catherine sometimes found herself wishing Phil would change his mind about dancing, but it was nice to have some time away from him, too.

* * *

One evening Phil and Catherine started talking about Benny over supper. Phil moved right along with her as she cleaned up the kitchen after the meal. He cleared the table, putting food away in the refrigerator and bringing her the dishes while she filled the sink with sudsy water. Phil wiped the table down and leaned against the counter telling her about his and Benny's trip to the auctions the day before.

Catherine finished washing up, noticing how easy she felt with Phil—like the early days. She was a little afraid Phil would see how pleased she was and be scared away.

The dishes done, they moved into the living room and Phil switched on a soft light, not enough to read by. Catherine somehow knew they would not be reading tonight.

Sitting on the couch, Phil began. "About the past, Catherine. Can we forget it and start over? Please?"

Catherine watched his face for a sign. Perhaps for a flock of birds flying across it, for something to tell her what she might say next. Phil's face was unreadable. No sign appeared.

She took a breath and plunged in. "Of course I wish I could forget it, too, but I have to talk about what happened or I'm afraid it will never really be done with."

Phil hunched down into the couch. He reminded Catherine of Blue during those first months after she brought him from the fair. Catherine took another breath.

"Everything I did was for the wrong reasons." She rushed on before her fear could stop her. "I never wanted to be with anybody but you. I didn't think I could live without you. I thought you'd go up to State and meet girls—prettier and smarter than me—and I was afraid of losing you."

"No need to have been afraid of that." Phil voice came out gruffly though he felt as tender as a newborn chick.

"I know that now, but then I didn't. So I suggested we date other people so if you did fall in love with someone else maybe it wouldn't hurt so much."

"That was your reason?" Phil was stunned.

"Yes, I never wanted to be with anybody but you. I thought you were probably dating girls up there, so when Mike asked me out I said yes. I didn't even like Mike. He was so full of himself. Then you called me from school. I could tell that nothing I could do would make you forgive me. I felt like I would die."

"Die?"

"Well, I may as well have died. The person that meant the most to me, the one who made me happy, the only person I could tell my dreams to and make dreams with—he is the one I hurt. It did feel like I died. Well, maybe not completely died right away, but over time I died. My dreams weren't strong enough to hold up without you holding them up with me."

Phil closed his eyes. Catherine watched him. After a few minutes he opened his eyes, took her hand, looked down at the rug and said, "What a fool I've been. I thought you were tired of me. When you suggested we date other people, I thought you were looking for a way to say goodbye without hurting my feelings too much."

"Oh, no! I was crazy about you."

"Then when Jake told me about you and Mike, I figured you loved him and not me."

"Love Mike? Like I said, I didn't even like him."

"Didn't even like him. Then why . . . ," Phil broke off. "When you stopped seeing Mike and acted like you were willing to see me again, I figured we could just go on like we had before."

"But it was never the same."

"No, it never was. But now . . . . Is it too late? Will you forgive me?"

"Forgive you? Of course, I will. Will you forgive me, I mean, not all at once, but when you can?"

"I wish I had been able to forgive you from the start. I love you, Catherine."

Phil reached over and held Catherine, tears running down his cheeks.

"I love you, Phil." His shoulder muffled Catherine's voice. Something tight let go in her, and she started crying, too.

Phil held her while she cried, feeling a protectiveness he had felt for her long ago and had forgotten. His own tears continued to fall as he realized that Catherine, the only one he had allowed to see him, could see him again because he would let her. The sadness washed through, and a weary peace took its place.

The irony of the moment amused Catherine even through her tears. For so many years she had hoped for this day. When she had finally given up hoping on Phil and started to build her own happiness, what she had been wishing through all the years came to her. After the tears subsided, they sat holding hands on the couch.

Catherine began tentatively, "Phil, do you remember we used to talk about what our life would be like?"

"That's a long time ago, but I remember. We wanted a house in the country and two kids, a boy and a girl . . . ."

"We never built our house. You wanted to, but I wouldn't."

"It would have been too difficult for you to be out there in the country with my mother so close."

"I could have made friends with her. I always meant to."

"No, she would never give way. Where do you think my stubbornness came from?"

Catherine laughed. "Yes, but look at you now. Your mom could've changed. You don't know."

"Maybe so, but it didn't happen that way. We're here now."

"Yes, and I do love this house. Don't you?"

Phil thought of his shop and his den and the porch. Did he love it? "I'm comfortable with it, I guess. Still hanker after the country though, to be honest."

"We can still make a change. You're retired, we have enough money set aside. We can do anything we want."

"You sound like you've been talking to Jaz. I've been thinking the same thing myself. Ok, so let's say we can do anything we want. What would you like to do?"

"Well, that's quite a question." She closed her eyes. "Ok then, just for instance," she said opening them again, "I'd like to go on a big trip. I've always wanted to travel."

Phil looked startled, and Catherine rushed to reassure him.

"Not out of the country, but all over the States and maybe into Canada."

"In the car?" Phil couldn't believe she had this idea but never told him.

"In a motor home. We'd buy a motor home—a used one to save money—and fix it up and take off on a trip. Then if we liked it, we could take off on another trip."

Catherine looked more like she had as a girl than Phil could have believed possible. She had crossed her legs at the knee and clasped her hands around one of them. While she talked he watched her foot swing up and down. Her eyes were bright in her soft wrinkled face. Another feeling he had forgotten rose in him. Catherine was his own dear girl. He felt proud to be married to her.

"So you want to take a trip. What else?"

"No, it's your turn. What about you?"

"Me, I don't know. I guess I'd like to take a trip, too, as long as there are plenty of places to go fishing along the way."

"That's just about everywhere. What else?"

Phil was quiet. "Well, I want to see Jack, Catherine. I miss Jack."

"Oh, Phil. Really . . . ?" Catherine felt the tears well up in her eyes again.

"There are a great many things I regret. As much as I've regretted holding back from you, I hated myself for turning my back on Jack. What can I do about it?"

"I don't know. I guess all you can do is let him know you want to see him. Then see what happens."

"You think so?"

"I know he's missed you, too." Catherine was quiet for a moment, then continued, "I have my own regrets, you know."

"You do?"

"The worst was the affair with Mike, but I've been grumpy to you all this time, to pay you back for not loving me anymore."

"I never stopped loving you, you know. And I don't think you were so grumpy. You've taken good care of me and the kids all these years."

"But without very many kind words to go along with it."

"Who can blame you? Who can be sweet day after day to somebody who mostly pretends you're not even there?"

"In any case, I'm sorry about it. I've been finding out it's easier to be nice than to be a grump. And that's not all that has me disappointed in myself."

"Really?"

"Even before I met you I had some plans. You remember, I wanted to go to art school and paint. I never did it, and I'm sorry about that, too."

"It's not too late. You've been painting with Jessica, and I liked what you did. You could take classes over at the college."

"At my age?"

"Why not?"

"I don't know. Go to school with a bunch of kids. What would they make of an old lady like me?"

"You said it yourself. We can do anything we want. If you want to paint, then paint. Remember that old gal, Grandma Moses. She painted, didn't she, and became famous for it, too."

She looked at Phil. "I've been painting some afternoons while you're out with Benny. Want to see?"

"Of course."

Catherine went into the bedroom to retrieve her paintings from under the sweaters. Phil sat back in the middle of the couch, stretching his arms out along its back, and looked around the room.

"Surveying my domain," he thought. He was amazed at how different he felt after the talk he and Catherine had had. She had never even liked Mike. She had been afraid she would lose him, Phil. That part didn't make much sense to him, but he had watched his own mind mess things up pretty well, so he couldn't hold that against her. He couldn't hold anything against her anymore. A feeling of lightness came over Phil. He thought he might float right up off the couch.

"Well, here they are." Catherine blushed as she handed the stack of paintings to Phil.

He looked through, taking time with each one. The colors were pure, and it looked like light was coming through the pictures from behind. He wondered how she did that.

"These are beautiful, Catherine."

"You think so?"

"Yes. Very beautiful. How did you do that with the light?"

"I don't know. It just happens."

"Well, I'll tell you, I wish you had gone to art school and been painting all these years. I wish I'd known . . . ."

"What good would that have done?"

"I don't know, probably none at all." Phil shrank back into the couch, discouraged again.

"I don't know that I would've kept it up if I'd started then anyway. I was ready to be married and have babies."

"But you could've gone back to it when the kids were in school."

"I didn't though, that's the point. What matters is that I want to do it now and I am. And if we go on a trip I can paint wherever we stop."

"While I'm fishing."

"Out in the boat."

Phil stopped. "The boat? You think we could bring the boat?"

"Why not? I've seen campers on the road with a boat the size of yours tied on top."

"This is beginning to sound so good I can't see what's to stop us." As soon as he said it, Phil could think of what might stop them. His mother wouldn't like their going off like that. She often said she didn't think she had much longer to live, that she wished the Lord would take her now, stuff like that all the time. Phil knew she would do everything in her power to keep them at home.

Catherine, on the other hand, floated on a cloud of possibility. They could do anything. All the years of frustration and disappointment melted away. The mountain between her and Phil was turning to honey before her eyes.

The next day dawned bright and clear. Phil had planned to meet Hank for lunch at the Iris Restaurant. They had often eaten there through the years when Phil was working at Kent. When he walked in, a couple of the waitresses called to him.

"Hi, Phil, how ya doin'?"

"Long time no see. Where you been keepin' yourself?"

"Hi Sherl. Hi Patti," Phil called back. Such a homey atmosphere. The restaurant was full as usual with business people grabbing a quick bite. He nodded to some Kent people as he walked to the back where he saw Hank waiting for him.

Hank half rose to shake Phil's hand. "Good to see you."

"You, too. How was your morning?"

"You know, same old grind." Hank winked at Phil. Phil knew that Hank had a pretty fun job and liked it.

"I hate to see you suffering. Good thing retirement's just around the corner."

"That's right. How's it going with your grandson?"

"Swell. He has a good eye and great hands for tying flies. We're building him a rod, too, and he's excited."

"Ready to be out there on the lake, is he?"

"Yep. You should hear him, Hank. He has as many opinions as a veteran fly fisherman. He'll have to test them out, but they're good ones."

"Hmmm, I wonder where those came from. Never been fishing but has opinions. Grandpa is helping him start thinking like a fish. Now whose opinions do you think he has?"

"Rest assured that I've warned him about settling on a fixed idea about method. I've made it clear that he'll want to experiment. He's already dreaming of a famous fly named after him."

"Must be a great kid."

"The best. He's going to put together a fishing display for the county fair. Says he'll enter it through his 4-H Club."

"Quite an enterprising young man."

Just then, Patti arrived to take their order.

"The usual?"

"Sounds good," Hank said.

"You remember what my usual is?" Phil asked.

"Of course. Pastrami on rye, dill pickles, chips, and a coke."

Phil shook his head. "You have me."

When Patti went to put the order in, Phil asked, "So Hank, how's it going for you? I mean, are you lonely?"

Hank shrugged. "Not lonely, exactly. As you know, Stella left me because we didn't spend enough time together. I'm really kind of a loner. Send me off by myself fishing, and you see a happy man. What about you?"

"Well, of course I'm married, but I always thought of myself as a loner, too. Catherine does her thing, and I keep pretty much to myself. That's been the way for a long time. But now . . . ."

"And now?"

"We're thinking of buying a camper and traveling around the country. Taking the boat and fishing along the way."

"Good going, my friend." Hank reached across the table and softly punched Phil's arm.

"You really think so?"

"Why not? Face it, you're not getting any younger. May as well go for it. Where would you go?"

"Well, that's the other thing. I haven't seen my son for a long time. He lives in Baltimore, so we're thinking of heading that direction."

"I didn't know you had a son. Your daughter lives here, right?"

"Amanda teaches school and lives south of town. Her Benny is my little fishing buddy."

"What about your son?"

"He left here after high school and hasn't lived here since."

"What does he do?"

"I don't know really." Phil stumbled. "Works for a newspaper I think."

"And you haven't seen him in a long time. Something wrong between you?"

"We've had our differences." Phil found it difficult to say what those differences were, but he went on anyway. "Jack's gay. He was only a kid when he told me, and I blamed myself and haven't seen or talked to him since."

Hank looked thoughtful. "I see . . . . That's a big thing. What are you going to do now?"

"I thought I'd talk to you about it, see what you think." Phil's voice trailed off.

"I don't know your situation, but if it were me, I'd say, life's too short to hold a grudge."

"That's what I've been thinking myself. I miss him, especially lately since I've been spending time with Benny. I keep thinking of Jack at Benny's age, and it about breaks my heart every time."

"So are you thinking of calling him?"

"On the phone? I thought a letter, maybe. To start anyway."

"That sounds good. Well, I hope it turns out the way you want."

"Only I don't know what I want yet."

* * *

When Phil came home, he found Catherine in the garden. She had stuck stakes at either end of several rows, strung twine between the stakes and was standing to one side, her garden journal and a pencil in her hand.

"Hi, how was lunch?"

"Good. Same as always, pastrami on rye."

"Your favorite."

"How about you?"

"Wouldn't you know, the first warm day, I'm out here in the mud checking the garden. As usual, I ordered more seed than the garden can hold. We'll just have to dig up a few more feet of grass to make room. Hope you don't mind."

"It'll do me good to do some digging. But not for a while yet. Ground's completely sodden."

Catherine lifted one foot to show him mud clear up to her sock. "You're telling me. One false step and look at me."

"I talked to Hank about Jack. I'm going to write him a letter, tell him I want to see him. What do you think?"

"If that's what you want . . . ."

"Hank reminded me that life is short. I figured that out when Benny had his accident, but I guess it takes a while for things to sink in with me."

"Sounds like Hank's a smart man."

"Congratulated us on our plan to buy a camper and take off for a while, too."

"Haven't even met the man, and already I like him. Maybe we could do something with him and his wife sometime."

"Hank's not married anymore, but I bet he'd come over and eat sometime. I'll ask him if you'd like."

"Do that."

"Well, I'm going to write that letter. Don't want to put it off another minute—twenty-eight years is long enough."

"I'm going out front to see if any of the bulbs are coming up yet."

* * *

Phil took some typing paper and a pen from the desk in the living room into the den and sat down to write to Jack. The letter wrote itself.

> Dear Jack,
>
> I've been spending time with Benny since his accident. We're building him a rod and tying flies together. Your mom is taking dancing lessons and painting pictures. The first warm day and she's already out in the garden. I finally cleaned up and got rid of the old barrels you used to play in when you were a kid. I can only guess how much I've hurt you. I'm so sorry, son. I miss you very much and hope to see you soon.
>
> Love, Dad

He folded the letter and sealed it in an envelope, wrote his return address on it, stuck a stamp on it, and propped it against the sugar bowl on the kitchen table.

CHAPTER

11

On the way out to the Home Place to see his mother, Phil considered telling her about the trip Catherine and he were thinking of taking. No plans had been made, but he found himself picturing what the trip might be like. He wanted to tell his mother, but he was afraid. His mother was as stubborn as an old rock. By the time he pulled into her lane, Phil had decided that he wouldn't tell her yet. To tell her would be downright foolhardy. She would probably die on the spot or kill him, one or the other.

He pulled up next to the barn, climbed the steps to the back porch, and stepped into the kitchen. The smell of ginger and the pan of cold biscuits sitting on the counter brought back his childhood. He walked through the house and found his mother in the front room.

She looked up from her book. "Why, it's you. It's good to see you."

Phil gave her a kiss on the forehead. "Good to see you, too." He kept the conversation light, telling her funny things Benny said when they were playing cards and how he was progressing with his fly tying and building his rod.

"Do you know how Grandpa got interested in fishing?" Phil asked his mother as they sat at the kitchen table over coffee.

"Your grandfather liked to tell stories. There was one about a time before he married Grandma. He had gone to spend the summer in the north country of Wisconsin with an uncle who needed help repairing a lake cabin. Every morning before they would begin the day's work, his uncle would take Grandpa out on the lake fishing. When they had what the uncle determined were enough fish, they would come back in and fry up their catch for breakfast. Then they'd eat cold any that was left over for lunch."

"I figured he'd started fishing as a boy like I did," Phil said. "He sure was eager to get me started."

"I guess he didn't start until then because he didn't have the opportunity," his mother said. "The uncle outfitted him with a rod and told him no self-respecting fisherman would use any fly but one he tied himself. Grandpa came home, so the story goes, and hooked up with the Isaak Walton League here in Henry County. First he learned everything he could; then he started teaching anybody who was willing to learn."

"Like me," Phil said. "As a boy I was convinced he was the finest fisherman ever to cast a fly on water."

"Well, he was a fine man. As to his being the best, I don't know. All I know is he kept us in fish the whole summer long. I learned about forty ways to make fish—had to or I would've gone crazy."

"It's funny, I don't remember having fish that much as a kid," Phil said.

"Well, you did. You can take my word for it."

As he drove home, he felt relieved he had passed a pleasant hour with his mother without her having mentioned Catherine. He was sure it was best that he hadn't tried to talk about their upcoming trip either. Plenty of time for that later.

* * *

One sunny day later that week, Phil was in the backyard stringing new rope between the clothes poles, and Catherine was thinning canes in the raspberry patch. The phone rang.

"I'll get it." Catherine left her pruning shears and work gloves on the back porch.

"Hello?"

"Mom, it's Jack."

"Jack! How are you?" There was silence on the line.

"Did your dad's letter come?" she asked finally.

"Yes. I've been thinking about nothing else since it arrived. What do you think I should do?"

"I don't know, Jack. You'll have to figure that out for yourself. I know your dad really wants to see you . . . ."

"I know. That's what he said in the letter." Jack was quiet again. "I've missed him, too, Mom. You know that. We've talked about it more than once."

"That's true." Catherine felt uncertain. What should she say to Jack? All she wanted was what would be best for Jack. She spoke quietly, as if to herself. "It's been a long wait, Jack. I know how hurt you've been. I know your dad doesn't expect you to forget all that. He misses you and wants to see you again. I don't think he expects anything."

"I know, Mom. I don't expect anything either. I wouldn't dare after all this time. But I don't want to open up old wounds either. What should I do?"

"I have enough trouble figuring out what I should do myself," Catherine said. "He misses you. He wants to see you. That's all. You say you miss him. Do you want to see him? Simple as that."

"I'll have to think about it."

"There's no hurry. Think about what you really want."

"Ok. Thanks, Mom. Love you."

"Love you, too, Jack. Bye bye."

"Bye, Mom."

Catherine closed the back door quietly, gathered her garden gloves and pruners and went back to the raspberries. Phil was on the ladder busy attaching the clothesline at the far end.

* * *

Later that week, Catherine had a long talk with Amanda. Jessica had continued to visit Catherine after school. Most afternoons they would paint. Jessica took all of her paintings home to put on the walls of her bedroom.

"She is so proud of those paintings she's been doing with you," Amanda said. "Last week she took a couple to show her art teacher."

"I didn't know that. What did the teacher say?"

"I didn't dare ask, and Jessica didn't volunteer the information," Amanda said.

"And how are things going at home?" Catherine asked. "Is she coming home from school on time?"

"More often than not. That's better, thank heavens, but she still has a cheeky attitude with me. I want her to show me respect, but I don't know how to make that happen."

"She respects you, don't you think? She's going through a stage is all. Don't all teenagers go through that?"

"I don't know. Did I?"

"You were a pretty easy kid, but then you had your books. You read five or six books a week, remember? Difficult to be mischievous when your nose is in a book all the time."

"I did read quite a bit, didn't I? Now I wish I had time for reading." Amanda sighed. "Just to sit down with a book for the fun of it. I didn't realize what a luxury that would turn out to be."

"I wish you did have time for yourself."

"I never catch up . . . as you know. My house is a disaster."

"That's not important. You love your family, and you're a fine teacher. Your house feels lived in, that's all."

Amanda laughed. "It's lived in all right."

"Now I want to let you know . . . ." Catherine took a breath. "Your dad and I are talking about buying a camper and going on a trip."

"A trip? Where?"

"To the East Coast. We might visit Jack for one thing."

"Daddy's going to visit Jack? When did this happen?"

"We've been talking about it lately. He wrote a letter to Jack a couple of weeks ago . . . ."

"What did Jack say?" Amanda herself was barely in touch with Jack. Most years birthday cards and Christmas cards with school pictures of the kids was all.

"He hasn't written your dad back yet, but I'm hoping he'll say yes."

"But it's a long way between here and Baltimore. Where would you stay?"

"Campgrounds, I guess. We haven't planned the trip yet, but we won't go straight to Jack's. We're thinking of exploring on the way, and your dad wants to take the boat so he can go fishing. It'll be fun."

"Fun? It sounds crazy," Amanda said. "You've never gone anywhere and suddenly you're thinking of driving all over the countryside. What if you have a breakdown on the way?"

"I guess we'll have it fixed." Catherine suddenly felt doubtful. "I thought you'd be happy we're going on an adventure."

"Well, I'm not. I wish you would stay here and keep on as you always have."

"But why?"

"Camping's dirty and I'm sure it could be dangerous. Bears or axe murderers or who knows what."

"People go camping all the time. It's perfectly safe."

"But what about the kids? They're doing so much better now. They rely on you and Daddy, and now you're leaving. What will we do?"

"We're not leaving until June. Nearly time for school to be out anyway. You'll have the things you want to do with the kids in the summer, just like always. We'll only be gone a month or so."

"A month? That's an awfully long time."

"You know how much we've enjoyed spending time with the kids this winter, and your dad and I both have some ideas we've been saving to do with them this spring. And we'll be back. You'll see. Time will go by fast."

"Do you have to go?" Amanda asked.

"It's not that we have to. We just want to, that's all."

Catherine drove home, puzzled.

* * *

The kick-off meeting for the Iris City Garden Club was scheduled for the first day of spring. Catherine had never considered herself a joiner. She was, she had to admit, terrified at the prospect of coming to the meeting as a newcomer with a plan and a request. She had been dreaming of a butterfly garden in the field she had befriended in the fall, and she was not about to stop now. With her catalogue and carefully made list of flowers that would attract butterflies, she went to the meeting.

The morning was beautiful. Spring had become more than a promise. The crabapples were in bloom and tight purple clusters of buds announced the coming of lilacs along the border between Jaz's yard and hers. The garden club met in the assembly hall at the public library. When she arrived, she found a group of women standing around a table at the side of the room talking. Catherine took a deep breath. The butterfly garden had taken up residence in her mid-section, and her palms felt sweaty.

She gave herself a lecture. "Now, Catherine, they aren't going to bite. Just go over there and say hello."

She found a coffee urn and a plate of sweet rolls on the table. While she was helping herself to a cup of coffee, she heard her name and turned to find Fern Barclay.

"How nice to see you here," Fern said. "I didn't know you were in the garden club."

"Actually, this is my first time at a meeting."

"I was in the garden club in St. Louis. When we moved here besides dance class, this was one way I thought I could meet like-minded souls. Anybody who loves gardening must be someone it would be good to know."

"Actually, I came to suggest an idea to the group," Catherine said. "I'm a little nervous about it."

"About the idea itself or about suggesting it?"

"The idea is wonderful. I'm scared I'll say the wrong thing or they won't like the idea, I don't know. I'm not very good at speaking in front of people."

Fern glanced around the room. "Everybody looks nice. It'll be fine."

One of the women called over the conversations, "Time to start the meeting."

"May I sit with you?" Fern asked. "It's my first time here, too."

"Sure, let's sit together."

The club was run informally, and, as the talk of last year, the weather and hopes for this year ebbed and flowed, Catherine found herself relaxing. She saw a few familiar faces; she guessed that was natural from living in the same small town for so many years. The big topic was the annual Iris Show which would take place in May as part of Springfest which always included retail booths, pony rides, displays and music in the town square.

Everything for the Iris Show was already in place. Gardeners from all over Southeast Iowa brought their irises, and last year's top prize had been won by a man from Fairfield, a town twenty-five miles west. This year everyone was certain Mary Granville's black beauties would win, especially since no one could believe they hadn't the year before. Mary, a tiny woman, sat on her hands and blushed during the speculation.

When the talk subsided, the chair asked if there were any new business they should discuss, and Catherine, taking another deep breath, raised her hand.

"There's a vacant lot, a small empty field really, at the corner of Monroe and Pine. I walk by it all the time, and the idea came to me to have a town butterfly garden there. I checked at the planning office and found out the field is owned by the city. It was originally set aside for a neighborhood playground, but, according to the mayor's office, there's nothing to keep it from becoming a community garden."

Several voices began at once.

"I know that lot," someone said. "There's a big open space and an old tree in the back corner. It's a perfect place for a garden."

"What would we grow?"

Catherine held up her catalogue opened to the pages on plants that attract butterflies. "Quite a number of flowers and flowering shrubs attract butterflies. Most of these will grow here."

"But how would it work?"

"I was thinking we could divide the field into several plots with paths in between. Two people could be responsible for each plot."

"What about water? Is there already water there?"

"I asked the city clerk when I went to check on the lot," Catherine said. "We'd have to petition for it, but it sounded like it would actually be easy for the city to put water in for us."

"We could have little plaques with the names of the people who were tending each plot."

"And a bench or two for people to sit on and watch the butterflies."

"And maybe a fountain or a little fishpond next to the benches."

"I'll volunteer to go over to Garden Florist and see what plants Paula suggests. I know she has several varieties of butterfly bush already."

Finally the chair stopped them by speaking a little louder than everyone else. "It sounds like everyone likes the idea. I think we should look into it and talk about it in two weeks when we meet again."

"But it's the end of March now," someone said, "and I think if we're going to do it this year, we'd better start now. We have extra money in the budget ear-marked for 'new projects.' In a few weeks it'll be dry enough to till the land if we're ready. I move we form a committee to go over there and look at the lot and report back next week. I think we need a special meeting to make this happen."

"I second the motion," Fern said.

"All in favor?"

Everyone raised their hands. A committee was formed with Catherine as the chair, and the meeting broke up after the committee planned to meet at the field the next afternoon. A special meeting of the club was called for the following Monday so they could hear the committee's report.

Catherine felt jubilant. They liked her idea. Unless something unexpected happened, Mount Pleasant would have a butterfly garden.

After the meeting, the president walked over to Catherine and held out her hand. "Coralee Burns. This is the most excited we've been in years. If there's anything I can do to help, please let me know."

Catherine and Fern walked out together.

"What a great idea," Fern said. "I keep thinking about our park in St. Louis this time of year. Let's go out to Oakland Mills and see if there are any wildflowers yet. I'm always surprised how early the first ones bloom."

They made plans for the next morning, and Catherine went home.

* * *

Though she had walked by the field several times during the winter, she hadn't stepped into it. Now, it would be a morass of mud and weeds, but she also knew that the sturdy green shoots pushing up out of the bulbs in her own garden must be mirrored by those she had planted in the field. She wanted to see what was happening there before the committee met the next day.

She found Phil coming up the basement stairs as she walked in the back door.

"Hi, how was the meeting?" he asked.

"Good. Will you come for a walk with me? I want to show you something."

"I have to finish something I started in the basement. I came up for some glue. I should be done in a few minutes."

Phil went back down to his shop, and Catherine went to change out of her skirt. She caught sight of herself in the mirror on the dresser and was startled as usual. Even as a girl, if a mirror caught her unaware, she would see her face and think, "That's not me. I don't look like that." Today what had startled her was a glimpse of the girl in her high school graduation picture.

"Come on," she said to herself. "You're sixty-five years old, not seventeen." But she couldn't be certain of anything anymore.

She moved away from the mirror and hung her skirt in the closet, but instead of changing, she sat on the chair in the corner daydreaming in her slip and stockings. So many things were changing. Forty-seven years might be falling away. She didn't know. Throughout her married life, Catherine had acted more grown up than she felt. She guessed the main reason for that had been her trying to make it look as though she had chosen her life as it was, as though she had known all along who she was and where she was headed. Catherine heard Phil calling.

"Coming." She struggled into her jeans and walked into the kitchen carrying her sneakers. "Here I am." She sat at the table and put her shoes on. "How are you coming with your fly tying?"

"Coming along. It's going faster than usual with Benny around, even with the extra time it's taking to build his rod."

They headed down the street on the way to the field. Phil didn't know where they were going. Halfway there he realized they must be on the way to the vacant lot where he had seen Catherine digging in the fall.

"Another mystery about to be solved," he thought.

At the field, Catherine led him on a faint track formed by her coming and going. When they came to the sycamore tree, she stooped and moved some dead stalks aside. A clump of strong green shoots showed where she had planted the bulbs in the fall. They were as advanced as the ones growing in the front yard at home.

She looked up at Phil. "We're going to have a butterfly garden here, and the field will have to be plowed."

"A butterfly garden. I see." Phil was relieved to find that Catherine had a plan. Her kneeling in the field in the fall still didn't make much sense, but he felt relieved anyway. "Thank goodness my wife's not crazy," he thought.

She showed him two or three more spots where green shoots pushed through the soggy brown weeds. "Do you think we can find someone to plow around them so they'll have a chance to bloom?"

"Well, it's early yet for plowing. Too wet by far. And look—aren't these daffodils?" He stooped by one of the bulb clusters. Yellow buds hung from slender stalks.

"They're early," Catherine said. "We'll have flowers here by next week. At least the daffies, but there are hyacinths and tulips here, too. They'll come later."

"You planted these?"

"Last fall."

"Whatever prompted you to do that?"

Catherine shrugged. "I don't know. I had some extra bulbs, and the field looked lonely."

"You know, I could bring the rototiller over here and plow this place under, being careful to go around the bulbs."

"I couldn't ask you to do that. That's a big job and this was my idea. I don't want you to have to rescue me."

"Rescue you? No such thing. I like helping out. The rototiller practically runs itself anyway."

"Would you really?"

"Easy."

* * *

After lunch the next day Catherine walked over to the field to meet the rest of the committee. She felt a little fluttery on the way. Would they still like her idea once they saw the field? She crossed Monroe Street and waved to Fern who was just parking her car.

"Hi, Catherine," Fern called.

"Hi. What do you think?" Catherine joined Fern and they stood on the sidewalk looking into the field.

"It's bigger than I expected," Fern said.

Susanne and Beth arrived together.

"Sorry we're late. No excuse, just late," Susanne said.

The four of them looked at the field. Susanne stepped one foot off the sidewalk and pushed the toe of her running shoe into the dirt. "Wet but pretty solid. It'll take work to make this field into a garden."

"Maybe so," Beth said, "but I think it will be beautiful."

"It will," Fern said. "It has a good feel."

"I didn't mean I don't like it," Susanne said, "but I think we should be realistic. Know what we're taking on."

"Phil will bring his rototiller over in the truck and plow the whole field," Catherine said. "He's my husband."

"Then we'll take over and make a garden," Fern said. "If we all work together we can do it. I vote yes."

"Yes," Beth said.

"Ok," Susanne agreed. "I'll polish my tools and do some push-ups so I'll be ready. When do we start?"

"We can report to the club, and I'll call the city and see if we can use the field," Catherine said.

* * *

The following Monday, Jaz joined Catherine for the garden club meeting where the members voted unanimously to petition the city for permission to establish a butterfly garden in Mount Pleasant.

"Any more news on when we'll have water?" Coralee asked.

"I spoke to the city again about installing the hose bib," Catherine said. "They said all we need to do is add it to our petition and they'll put one in."

"I think the field is too big for one bib," Susanne said. "Let's ask for two."

"Before I moved here I worked as a grant writer for a non-profit," Fern said. "I could write the proposal for the city council if you want."

"That would be wonderful," Coralee said.

"I can also write a piece for the *News* inviting people to take a plot," Fern added.

"Great." Coralee glanced at Nancy, the recording secretary, who was busy taking notes. "How long will it take the city to respond?"

"The city council meets next Tuesday," Catherine said. "They can put our petition on the agenda if they receive it by Friday."

"That will be easy," Fern said. "It would be good to have the committee check it over before we submit it. Can we have a brief meeting at my house on Thursday?"

"Thursday works for me," Beth said.

"I'll be there," Susanne said.

Catherine nodded to Fern. It was all coming together.

* * *

Fern wrote the proposal for the city council, and Catherine brought her crumb cake to the meeting. She hadn't been to Fern's house before and arrived early. The house reminded her of Fern. A low sprawling stone and wood bungalow, it was set back from the street among a grove of evergreen trees. A winding flagstone path led to a red front door. Schnappsy started barking the moment Catherine knocked on the door. Fern answered, holding Schnappsy by the collar.

"Hi. Come on in." She hushed Schnappsy.

Seeing the cake Fern said, "That looks good. What is it?"

"My mother's crumb cake."

"Great. I'm making tea," Fern said.

"Can I help?"

"Come on out." Fern led the way to the kitchen.

What a contrast Fern's house was to Jaz's. Everything was sleek and simple. Large kitchen windows looked out on a deeply wooded backyard. Birds came and went from a feeder near the house.

"I like your house," Catherine said. "It reminds me of you."

Fern laughed. "I love it. It's the closest to a dream house I've ever lived in." She listened. "I think I hear Susanne and Beth." She let Schnappsy out the back door, then carried a tray to the living room. Catherine went to the door. Other than Alice, she'd had few friends through the years. This felt like another new beginning.

"Hi." She opened the door wide and led the way into the living room. They sat on low couches around the coffee table where Fern had set the tray with the tea and cake.

Fern passed copies of the proposal for the city council.

"This is so professional looking," Beth said.

"Shall I read it to you?" Fern asked. "I think that's the best way to see if it's complete." Fern read the proposal aloud as they followed along.

"Clear and to the point," Susanne said. "I think we should present it as it is."

"All in favor?" Catherine asked. They all agreed.

"Here's the article for the paper, too," Fern said. "I figured while I was doing the proposal I might as well go ahead and write the article."

"Will you read that to us, too?" Beth asked.

Fern read the article aloud.

When she finished, Susanne said, "You make signing up for a plot sound inviting. I bet we'll have a good response."

"I already talked with Sue Waters at the *News*. She said she thought they'd run it in Wednesday's paper. That way they can include the city council's response to our petition."

"She sounds convinced the city will say yes," Catherine said.

"Of course they will," Fern said.

CHAPTER

12

The next morning when Catherine walked into the kitchen, she was greeted by first light dawning through the window. She whistled to Blue as she took the cover off his cage.

"Pretty bird. You are the prettiest bird, the very most beautiful bird that ever was."

Phil came in while she was talking to Blue. "You're right, he has turned out to be a pretty bird. After how he looked when you brought him home, who would have thought it?"

He walked over to the cage whistling his favorite tune. Blue cocked his head and looked from Phil to Catherine.

He opened his tiny beak. "Cheep."

Phil whistled again.

"Cheep, cheep."

Phil and Catherine went about their morning routine. Phil, to the front porch to look for the paper, while Catherine started the coffee and cut up some oranges. The moment they took their attention off Blue, he started to sing. Great strings of notes filled the air.

Phil came in with the paper. "Listen to him sing. A big song for that little bird."

"He is a darling, isn't he?"

During breakfast they talked about the day. Catherine would meet Fern at the park. Since it was the first day of spring vacation for Amanda and the kids, Phil would gather the fishing gear and take Benny on their first actual fishing excursion.

"I'm a little nervous," he admitted. "I hope I haven't pumped Benny up too much. Fishing's mostly sitting, as you know."

"Benny has staying power. I bet he'll like fishing just fine."

"That's what I thought when Jack was a kid. He could sit in his room with a book or up in his tree for hours but take him out on the lake and watch out. He couldn't sit still no matter what."

"Benny's a different boy altogether. He'll have fun out there, you'll see."

"I hope so. Well, guess I'd better be going. The only way I'll find out is to go. Fish will stop biting before long."

"Well, go on then. You two always have fun together. It'll be fine."

Phil went to the basement, and Catherine went out on the front porch to see how chilly it was. Even so early in the morning the air felt almost balmy. It was sweater weather at last.

***

Phil put on his old fishing hat and stowed the fishing gear in the back of his truck. He packed Benny's new rod in its case and laid their rods together in the truck bed. He brought along both his old tackle box and the banged up toolbox they had found at the auction for Benny to use. The tackle boxes were outfitted with flies, tools to tie a quick fly if necessary, and an assortment of hooks, feathers, floss, and tinsel. He filled the picnic cooler with cold sodas and the sandwiches he had made the night before, dropping in a few oranges and apples at the last minute.

Despite Catherine's reassurances, he continued to feel nervous on the drive to Benny's. When he pulled into the drive, Amanda was hanging wash on the line. "Just like her mother," he thought.

"Hi, dad," she called. "I couldn't bear to put these in the dryer. Such a beautiful day."

"Nice to have a few days off?"

"It's a long haul between Christmas and spring break, but we all survived."

"Good thing. I'd hate to have to come visit you in the clinker after you'd offed a kid," Phil said. "Where's Benny?"

"Throwing a stick for Goldie behind the barn. He's training her to fetch."

"Too bad we can't take her fishing with us. I can picture us out there with that half-grown pup. We'd probably end up in the water. Maybe when she mellows out we can try her."

Phil walked around the barn. Goldie's long fur shone in the sunlight and her ears flapped when she ran. She was turning into a nice looking dog, Phil thought. He smiled to see the change in Benny in the past few months. The timid boy who had come home from the hospital had disappeared, and the old Benny was back. But even better now. They were pals. They had spent more time together in the past three months than during Benny's whole ten years of life until now.

"At least I didn't miss it altogether." He shook his head. "If Benny hadn't needed me . . . ."

Benny saw Phil coming across the field. "Hey, Grandpa. Watch what Goldie can do."

Benny had a chunk of tree branch in one hand. Goldie started running as soon as he took his arm back to throw. She over ran the stick, wheeled around and scooped it up. She brought it straight back to Benny and dropped it at his feet.

"Isn't she the smartest dog you ever saw?"

Benny and Goldie ran over to where Phil stood watching. Goldie jumped up on Phil to be petted.

"Hey, girl, easy now." Goldie wiggled all over when she wagged her tail.

"She likes you, Grandpa," Benny said. "She misses you when you're not here."

"I like her, too. You've done a good job teaching her to fetch. Are you ready for our first morning on the lake? See if you can catch some bluegills?"

"I'd better put Goldie in the house. Otherwise she'll want to follow us."

"Good idea. I have a surprise for you in the truck. Want to see?"

"Course I do." Benny ran to the house with Goldie at his heels.

Amanda had finished hanging the wash. "Are you off?" she asked.

"We want to be out there as soon as we can," Phil said. "Fish are biting now. I can feel it."

"Just a second." Amanda went into the house and came back with a paper sack. "Chocolate chip cookies. I made them last night."

"Yum," Benny said.

"Thanks, Amanda. We'd better be going. Don't expect us before three," Phil said. "I packed a lunch so don't worry, we'll be fine."

Benny ran ahead, and Amanda caught Phil's sleeve as he turned to join Benny.

"He'll be safe in the boat, won't he?" she asked.

"I have a life jacket just his size," Phil said, "and I promise you, he'll be wearing it before we put the boat in the water. How does that sound?"

"Good. Well, have a nice time." Amanda climbed onto the porch and turned to wave.

Phil opened the truck door and handed Benny a blue fishing hat. "Here's your surprise."

"Oh boy, a hat! Now I'll be a real fisherman."

"Let's see." Phil put the hat on Benny's head and adjusted the tab in the back until it fit.

After a short drive, Phil pulled into the deserted parking lot at the lake. "Looks like we'll have the jump on the fish today."

He grabbed a life jacket from the truck bed and snapped the buckles over Benny's chest, noticing that Benny did not ask why he had to wear the jacket.

"Can you carry these?" Phil handed Benny his rod and tackle box.

"Easy, Grandpa."

Phil led the way down a path to the lake edge where the aluminum skiff had spent the winter.

"Is that your boat, Grandpa? Awesome."

A slight breeze rippled the water. A few puffy white clouds made the sky seem even bluer. Phil turned the boat over and, pleased with himself, thought, "Same as ever." His old wooden boat became waterlogged and then cracked when it dried out in the winter. Then it leaked all summer. When it was time for a new boat, Phil had decided on aluminum and never regretted it. Being a purist with respect to fishing methods did not extend to his boat. Phil and Benny went back to the truck for the oars and the cooler. After stowing their gear, Benny pushed while Phil pulled the boat neatly into the water.

"Come on buddy, in you go." Phil helped Benny climb into the stern, then shoved off, hopping in himself. He settled himself amid ship and set the oars.

"Are you going to row us out? What about the motor?" Benny asked.

"If we need it, we'll use the motor, but I usually row. I like it better."

"How come?"

"Quieter."

"Oh." Benny settled himself in the middle of the thwart and held onto the gunwales with either hand.

Phil watched Benny while he rowed to the middle of the lake. The boy looked at everything. The fact that he was quiet Phil took as a very good sign. Benny turned to watch the wake trail behind the boat, but he was careful not to rock the boat when he did it. Phil's hopes rose, and he began to relax.

Phil headed for his favorite cove and pulled close to shore where the bank was grassy. That way, Benny's line wouldn't end up tangled in branches and frustrate him on his first day. Benny had been quiet all the way to the cove, and Phil hadn't had to tell him that fish might be scared away by noise or sudden movements.

Phil took a popper from his tackle box and tied it on his line. Benny did the same. Phil made a couple of experimental casts. Benny watched closely, then picked his rod up and made a near perfect cast letting his popper settle in near the shore.

"Good job, son. We'll see if the bluegills are hungry this morning."

Benny's popper sat on the water, gently moving up and down. He watched it intently, and within moments felt rather than saw a tiny nibble. Then, splash, the fly went under and the rod bent. The fish had taken his bait and was running with it.

Phil sat and watched, ready to say something if Benny needed help or a suggestion to land the fish. But Benny didn't need help. He was a natural. And he was having fun.

Benny pulled back on the rod, reeled in a little line. He let the line go slack a moment. Then he pulled the rod and reeled again until only a couple feet of line hung from the end of the rod and a nice-sized bluegill flapped from the end of his line. Phil helped Benny remove the hook from the fish's mouth. Benny slid the green gold fish into the bucket of water prepared for their catch.

"Good job, buddy. Good job." Phil spoke quietly but the pride in his voice was clear.

"I caught him, Grandpa!" Benny's face glowed with fishing exultation. "Can I catch another one?"

"Of course you can."

The lake gently rocked the boat. The swish of line as Benny cast, the clicking of his reel as he took in line were the only sounds. Benny was a quiet fisherman. He caught five more fish that morning. Phil watched Benny's intense concentration with growing satisfaction. After Benny's third fish, Phil started fishing himself. After catching four, he put his rod aside.

"I'm always hungry out here earlier than at home," Phil said. "Would you like an early lunch?"

"I'm starving. Let's eat now."

They took their time eating, saying little.

Phil thought. "He'll make a fine fisherman."

While they ate, Phil showed Benny his favorite tree. "See that willow tree over there? Look how its branches are all the same length and how they nearly drag in the water but not quite."

"Yup."

"See the tiny buds along the branches. I'll bet next time we come they'll have opened. Would you like to explore the shoreline before we head in?"

"Can't we catch some more fish?"

"We have enough for today. This is enough fish to clean, and there's plenty for supper at both houses," Phil said. "We can always come back."

"All right. Can I row?"

"Go ahead, have a try."

Phil traded places with Benny who, after a few tries, headed the boat along the shore in a fairly consistent way. Phil loved to look in under the bank where tree roots wound their way down into the water. As they trailed along the shore, Phil pointed out an occasional hole where some animal might live. When they found another cove, they pulled in to rest. Phil tossed an old boat cushion to Benny and lounged back on one himself. He took off his hat and covered his eyes with it. Peeking, he saw that Benny did the same.

"The only thing better than a day on the lake is a day on the lake with Benny," Phil thought.

* * *

When they arrived at Benny's house, Goldie ran out to greet them, barking. The noise brought Amanda out on the porch.

"How'd it go?" she called.

"Mom, Mom!" Benny called. "I caught six fish."

"That's great."

"He's a natural," Phil said. "Say, do you have a knife we can use to clean the fish?"

"Well, of course I have a knife, but where do you plan to clean those fish?"

"I don't know," Phil answered. "How about on the steps?"

"On the steps? These steps? Oh, no you don't," Amanda said. "How about on the old well platform?"

"Ok by me," Phil said.

Phil was surprised to find Benny not only willing but doing a pretty good job of cleaning the fish. As far as he could see, this was the last test. Benny could wrap a rod, tie flies, cast, land a fish, row, and, best of all, he was quiet. Apparently he didn't mind cleaning the fish either.

"Grandpa, when can we go again? How about tomorrow?" Benny asked.

"Had fun, did you? Maybe the next day. I wouldn't want you to become tired of fishing."

"That will never happen. I could fish everyday."

"Well, day after tomorrow then. Your family and Grandma might get tired of all the fish we catch even if we don't."

* * *

Fern was sitting on a bench when Catherine arrived at the park.

"Hi. Sorry to keep you waiting," Catherine said. "I wanted to show you this Iowa wildflower book, but I forgot it and had to go back."

"I love having a few minutes to sit." Fern looked through the book.

"I like the way it's laid out," Catherine said. "They show the flowers in the order they bloom and tell their uses. Most of them are for healing or cooking—or both. They tell how the Native Americans used them, too."

"That's intriguing. I like thinking about the time when Indians lived in these woods and what their lives might have been like. Seems like they found a use for everything." Fern held out the book. "Do you want to bring this along?"

"Yes. I wish I had my own copy so I could write in it when and where I see different flowers. At least it doesn't have to be back at the library for a couple more weeks. I brought a little notebook to keep track of the flowers we see."

Catherine put the book in her shoulder bag, and they set off down the trail looking closely at the forest floor on either side of the path. Bits of green began to catch their attention, and then they noticed a patch of lavender wildflowers, delicate first blooms of spring. Crouching down they examined the flowers, and Catherine took out her book to identify the pale blossoms.

"Here it is. *Hepatica americana*. It's in the same flower family as buttercups. The Chippewas made a tea and used it to cure children with convulsions. It grows in dry leaf-covered soil in the woods." Catherine looked around her. "This is the place."

"Look over here. It's trillium. Easy to remember because it's a lily with three petals and three leaves."

Catherine found the picture in the book. "'Rich, moist woodland soil,'" she read. "Look at all the uses the Indians found for that. Everything from a dressing for wounds to treating ear infections."

As they walked they saw more flowers. Catherine found them in her book and wrote entries in her notebook.

"I guess our eyes are becoming used to looking for them. I didn't see any at first, and now they're everywhere," Fern said. "Look at these." She squatted by the path and pointed out a patch of flowers on slender stalks with clusters of white blossoms.

"I know those," Catherine said. "They're Dutchman's breeches. See how the flowers look like little britches hung upside-down? The leaves look like fern."

"My namesake," Fern said. "These are my favorites so far."

Walking along they found green shoots which might lead to flowers later on. Some had buds already.

"We ought to come back every few days so we won't miss anything," Fern said.

They turned a corner and came upon Catherine's favorite spot, a glade surrounded by arching trees.

"Right in the center there, a little later on, there will be a ring of flowers," Catherine said. "I didn't know their name until now." She turned the pages and showed Fern a group of tiny white flowers with violet centers. "They're called 'blue-eyed Marys'. Every year I watch for them. When I see them I think of fairies dancing under the stars."

Fern leaned over the book. "They're pretty. Wildflowers are so quick that they're easy to miss."

"I know what you mean. I love finding the little wild rose hips in the fall, but so many years I miss the roses in the spring. Seems like they bloom for about a week and that's it."

"Mmm, and a lovely scent. So much more delicate than garden roses."

The path wound back to the parking lot. They agreed to walk together every week to watch the progress of spring in the woods. Some of the trees already showed a feathery green while others had tight buds that looked like they'd never open.

* * *

A couple of weeks before Benny's birthday, Amanda called Catherine. "Hi, Mom. I'm planning a party for Benny and I'm wondering what you think. He still seems a little shy at school since his accident. Do you think it would be too much to have a really big party out here?"

"How big do you have in mind?"

"Well, I was thinking of inviting his class plus the kids he grew up with—you know, Joanne, Marcy, and Linda's kids plus a few of the boys his age in 4-H."

"Why so big?"

"I don't know. I guess I thought if he had the kids from school, he might start playing with them again. He used to have a friend over or go somewhere to play a couple of times a week. Now he spends all his time by himself or with Dad. Not that I think that's a bad thing."

"No, of course not. I didn't realize things had changed so much. What about Joey?"

"They've been friends since pre-school, but since the accident I don't think they've played together more than two or three times. Benny said 'no' so many times that Joey gave up calling. I don't know what to do."

"Do you think a big party might be overwhelming for him?"

"That's what I wondered. I thought we could have Mr. Chalmers come with his puppet show. I know he hires out for parties. And Greg across the road already said he'd bring his pony over for the kids to ride."

"That sounds like fun, but isn't Benny too old for that?"

"Mr. Chalmers has a show geared to older kids. He came to school this winter and the kids loved it. Maybe Greg will bring a horse instead of a pony. He has a gentle old mare."

"That sounds good. What about inviting a smaller group?"

"I guess you're right. Maybe we can ask just the kids he's been friends with in the past."

"What about letting Benny make the list?"

"I asked him and he said he didn't much care who came." Amanda sounded discouraged.

"Maybe your dad and he could make the list." Catherine hated to see Amanda disturbed.

"That's a good idea." Amanda's voice brightened. "Tomorrow when Dad comes out I'll ask him to help Benny think of who he'd like to invite."

"I can help you with the party."

"Really? That would be great. Well, I have papers to grade so I'd better go."

"Bye, Amanda, love you."

"Love you, too. Bye."

Catherine felt elated. She slipped a CD into the slot on the stereo system and danced herself around the house. Phil heard her and came up from his workshop. He stood in the kitchen doorway watching a full five minutes before Catherine saw him.

When she did, she fell on the couch laughing. "I forgot you were in the house."

"You're a vision," Phil said. "What's the occasion?"

Catherine shrugged. "Nothing. I'm just happy."

"That's good. That's very good."

* * *

Catherine and Jaz tended their seedlings with growing anticipation. If the spring rains held off, soon they could begin planting. Catherine tried to curb her excitement by remembering April of two years before when a couple of frigid days had frozen the lilac buds all over town.

Certainly, she thought, it was safe to plant peas. A couple of sunny days later she pulled back the compost from the first row. She gingerly worked the soil with her spading fork, set stakes in the soft earth at either end of the row, strung twine between them, and planted the sugar snaps, her favorite pea, in two straight rows to either side of the twine.

The next week Phil dug up sod at the end of the garden to make space for Catherine's new vegetables. Then he dug a good wide bed under the kitchen windows for Jessica's wildflower garden. He spent the afternoon working the soil by hand so it was soft and ready for seeding. Catherine raked the compost off several more rows in the vegetable garden and spaded the soft earth under the compost. While they were working, Jaz came out of her back door.

"Hi," she called over the hedge. "Thought I'd plant something. Is it too early to plant garlic? I keep seeing new recipes, and they all have loads of garlic. I'm taking it as a sign that I'd better plant even more than I think I can use."

"Garlic? I usually don't plant garlic until May," Catherine said. "The soil is still pretty damp and we might have one more frost. You never know."

"What can I plant now?" Jaz asked.

"Peas. Probably lettuce. Greens," Catherine said. "Radishes, of course."

"Radishes? I forgot all about them," Jaz said. "I have a packet of seeds somewhere. I'll go look."

Jaz came back with the seeds. "Seeds but no trowel. Since I turned the garden shed into a pottery studio I can't find half my garden tools."

"I'll find you one," Phil offered. "I'll bet we have three or four in the garage."

Phil handed Jaz a trowel over the hedge. "Thanks. I'll return this one when I find mine."

"That's ok," Phil said. "Keep it. We have plenty."

Phil put the rototiller in the back of the truck and took it to be serviced. He didn't want to be in the middle of plowing Catherine's field and have it quit.

* * *

Jessica came over after school the day after Phil prepared the wildflower bed. Catherine was on her knees in the garden.

She stood with difficulty. "Whoa, sore back. I'd better do some stretching or I'll be a mess before the garden's planted. How was school?"

"Same as usual. I had a test in biology. I probably flunked it."

Catherine washed her hands with the hose and dried them on her jeans. "You think so? I'll bet you did better than you think. That's usually the way."

Jessica put her backpack on the steps, and Catherine showed her the beginnings of the vegetable garden. "You did all this since the last time I was here?"

"Grandpa's been helping," Catherine said as Phil's truck turned into the driveway.

He hauled a couple of good-sized rocks out of the truck bed. "Hi Jessica. Come and see your new garden." He added the rocks to a border he was making between the garden and the yard.

"Can I start planting now?" she asked.

"You can plant some this afternoon before dark," Catherine said. "How about a snack first?"

Jessica and Catherine went in the house while Phil brought more rocks from behind the garage to finish the border for Jessica's garden.

* * *

Phil came back from his second fishing excursion with Benny with another mess of bluegills. It was a good thing Phil liked to cook fish. He always did it the same way—sautéed in butter in a cast iron skillet. After supper Phil sat back in his chair. Catherine detected mischief in his posture.

"Want to go for a ride?" Phil asked. "There's still some light left."

She looked at him suspiciously. "Let me put my sweater on."

Phil held the back door open for her, and Catherine walked out to the car.

"Let's take the truck instead." Phil headed for the passenger's side and opened the door for Catherine.

Then he climbed in, started the engine and backed out of the driveway.

"Where are we going?" Catherine asked.

"You'll see." Phil turned on the radio and tuned in the oldies' station.

As they drove south through town a familiar tune from Jack and Amanda's teenage years filled the truck.

When it ended, an energetic disc jockey announced, "And that was 'Got a Hold on Me' by Christine McVie. Next is 'Dancing in the Dark' by Bruce Springsteen."

Phil followed West Clay to Oakland Road and headed west into the soft light of an Iowa sunset. Catherine thought Phil was taking her to the county park but when they reached the turnoff, he crossed the Skunk River and headed south toward Salem.

A sinking feeling in Catherine's stomach caused her to turn the music down so she could talk. "You're not taking me to visit your mother, are you?"

"Just wait and see."

"Because I need some time to prepare myself, if that's what you have in mind."

"Now, don't worry. I wouldn't do that."

"Ok, then." Catherine turned the radio back up and started to relax. It had been a long time since they had gone out for a drive. In the beginning, it seemed like that was all they did. Out for a drive, radio blaring, on one country road or another. Catherine laid her arm along the window ledge and began watching for familiar landmarks. There was the farm with twin silver silos and the barn with a diamond-shaped window in the peak. Here's where the road dipped down and crossed Fish Creek, and here was the gravel road which led to the Home Place where Phil had grown up.

Phil braked and turned into the gravel road and when Catherine saw the battered 'Gravel Ends' sign she turned to him. "I thought you said we weren't going to your mother's."

"We're not. Trust me."

Catherine sat back, but didn't relax this time. She was watchful. Phil's mom had hurt her. At their wedding she had told Catherine she would never really be part of the family so she might as well not try. Catherine tried anyway, but everything she did only seemed to make things worse. As far as Catherine knew, Phil's mom had never told him what she had against Catherine. She thought this was a shame because if only she had known, certainly she could have changed whatever it was, become the daughter-in-law Phil's mom wanted. Now, here they were, within a mile of the Home Place and gaining on it every moment.

Phil drove past the house and turned onto a faint track into the woods about half a mile down the road. The lane was nearly indiscernible, and Phil switched the lights on. Once Phil stopped the truck to pull a fallen tree aside, but now Catherine knew where they were going. She felt an unexpected surge of happiness. Phil was taking her to their special place, the clearing in the woods where they had planned to build their house. After the fiasco with Mike, Phil had never brought her here again. All through the year before they were married she had wanted him to bring her here with all her heart, but she could never bring herself to ask him.

This was her first visit in nearly fifty years. She looked about her in the fading light of early evening. Nothing had changed. Perhaps the trees were larger, but when they came to the end of the lane, the clearing was much as she remembered it, a small glade in the woods, perfect for a house and a family.

Phil swung the truck around to face the lane as he always had, turned off the engine and the lights. He sat motionless, hand still on the keys, for several moments. The silence of the evening gathered around them. Catherine's eyes adjusted to the dusk, and leaning against the door, she turned toward Phil and watched him. He sat back looking straight ahead. Suddenly she saw them as they were so long ago. Then she had sat with her back against the door, legs stretched out, her feet in Phil's lap.

"Catherine," Phil began. "I don't know what to say. I want to start over, but it's too late. We're old. We had so many things we wanted to do and we didn't do any of them. Except have two kids, and look how that turned out. I feel like I threw it all away. The chance to do what we wanted to . . . ."

"I know, I feel the same. We could've been so happy. What a waste. What a mess I made of everything."

Phil reached across the seat and took her hand. "No, it was my fault. I was too stubborn to tell you how I felt. I was hurt, but I loved you as much as ever, and I couldn't let you see it. I was locked up so tight even I couldn't find myself. And I refused to forgive you. Now it's too late."

"Do you really think so? We're not that old, you know. There's plenty of time yet."

"If I'd known then what I know now . . . . I wish I could go back and do it all again. Not just how I treated you but the kids. I wish I could raise them all over again. I'd do it differently, let me tell you." Phil stared out the windshield into the gathering dusk.

"You know, Phil, I'll bet most parents feel that way. Hindsight being what it is. And probably most people would do their marriages differently, too, given the chance. There's nothing we can do about that. The only thing we can do is to see where we are now and, if we want to do things differently from now on, we can. We've already started doing that anyway. How about that letter you wrote to Jack?"

"I guess you're right, but I don't know what's going to happen."

"Nobody does. I think it's going to turn out fine." Catherine reached over and touched his knee.

"I hope so. But what about us? Can we put ourselves back together? It's been so long since we were even friends."

Catherine laughed. "That used to be true, but what are we doing talking like this if we're not friends?" Catherine kicked off her shoes, leaned against the door, swung her legs up onto the seat and nestled her feet into Phil's lap.

He took her feet in his hands and leaned his head against the back of the seat. Darkness settled into the woods while they sat silent.

Finally, Phil said so quietly Catherine couldn't be certain she heard, "I guess it's going to take time, but I'm willing to do whatever it takes."

"Hmmm?"

"I love you, Catherine."

"I love you, too, Phil."

They sat a little longer until the chill of the April night crept into the truck. Phil squeezed Catherine's feet which he still held.

"Guess we'd better go home."

They rode home in silence, and Catherine watched the stars filling the clear night sky.

CHAPTER

13

One afternoon just after Phil left to take Benny to the lake, the phone rang. When Catherine answered she heard Amanda's voice.

"Mom?"

"Hi, honey, what's up?" Amanda sounded upset.

"We have to talk. Can I come over now? I'm at school and I could be there in a few minutes."

"Come on over. I'll put some water on for tea. See you soon."

"Bye."

Catherine put water on, arranged cookies on a plate and put cream and sugar on the table, all the while trying to figure out what Amanda might be upset about. Could it still be that she and Phil were thinking of traveling? That was the only thing she could think of.

Amanda's car drove up in front. Catherine greeted her and led the way to the kitchen. Amanda sat down at the table.

"What kind of tea would you like?" Catherine asked.

"Anything." Amanda looked distracted. "Whatever you're having."

Catherine put teabags in two mugs, poured boiling water over them, brought them to the table and sat down across from Amanda.

She took a deep breath. "You wanted to talk. What's going on?"

Amanda started talking fast. "It's Jessica. All I hear morning, noon, and night is 'Grandma said this' and 'Grandma did that.' She'd rather be with you than me any day of the week."

"But, honey, I had no idea. We've enjoyed having her around so much, I assumed she was easier for you, too. But she's not, is that it?"

"Well, sort of. She won't talk to me any more now than she ever did. I feel like a complete failure as a mother. She thinks everything you do is wonderful. She brings something home from your house nearly every week—a painting, some clay thing, whatever."

"I thought that was what you wanted, wasn't it? I mean, you wanted her to be interested in something besides hanging around with those older kids. Is she still doing that?"

"I don't think so. She's been coming home on the bus except when she's at your house or when she goes to 4-H straight from school. It's not that. I want her to do things with me, that's all."

"And she doesn't? When I offered to let her make cookies over here, she told me she wanted to save those for when she could do them with you."

"Oh." Amanda had been sitting forward in her chair. Now she sat back. "There's never any time. During spring break I had papers to grade and lesson plans to write. I'm so far behind, it's all I can do to catch up when I have a few extra days."

"I know. There never seems to be enough time. Especially when you were a teenager, I kept thinking we'd make some wonderful meals together, and you remember the time I tried to teach you to sew?"

"I remember all right." Amanda looked into her mug, then looked at Catherine sheepishly. "I guess it's never easy raising kids, is it?"

"It wasn't so bad, but then, I didn't know how to reach you either. You were in your own world most of the time."

"It was a pretty lonely world. I don't want Jessica's life to be like that."

"I didn't want yours to be like that, either," Catherine said sadly, "but there didn't seem to be much I could do about it."

"I want it to be different with Jessica. It has to be."

"Honestly, Amanda, I'd like nothing better than for you and Jessica to be close."

"I know that. I'm sorry. It's true that spending time with you has been good for Jessica."

"You think so?"

"Well, she's definitely happier. In the fall I was beginning to think she was depressed. I do think its good for her to have you."

"I love having her here."

"Well, I'd better go home. Jessica's bus will be along soon, and maybe we can make cookies before supper. Grading papers can wait. Thanks for the tea."

"Anytime."

Amanda put her jacket on and slung her purse over her shoulder. She gave Catherine a hug. "Bye, Mom, I love you."

"Bye, honey, I love you, too."

* * *

After Amanda left, Catherine felt suddenly tired, went into the bedroom and laid down. Between sleeping and waking, Catherine's mind worked along the old paths. She might as well face it—she had never understood Amanda. Even having Jessica over had at least been partly so Catherine would feel better about not having been much of a mother to Amanda. Not that she hadn't tried. Catherine had made sure Amanda had nice clothes like the other girls. She hadn't had to wear dresses made out of feed sacks as she had. Catherine saved so she could give Amanda a canopy bed and whatever else she wanted, but apparently there had been something she had not known how to ask for. What was it that Amanda wanted?

Her mind switched to musing about the drive with Phil. She knew what she herself wanted, even now. She wanted what Phil had given her in the early days, what she had never been given as a child. Phil had seen her, Catherine, as she was and loved her for being that person. His seeing her had filled a hole in her. She imagined everyone must want that same thing. Not only did she want to be seen again. She knew she could do a better job seeing Phil. She was determined to do that.

Amanda, too. During Amanda's childhood, Catherine had been trying with all her might to be the wife and mother Phil wanted so he would love her again. She had tried to prepare Amanda to be the perfect wife herself so she would be loved and not rejected as she had been.

Now, as she lay between waking and sleeping, Catherine thought that most likely Amanda had wanted her mother to see her as a person, individual and special, like no one else. And, too, maybe Amanda would have liked to paint pictures with Catherine or plant a wildflower garden, but Catherine had carefully kept even herself from knowing what she liked to do. She certainly never thought to share those dreams with her daughter.

One very good thing came to mind. Amanda had married a man who was good to her, a man who was thoughtful and kind. Catherine imagined he saw her and loved her for being uniquely Amanda. And from now on, she, Catherine, pledged to look and see, listen and hear her beautiful daughter.

Catherine found herself smiling. She nestled her head into the pillow and fell asleep.

* * *

When Phil came home from fishing he found Catherine sleeping. As he walked into the room she woke up.

"Hi. Having a nap?"

"Guess I was tired. What time is it?"

"4:30, thereabouts."

"How was fishing?"

"Great. Benny caught his first bass, about a three pounder. He was so excited I thought he might jump out of the boat. Amanda looked a little dubious about it until we cleaned it. They'll eat well tonight."

"Amanda came over this afternoon."

"She did? Well, that's nice."

"She was pretty upset when she arrived."

"Upset? About what?"

"Well, it seems Jessica does nothing but talk about what a good time she has over here, and she still won't give Amanda the time of day. Amanda was all in a flurry about it."

"But I thought that was what she wanted, for Jessica to be busy. I'd think she'd be happy about it."

"That's what I thought, too. She doesn't want to disappoint Jessica, that's all."

Phil sat down on the bed. "And she thinks being over here will keep the two of them from being close?"

"She's so busy with school, she feels like she doesn't have enough time for Jessica. She talked it through, though, and by the time she left I think she felt better. She was going home so they could make cookies together."

"Well, let's wait and see. We never know how things are going to turn out." Phil squeezed Catherine's hand.

Catherine squeezed back. "Guess I'd better start dinner."

"Want some help?"

Catherine started to say no but changed her mind. She was beginning to like having Phil in the kitchen.

* * *

The day of Benny's party dawned clear and crisp. As Catherine drove down Cherry Street she saw Mr. Peabody walking his bulldog, Peaches. She checked the clock. 8:02. Mr. Peabody stepped out of his door at eight every morning. You could set your clock by it. Catherine waved and turned the corner onto Washington Street. She stopped at the store on her way out to Amanda's to pick up party supplies. When she arrived, Tom and Amanda were setting up two picnic tables next to the barn. After greeting them, Catherine spread table-cloths and arranged party plates, napkins and cups.

On her way to spread blankets on the ground for the puppet show, Amanda stopped to talk. "Thanks for coming early, Mom."

"It's good to be here."

"And Mom, I'm sorry I was so upset about Jessica the other

day. It didn't have anything to do with you really."

"I know. It's ok."

"I'm just frustrated that I have almost no time for her."

"I know, honey. How'd the cookies go?"

"Great. We made enough for the party, too. They're on a plate in the kitchen if you'd like to try one." Amanda carried the stack of blankets to the puppet stage, and Catherine went off to the kitchen.

* * *

The party went better than any of them had dreamed. Benny sat with the other kids and laughed at the puppet show. He especially liked the horse, Daisy. Watching him ride, Phil marveled that they hadn't thought of giving Benny a horse. He remembered how important Prince had been to him. But then, he reasoned, neither Tom nor Amanda had grown up in the country. It wasn't really surprising Benny didn't have a horse. Yet that could change. Maybe when he and Catherine came home from their trip . . .

Catherine took pictures of everything with her old camera. When the pictures were developed, she took them straight out to Amanda's.

Amanda held out a photo for Catherine to see. "Look at this one of Benny with his cake. Look at that smile."

"He's smiling in all of them. Look at this." She pulled out a photo of a gleeful Benny on Daisy.

"You're right. He looks like our old Benny."

* * *

One evening at dinner Phil said, "Let's look in the Sunday *Register* and see if there are any used campers for sale. I wouldn't mind driving up to Des Moines to look for one. I'll bet there would be more to look at up there."

"You've really been thinking about going?" Catherine asked. "I thought you'd forgotten all about it."

"I do want to go. Once we can see that Benny's back to his old self, I say, let's take off for a while."

"How long do you think?"

"I don't know. Say, six weeks or so."

"Six weeks? That's a long time."

"The longer the better."

"But when should we leave?"

"How about . . . early June?"

"But what about the garden?"

"I bet Jaz and Jessica could handle it."

"That is, if Amanda has the time to bring Jessica over here."

"I don't see why she wouldn't. I'm sure she'll do it."

"You really want to go?" Catherine asked again.

"Of course I do. We'll have a great trip."

Catherine started to clear the table, and Phil hopped up to help her. Coming back from the sink she nearly collided with him. He stopped her and gave her a quick kiss on the lips. Surprised, they both laughed.

* * *

The next morning Phil announced at breakfast that he was going out to visit his mother. "I'll be coming back in past the grocery, and I can stop if we need anything."

"Thanks, but I'll be out myself. I have a pretty long list so I'll stop." Catherine couldn't believe that Phil was now offering to go to the store for them, or that he was telling her he was going to visit his mom.

Through the years Phil's mom's rejection had piqued Catherine's anger. She had said her share of negative things about her mother-in-law, too. Maybe that was why Phil rarely told her when he was going out there.

Now she merely said, "I hope your mother's doing well. Have a nice visit."

* * *

On the way to his mother's Phil rehearsed what he would say about the plans for buying a camper and traveling. He wasn't looking forward to that part of the visit, but figured he might as well tell her now as wait and stew about it.

It was one of those perfect days in mid-April when leaves were unfurling on every side. Maple, oak and hickory trees softly dressed for summer. Wildflowers were popping up along the roadsides with the first hint of balmy days. Masses of white clouds billowed in a deep blue sky.

Phil found his mother on the front porch wrapped in a rose-colored shawl with a blanket over her knees. Busy with Benny and helping Catherine with the garden, it had been a few weeks since his last visit. He was taken aback to find his mother more frail than he remembered. When he took her hand in his, the blue veins stood out on her nearly transparent hands. When he leaned over to kiss her brow, there was a smell of age about her that he had never noticed before.

His sister had told him that Lucy was having to do more and more for Grandma. From the careful way the blanket was tucked around her knees, Phil could see that Lucy must have helped her settle in her chair on the porch. Phil sat in the chair next to hers, sad that what he would tell her would make her mad.

She didn't greet him when he arrived. She looked so peaceful and quiet that he didn't say anything for a while either. They sat as they had so many times before on the wide front porch looking out over fields being plowed one by one as the dampness dried out of the soil. The rich earth smell of the freshly plowed fields always spoke to Phil of new life, of spring.

As they sat, Phil felt a thrill and broke the silence. "Spring's coming on."

"Thank heavens. I thought winter would never end," his mother said. She added, "Nice you came by. I always like seeing your truck turn into the drive."

Phil looked at her and listened to her words again in his head to detect if there were any sarcasm in them, but no. As usual, she was happy to see him and never begrudged the time between visits, long or short.

"I've been so busy with Benny and fishing lately, time is disappearing on me. Plus I've been helping Catherine make room for some new things she wants to plant."

"That Catherine. She always was one for trying some new-fangled thing or other." Phil's mother looked away and spoke so quietly he nearly missed it, "Never could abide that girl, anyway."

Phil took a deep breath. He never challenged his mother when she started in on Catherine, but today he couldn't bear it.

"Catherine's all right. She's planting some heirloom varieties, going back to the old time vegetables. She has Jessica planting a wildflower garden at our place, too. She's doing Jessica a world of good."

"Is she now?" his mother said. "Well, what else is new?"

Again Phil took a deep breath and plunged in. "Catherine and I are looking to buy a used camper and take off on a trip for a few weeks."

His mother looked but said nothing.

"I mean, here I am retired, and we've never done much traveling. We're thinking of heading out to see Jack."

"I bet I know whose idea that was. That Catherine . . . ."

"Now, Mother, that's enough. If you have anything mean to say about Catherine I don't want to hear it. Ever again. Is that clear?"

"'Mother,' is it? I'm barely able to move from my bed to the john and you're going gallivanting around the countryside. Go ahead. I'll probably be dead by the time you come back."

"Oh, Mama, I love you. You know I do, but I have to go on and live. Time to do some of the things I've been wanting to while I still can. You have Lucy to watch out for you. She's taking good care of you. And we won't be gone so long, you'll see. We'll be back before you know it."

"When are you leaving?"

"Probably early June. A while yet. I'll come see you more often between now and then. So often you'll probably be sick of the sight of me. How's that?"

"Well, if you'd rather go off with that woman than be here in case something happens to me . . . ."

"I meant what I said." He felt his jaw tighten. "No more snide remarks about Catherine. Period."

"All right, I heard you the first time."

For some moments they eyed each other like boxers about to enter the ring. Then Phil's mother dropped her eyes and pulled her shawl around her shoulders.

"Are you chilly?" Phil asked. "Why don't we go in and I'll heat up some coffee and make some toast? Could do with some myself."

Phil helped her into the house. He could hear his niece upstairs vacuuming. The house looked and smelled clean.

His mother was on her best behavior for the rest of the visit, barely daring to discuss anything. Not only did she not complain about Catherine, but her other usual topics for complaining—Lucy and the way she took care of her, her health, the weather—didn't come up either.

Phil left after promising to come again soon, giving her a long hug and settling her into an armchair by the window in the living room. Rather than driving back into town right away Phil went for a drive further into the country, taking back roads. He didn't pay attention to where he was going. Didn't have to. He knew the countryside south of town by feel.

Guilt rose in him like sludge. Yes, his mother had his sister and Lucy, but it was Phil she counted on. He knew that, and he hated to leave when she was growing more frail all the time. She would be eighty-nine in July—while they would be gone. Maybe they should postpone their trip, stay for her birthday. But no, he had been waiting all his life to go back to the beginning with Catherine. Now was his chance, and his mother would be fine. The later he waited, he felt certain, the more difficult it would be to leave her.

He almost wished they were leaving tomorrow. His mother might live to be ninety-eight, or she might die tomorrow. There was only one thing to do. He finally knew what he wanted. He wanted to love Catherine and be loved back. He wanted to live every bit they could salvage of their dreams.

But what about Jack? Why hadn't Jack responded to his letter? Catherine had tried to reassure him by saying she thought Jack needed time, but deep down Phil doubted Jack would forgive him for his cruelty—and why should he?

"I don't deserve to be forgiven anyway," he thought. "My heart's nothing but a stone."

He had done what he could to open the door between himself and Jack, said he was sorry, but who was he kidding? If Jack wanted to see him, wouldn't he have written or called by now? And his mother. She was so sweet when he came around. She at least was always glad to see him. He could do her good by coming around more often. Maybe he should forget this trip idea.

The road turned a corner, and as the truck made the turn, a hill in the distance caught Phil's eye. The hill was greening up with new grass and masses of white clouds piled high in the sky above. Shafts of sunlight streamed down on the hillside. Driving on, Phil knew he would go through with what he had begun. He and Catherine would go on the trip. If Jack didn't write or call soon, Phil would write again.

* * *

Before Catherine left the house, she tucked several packets of wildflower seeds into her pocket. The park was a haven on a perfect April morning, and she wandered the paths, not caring which fork she took when a choice presented itself. Sunlight filtered through the delicate green overhead. Catherine walked into the beauty with a quiet mind.

When she came to the first bridge, she stepped from the path. Kneeling on the sunny bank, she planted small batches of each variety of the native flowers she had ordered for Jessica.

Amanda came to mind. Sitting back on her heels, she gazed into the water as it rushed down to the Skunk or the Mississippi, she supposed. The stream flowed fast and high with the spring thaw still in it. When Benny had fallen into the frozen river, Amanda had saved him. For the first time, Catherine clearly saw how strong, courageous, and capable her daughter was. In a spring thaw of her own, she was at last seeing Amanda as she was.

She brushed the leaves and dirt from her skirt and stepped back onto the path. She felt clear-headed and walked briskly.

Climbing uphill out of the woods she noticed that someone had straightened the birdhouse pole. It was now awaiting a pair of birds to build a nest and take up family life there.

* * *

When Catherine drove into the driveway, Phil came out to greet her and, as easy as if they had been happy to see each other all these years, they came together in a warm hug. Then, Catherine couldn't believe it, Phil gently took her chin in his hand, raised her face and kissed her as tenderly and long as when they were kids. When they finally drew apart, Catherine felt embarrassed and laughed.

"Well," she said.

"What's for lunch?"

Catherine saw his unruly hair and the mischievous glint in his eye. Phil was back.

* * *

The evening Hank came to supper was at the end of a lovely spring day. Catherine had been drawn to the park, and on her walk, an easy supper presented itself. Phil had caught a good-sized bass that morning and she had plenty of baby greens from the garden. She'd put some potatoes and an apple crisp in to bake at the same time. When she came home, she thinned the lettuce patch into a basket before going inside. When she opened the back door, Phil heard her and came up from the basement.

"Hi. Where have you been?"

"Out to the park. I couldn't resist."

"No need to resist. What shall we have for supper? Remember, Hank's coming tonight."

"Don't worry, I didn't forget. Will you cook the bass you caught this morning?"

"Fried in butter?"

"Sounds fine to me. What time is Hank coming?"

"Around six."

"Let's eat as soon as he arrives. Then we can take a walk after supper."

Catherine recognized Hank when he arrived, though they'd never spoken. It was unusual for her to have a man in the house other than Phil. When Phil brought him into the kitchen where she was tossing the salad, the room seemed suddenly small. She held out her hand, and Hank's handshake was warm and firm. She liked his smile.

At supper, Catherine watched while Phil and Hank talked about fishing. They were as lively as boys.

After dessert, Phil said, "Hank and I will do the dishes."

Catherine started to protest, but instead she sat on the couch and tried to read. Copious laughter and the sound of splashing drew her attention to the kitchen, and she wondered if the kitchen would survive. When they finally came to the kitchen door, their shirt fronts were soaked.

"All done," Phil said. "How about that walk?"

Catherine closed her book. "All right. I wonder if we'll need jackets."

Hank opened the front door to check. "A sweater maybe. It's cool but not really chilly."

They strolled down Monroe Street to the corner of Pine where the newly plowed field waited in the moonlight to become a garden. Neither Phil nor Catherine commented on the garden, and the three of them walked on.

* * *

Early the next morning, Catherine and Jaz walked over to look at the field. How different it looked in the sunshine with the weeds churned up.

"This place needs work before it'll attract butterflies," Catherine said.

"True, but we can do it," Jaz said. "Why don't we start right away?"

"Good idea. After we clear out the weeds, we can lay out the plots and paths. It'll come together eventually."

"Pretty fast, I'd say."

"Let's divide the list and call everybody. Do you think tomorrow is too early to start?"

"The sooner the better. Everybody will want to help."

The next day cars lined the usually quiet street. A team of women raked, hoed, broke up chunks of earth, and shook weeds loose. They piled the weeds along one side of the garden to start a compost pile.

Catherine worked under the tree, carefully weeding and loosening the earth around the bulbs she had planted in the fall. She was especially careful as she tended the spots where she had planted the flower seeds. Kneeling on the damp ground in her overalls, she felt the pulse of the field flowing into her hands. She listened to the women laughing and talking to one another while they worked. A good bit of progress had been made by lunch time, but there was still a long way to go.

Coralee stood in the center of the garden rubbing the small of her back. "Hey everybody. Let's go out to the Golden Dragon for lunch and come back afterwards for a couple of hours."

"That sounds good. They have a great buffet," Fern said.

After lunch they continued to work the soil, and the next day they came back again. By the third day the garden was ready to divide into plots. Catherine brought string and stakes and they divided the space into twenty-four plots with paths between.

"How will we decide who has which plot?" Beth asked.

"Why doesn't everybody go and stand by a plot?" Coralee said.

The women spread themselves out over the garden.

"People have been calling all week," Fern said. "The article in the paper will take care of the rest."

"Judy and Grace are at work. So are Amy and Patricia," Coralee said.

Catherine and Alice had the plot nearest to the tree.

* * *

The following week the city crew put in two hose bibs, and Susanne arranged for a truckload of wood chips to be dumped at the site. The women raked the chips evenly on the paths, and the garden took shape.

* * *

Late one afternoon after spending the day in the butterfly garden, Catherine sat at the kitchen table feeling pleasantly tired. Phil made them each a cup of tea.

"I wish we had a sign," Catherine said. "That's all the garden needs except the planting."

"A sign would be nice," Phil said. "Will the city put one up?"

"No. We asked and they said no."

Phil spent the next afternoon down in his shop. Catherine was in and out working in the vegetable garden. She didn't give Phil much thought.

"He's probably making flies or just fussing with stuff down there," she thought.

When she called him to supper, Phil came upstairs carrying a large wooden sign. Carved into the wood were the words Iris City Butterfly Garden. A butterfly stood out from the background on either end.

Catherine had forgotten that Phil used to carve when they were kids. He carved animals then, small horses, dogs and cows. Once he had given her a lioness and a pair of cubs. He had a set of chisels down in his shop, but as far as she knew, he hadn't used them for anything other than fitting out a new door a couple of times since they'd bought the house.

"Phil, it's wonderful. How did you do it?"

"Easy."

"And so fast. Everybody will love it."

Phil shrugged and went to wash his hands for supper.

* * *

The next afternoon, Catherine, Jaz and Alice drove over to Angelika's Greenhouse to buy plants for their plots.

Angelika lived in the country about half an hour northwest of Mount Pleasant. There were closer nurseries, but, years before, Catherine had followed the sign to Angelika's nursery one day. As soon as Catherine began wondering about plants that attract butterflies, she thought of Angelika.

"Let's plant as many perennials as possible," Catherine said. "Then we won't have to do as much weeding."

"Or as much watering," Alice said.

"Let's plant flowers that smell good," Jaz said.

"Roses, of course." Alice turned to Catherine. "Do roses attract butterflies?"

"I don't really know," Catherine said.

"You don't?" Alice asked. "When you had the idea for a butterfly garden, I thought you must know all about butterflies."

"No, nothing," Catherine admitted. "Except how beautiful they are and how they make me feel. When I was a little girl a butterfly landed on the back of my hand. I held my breath until it flew away."

"Let's hope Angelika knows," Alice said.

"She will," Catherine said. "She knows everything about plants. You'll see. Keep an eye out for the sign. It's easy to miss."

"Maybe I'll buy some plants for my garden at home," Alice said. "Now that Marvin's at day care I have more time."

"There's the sign," Jaz said, pointing.

They turned off the main road. The narrow gravel lane led past a cottage with greenhouses behind. Angelika, a woman in her fifties dressed in flowered overalls, came to greet them.

"Catherine." She pulled off her garden gloves and extended her hand. "Good to see you again."

"You, too. These are my friends, Alice and Jaz."

Angelika shook hands with each of them.

"We came for flowers that will attract butterflies," Catherine said. "We're starting a butterfly garden in Mount Pleasant this spring."

"Let's see. Butterfly bush, of course, all colors. Yarrow, day lilies, echinacea, cornflower, coreopsis . . . ." Angelika ticked them off on her fingers. "I assume you want perennials."

"Definitely," Catherine said.

"As long as they smell good," Jaz added.

"Most perennials are fragrant," Angelika assured her.

They followed her through a greenhouse and into the garden.

"Here are the hollyhocks and malva," Angelika said. "Both good for butterflies. Tall though so plant them where they won't block your view."

"Hollyhocks." Alice sighed. "When I was small my mother grew hollyhocks as tall as the house."

"Just plant them where they'll have plenty of sun and there's a trellis or side of the house. They'll grow, maybe, seven feet tall."

"I'd like some for the butterfly garden and my garden at home," Alice said.

Angelika brought a cart from outside the greenhouse and pulled it rattling inside. "Here you go." She helped Alice load a flat with hollyhocks.

Jaz wandered along. "What's this?" She pointed at a tray of plants with gray green leaves and spiky red flowers. "Smells familiar."

"Ah, that." Angelika joined her. "Pineapple sage."

"Pineapple? It smells just like it. And so pretty."

"All the *salvias* attract butterflies." Angelika led the way to a group of plants in pots, some with purple flowers, some with pointy leaves, some with rounded leaves.

"That's the sage I have growing in my herb garden," Jaz said. "I make a great Tuscan tomato soup with it. Are all of these sage?"

"Yes. There are quite a few varieties."

"But they're so different. I can't imagine pineapple sage and garden sage being from the same family." Jaz carried an armload to the cart.

Catherine had gone off on her own. She wandered through the green-house and out into the sunshine. She stooped to smell a flower, read a tag, feel a petal or leaf. One plant caught her attention. Catherine checked the stem. "Square, definitely a mint."

Angelika came up. "Bee balm. A perfect butterfly plant. There aren't any flowers on it yet, but just wait. Well, I hear a car. Just wander around and see what you like."

Alice walked out of the greenhouse blinking in the bright garden.

Jaz came behind pulling the garden cart. "Already half full."

They wandered in and out of the greenhouses, adding to the cart as they went.

"Good thing this cart doesn't look any bigger than the trunk of my car," Catherine said.

When they got back to the parking lot, they found Angelika talking with a woman next to a jeep. A little girl stood on the running board knocking on the window while a yellow lab pup sat on the inside and whined.

Catherine overheard Angelika say, "It's fine with me. You can let him out."

The child opened the door and the pup tumbled to the ground. It picked itself up, shook its head, looked around, and ran straight for Alice. What happened next surprised Catherine even more than that. She knew for a fact that Alice didn't like dogs; never had, never would. Or so she had said.

Now here was Alice squatting down laughing while the puppy jumped up and licked her face. The woman whistled for the pup but it ignored her. She went off with her little girl to look at plants. When Alice stood up, the pup sat looking expectantly up at her, then followed her to Angelika's office where the three of them paid for their plants.

They loaded the plants in the trunk of the car and settled in themselves, but the pup sat to one side and cried.

Sitting in the back seat, Alice turned to watch the pup until the car turned the corner in the lane. "It's watching us the whole time," she said. "Poor little thing."

"But Alice," Catherine said, "I thought you didn't like dogs."

"Well, I don't as a rule." Alice chose her words carefully. "Just lately, I've been thinking a dog would be nice."

"Nice?" Catherine asked. "Nice for what?"

"For me," Alice said. "To keep me company. Marvin's not much company these days, and I thought a dog would do me good."

"I think it's a great idea," Jaz said, "and if that puppy's any judge, a dog will love you."

"You think so?" Alice asked.

"Of course. Look at the way it followed you around."

"Are you thinking of getting a puppy?" Catherine asked.

"I don't know. Maybe a dog from one of those rescue organizations," Alice answered. "I haven't decided yet."

They were quiet the rest of the way home. Catherine dropped Alice off, and she and Jaz drove home. Phil came out to help unload the car, setting the plants in the lee of the garage.

It was dusk when they finished. Jaz said goodnight and took the short-cut through the gap in the hedge.

* * *

Phil and Catherine walked into the house together. She was amazed to smell dinner cooking.

"I went fishing today so I put some potatoes in to bake along with a bass I caught. I chopped up some almonds and squeezed lemon and salted it good. Hope it turns out ok." Phil picked up a fork to test the potatoes.

"It smells good."

"Well, it's nearly ready. I have a salad in the fridge, too." Phil opened the refrigerator door to show Catherine.

Then Catherine noticed that the table was set with the good china. A vase of lilacs sat in the middle of the table with the glass candlesticks on either side.

Catherine let Phil serve her. He took the salad from the refrigerator, poured oil and vinegar on, and tossed the salad in the air.

Phil lit the candles. They ate dinner with stories back and forth about their day.

"You know I like to be on the lake early in the morning," Phil said. "This morning was perfect. The lake was like glass."

Catherine took a bite of fish. "This is really good. Where did you find the recipe?"

"No recipe. I made it up." He took a bite. "It is good. How was the trip to the nursery?"

Catherine told the story about the pup tumbling out of the car and heading straight for Alice.

"He couldn't have been more than eight or ten weeks old."

"No leash?"

"None. He ran right up to Alice and sat at her feet looking up trustingly like he knew her from somewhere. You know, Alice has never much liked dogs, never has had a pet, but she was taken with the little guy. He followed her around the whole time and cried when we left. None of us knew what to make of it."

"Alice always looks a bit bewildered to me. I can just about see her with that pup."

"Then on the way home, Alice told us she's been thinking lately about a dog for company. You know since Marvin's stroke she barely leaves the house, and you can imagine how lonely she is."

"Who was with Marvin today?"

"He goes to adult day care a couple of days a week now. They pick him up in a bus and even give him lunch. It's a godsend for Alice. Anyway, she's thinking of getting a puppy or one of those rescue dogs."

"A puppy is a lot of work."

"That's just what I told her. I told her if she wanted to, I'd go with her to pick a dog out tomorrow."

"It's a great idea," Phil said. "But what about Marvin? Will he mind?"

"No, I'm sure he won't. He hates being a burden on Alice. He'll be glad she has a dog."

Phil had a story of his own to tell.

"Wait 'til you hear this. When I went out to the lake this morning, Hank was out there. You'll never guess. He was playing hooky from work. Called and told them he needed a 'well day.' I asked him, 'What's a well day?' And you know what he said?"

"No idea."

"He said, 'Why wait 'til you're sick to take a day off? Better take it when you're well and can enjoy it.' Did you ever hear of such a thing?"

"No, but it's a good idea. I wish Amanda would take some of those."

"Anyway, Hank and I decided to go fishing together one day.

I don't know how I'll like that. With Benny it's fine. Being with him is like being with myself all over again. But Hank is a talker. Not bad, mind you, but he has plenty to say for himself. Still, think I'll do it."

After dinner, Phil said, "Let's leave the dishes and go for a walk."

They walked east and found themselves on the corner by the butterfly garden. The sign Phil made sat at an angle in the front corner of the garden.

Phil and Catherine walked back through the garden and sat on the bench under the tree. It had grown chilly. Phil put his arm around Catherine, and she leaned closer.

"This is nice," he said.

"It is." They sat quiet in the soft evening air.

They gazed over the garden in the semi-dark. Catherine began to feel rather than hear the gentle song of the field.

"What's that?" Phil asked.

"Do you hear it?"

"Sounds like some singing but far away."

"It's the field. It does that."

"What do you mean, 'It does that'? I've been in a lot of fields in my time, and I've never heard one sing before. What is it?"

"I don't really know, but I like it, don't you?"

"Very much."

* * *

The evening grew colder. They made their way back through the garden and walked home holding hands.

At home, they hung their jackets by the back door and did the dishes. As he dried the last plate and put it in the cupboard, Phil asked, "Want to turn in early? I'm bushed."

"I guess so," Catherine said, wondering.

When they were both in bed, Phil turned to her and Catherine moved to meet him. Quietly, tenderly, in the early night, they made love as if for the first time.

CHAPTER

14

By the beginning of May, Jessica's wildflower garden was in its glory and the vegetable garden was bringing in lettuce, greens, peas and radishes. Early mornings found Catherine on her knees, thinning, weeding, mulching. Best to be in and out of the garden before the sun rose in the sky and it was too warm. By May in southeast Iowa there were already some muggy days. Spring was a short breath between winter and summer.

Something happened to Catherine when she put her hands in soil that happened nowhere else, a definite settling in. She guessed she was what some people called 'grounded' by it.

Usually after finishing in the vegetable garden she would survey all the gardens to see if any cleanup needed doing, and also to pick flowers for the table.

One morning she had picked as far as the front gardens when the mailman arrived and handed her a bundle of letters and one of Phil's fishing magazines.

"Hi Pete, how's it going?"

"Great, Catherine, nice weather. Awful busy though."

"Why's that?"

"My wife opened a cafe down in Donnelson, and I've been helping her out. You should come down. Best raspberry pie in the state."

"What's the name of it?"

"The Bramble Rose—her name's Rose. It's right on Main

Street. You can't miss it."

"Good name. What do you do?"

"Believe it or not, I wait tables on Tuesdays, so come in then. We have the fried chicken special that day."

"I'll do that. My favorite antique store is down that way. Maybe I'll see you next Tuesday."

"Well, better keep moving."

Catherine looked through the letters. Jack's handwriting caught her eye on a letter addressed to Phil. Catherine's stomach knotted, and she went into the house to call Phil up from the basement.

She stood at the top of the basement stairs and called down, "Phil, a letter from Jack for you."

Phil came upstairs, took the letter and examined the envelope. Jack's return address and his own address, plus a stamp canceled in Baltimore. No clues. Phil opened the letter standing in the kitchen, and Catherine, feeling self-conscious, busied herself at the sink, washing dirt off the roots of the greens she had thinned out of the garden. Baby greens were a bonus as the garden filled out and she had to thin so many plants to give them room to mature.

Phil found himself remarkably calm as he opened Jack's letter. He had waited so long, that now that it had arrived, he felt relieved. The letter was handwritten on letterhead stationary.

Dear Dad,

I'm sorry it's taken me so long to respond to your letter. You can imagine it came as quite a surprise to hear from you after all this time. I had to sit with it for a while to see how I feel. Here I am finally, and I want to tell you what I've been thinking.

Except when I was pretty young we were never very close. Nonetheless, I've missed you, too. You're my dad and I want to know you again. If that's what you want, let's see each other soon.

Mom wrote and told me you are thinking of buying a camper and taking a trip East. I talked to Jeff and we'd like to have you come for a visit and stay with us.

In all honesty I feel a little nervous thinking about seeing you again because it's been so long, but I want you to come.

Let me know.

Jack

Phil handed Catherine the letter.

"Think I'll go fishing."

Phil dragged the boat into the water and rowed fast, paused at the right moment, and turned the bow toward the willow cove. Once in the cove, he began to feel more settled and his rowing slowed. The boat drifted the last twenty feet and came to rest against the bank. Phil guided the bow under the overhanging willow, tied the line to a branch and settled in.

Even fishing would have been too much of a distraction, and he needed to think clearly. When he wrote the letter to Jack he had thought of Jack alone, picturing the gangly college kid he had last seen. The mention of Jeff in Jack's letter was a shock. Not only was Jack gay; he had a partner. When he thought of Jack and Jeff together his chest tightened up. He hated that feeling and wished it would go away.

Looking back on the past few months he could see how much his life had changed. Benny had started it. No, before that . . . . Catherine had started changing, doing things that were out of character. Or so he thought. Then he started remembering her as a girl—more sprite than girl, really. When he thought of that girl, he could easily picture her rescuing Blue from the fair or befriending a field which sang to her. What astonished him most, however, was that one day, after all the stubborn barren years, he had seen her, his Catherine, the girl he loved and would always love. Just to love her. That would be enough.

And Jack. He wanted to put his family back together. He

knew he couldn't go back and make it up to Jack for sending him out of his life, but he wanted Jack now. Even if that meant Jack as a man of forty-seven. It was easy for him to remember how old Jack was because Phil had been twenty when Jack was born. Catherine had been eighteen. How had he thought he was old enough to have a child then? Yet, he had. Now, the idea of Jack, a forty-seven year old man with a life Phil knew nothing about . . . . How could he go to Jack's house, actually, Jack and Jeff's house? To walk in and be there, in the midst of Jack's life.

Catherine had gone to visit Jack—maybe he could ask her what it was like with Jack and Jeff. Maybe they would kiss each other in front of Phil. What would he do then? He would die, that's what. Thoughts swarmed in his head like a flock of sparrows.

"I'm growing older every day," he thought. "Before I know it, I'll be dead. Maybe not soon, but I'm creeping up on it. No telling when." If he didn't face this fear of Jack and Jeff, he might lose his son forever. There was no doubt in his mind: he didn't want to do that. He would have to go forward. Jack had invited them to stay at his house. Phil could say he would come but stay in the camper, or at a hotel—they could afford it—and visit during the day or go out to dinner. Anything so long as he didn't have to be there when it was time to go to bed at night. He wasn't ready for that.

He could go to Jack's and see. And Catherine would be with him. He wouldn't have to go there alone. His mind let go. He breathed in the spring sunshine laden with the scent of hot leaves, grass and lake. He noticed how the water gently lapped the sides of his little boat, how he felt here. He fit perfectly in this spot, as much as the tree, the sun, the lake.

* * *

Phil rowed slowly back to the clubhouse. The sun had climbed high, and he was hungry. He hadn't fished at all, and he felt amused as he stowed his gear into the back of the truck. A couple of cars in the parking lot looked familiar, but he hadn't seen anyone out on the lake. Not the best time of day for catching fish. He had one foot in the truck when Greg and Art came around the corner of the clubhouse and saw him.

"Hey, Phil. How are ya buddy?" Art called.

Phil turned around. "Good. And you?"

"Not too bad," Art said. "You catch any this morning?"

"No, too hot. Fish are lazing pretty deep."

"Say, a bunch of us are going on a big fishing spree in Montana in June," Art said. "You want to come?"

"Cold streams, plenty of shade, fish any time of day, as much cold beer as you can drink," Greg added.

"Thanks, but my wife and I are taking off on a road trip then," Phil said.

"You're kidding. Maybe you didn't hear right—I said, 'fishing spree,'" Art said. "You can always take a trip with your wife. This is the real thing, a once-in-a-lifetime deal."

"It sounds good . . . , but nope, already have plans." Phil hesitated. The fishing trip did sound good. He shook his head. "Thanks anyway."

"Are you crazy?" Greg asked.

"Maybe I am." He shrugged. "Well, I'm off. See you."

"Bye, buddy."

On the way home Phil wondered if he were nuts after all. He had never had the time to take fishing trips with the Isaac Walton guys when he was working. Since he retired and sat on the porch they hadn't thought to ask him. Maybe he should take this chance and go fishing.

He had always wanted to fish the legendary trout streams of Montana. Then he wouldn't have to face the reunion with Jack. And he wouldn't have to meet Jeff. This thought was followed immediately by a moment of clarity. Going to Montana would be running away, and he had done enough running. No, he would go ahead with the plans he and Catherine were making. He suspected that he would be glad he did.

* * *

As late spring crept toward early summer, Catherine became more and more busy. She was dizzy with it and talked to Blue.

He was still her best counselor—didn't say a word but watched her with bright intensity. She thought he must understand and sympathize with everything she said.

Many mornings while she worked in the garden, she found Jaz working just across the hedge. They talked gardening— What was eating the leaves on the cucumbers? How often should they re-seed the lettuce? What could they do with five hundred radishes?

The butterfly garden was a success. Alice and Catherine tended the plot near the tree. The article Fern had written for the paper brought so much response that every plot was taken. Jaz had a lawyer helping her, a man who lived in a townhouse with no garden space. Because of her inspiration for the butterfly garden, Catherine had been asked to serve on the panel of judges for the annual Iris Show later in the month.

Jessica came over two afternoons a week to tend her wildflower garden and so she and Catherine could paint or work with the clay in Jaz's studio.

* * *

Catherine was faithful to dance, too. The class was preparing to go to a dance party in Burlington the coming weekend. Dancers from all over Iowa were coming, and Catherine made a new skirt with a matching scarf for the party.

Fern, Frank, and Whit picked her up. Fern sat in back with Catherine and gossiped about the women in the garden club.

"Did you know Amy is leaving her husband?" Fern asked. "She has two little kids and works two jobs. I don't know how she has time for everything as it is, but to go it alone. I could never do it."

Catherine listened, feeling increasingly uncomfortable. She changed the subject to Jessica's wildflower garden.

Catherine and Fern had continued walking in the park until Catherine became too busy with her own garden. Fern was busier, too, as she became acquainted with more people in town. The last couple of times they had tried to set up a walk, it hadn't worked.

Catherine had continued walking alone. She stayed close to the woods all during the year. It kept her sane. Every time she walked she looked into the tiny glade where the blue-eyed Marys grew. The other day she had seen tiny shoots and slender stems.

"Let's walk at least one more time this spring before Phil and I leave so we can see the blue-eyed Marys together," she said to Fern. "Remember we saw their glade that very first time we walked together?"

"Of course. Schnappsy and I've been watching for the flowers every time we go out there. I didn't know you and Phil were going away."

"Didn't I tell you? We're buying a camper so we can take trips. We leave for the East Coast in early June."

"But what about the butterfly garden? You can't leave now. The garden's barely planted."

"Of course I can. There are plenty of people to keep the garden going. Alice will keep track of our plot and Jessica will help her. It'll be fine."

Whit had overheard them. "But what about dancing? We start having competitions next month, and I thought we'd be dancing together. You can't leave."

Suddenly, Catherine felt confused. Gardens? Dance competitions? What about her and Phil? That was what mattered. "Well, I'm sorry," Catherine said evenly. "Our plans are all made."

"It's not fair." Whit's voice rose. "You should've told me from the beginning. If I'd thought you wouldn't be here, I would have found another partner. Now it's probably too late for that."

"Maybe not," Catherine said. "Anyway, we didn't have any idea we'd still be taking classes now, much less entering competitions. You'll figure something out."

Fern's husband, Frank, had his own remarks to make. "Fern and I thought about buying a camper. Rented one for a trip to the Grand Canyon once. Eaten alive by bugs. Most miserable two weeks of my life."

Catherine sat silent the rest of the drive to Burlington, determined, at least, not to cry. Tears pushed at the back of her eyelids. Then she remembered where she and Phil were going and why.

They were in love. They were going on their honeymoon. This was the first time she had used that word to herself, but it was true. They were off to a new start.

They would see Jack together. She had wished and prayed for this day. Gardens, dances, a few bugs, what were those? Nothing. Never mind what anyone thought. She was doing exactly what she wanted. And it was about time.

* * *

One heavy thought still hung in her mind. Amanda. When she had taken stock of her relationship with Amanda, Catherine had seen there was still something more she could do, but she had been busy and she was scared of the talk she knew they needed to have. Finally she called Amanda and invited her to go for a walk in the park.

Catherine felt sure the park would lend a softness to their conversation. She herself had found so much healing there and she hoped for the miracle of a new beginning with Amanda.

The day was overcast and windy, threatening rain. Catherine arrived at the parking lot early and leaned against the wooden fence gazing into the woods. The wind whipped the leaves on the trees inside out so they looked more gray than green.

Catherine welcomed changes in the woods—the different weather, times of year, times of day. No matter what, the woods always renewed her hope, and when she heard Amanda's car drive up, Catherine went to meet her with a lighter heart.

Amanda walked quickly to meet Catherine and hugged her. "Hi, Mom, thanks for calling me. I've been wanting to come out here before the spring was completely over."

"Me, too. Let's walk, want to?"

"Sure."

They set off down a wide path through the woods. An old wood and wire farm fence ran along one side, bordering a ravine with a sluggish stream at the bottom. Wildflowers and berry bushes twined through the fence. On the other side of the path, the forest climbed a gentle slope.

Catherine gazed into the woods. "See how the wind turns the leaves. They barely look green. I love that."

"Hmm, pretty." Amanda stopped and looked.

They walked on for a while in silence. Catherine was aware of Amanda walking by her side—the yellow sweater over the crisp white blouse. Her jeans brushed together as she walked making a soft swishing sound which, despite the wind in the trees, Catherine could hear. Her tread mirrored Catherine's own. Amanda's face, mostly hidden by the shower of curls which Catherine could see out of the corner of her eye, bobbing and swinging with Amanda's stride . . .

"How I love her," Catherine thought.

Amanda stopped to pick a buttercup.

"I need to tell you something. Is it all right?" Catherine asked.

"Of course." Amanda twirled the buttercup between two fingers.

Catherine took a deep breath and began. "When you were a kid I was so wrapped up in my own story that I barely listened to you when you did try to talk to me. I'm not sure it's been much better since you grew up."

"Come on, Mom. You weren't that bad."

"No, it's true. Feeling sorry for myself was my full-time job most of my life."

"But you did the best you could. Don't be so hard on yourself."

"You're trying to let me off the hook. I just want you to know that I know what I did. I never saw you as you are. I wanted you to be like me. And you're not me, you're you. I thought that was what I was supposed to do, turn you into me."

"You might have known that wouldn't work."

"When Benny nearly died and you saved him, it was like I was seeing you clearly for the first time. You are a strong, courageous woman. I love you the way you are and I'm proud of you. I don't want you to be like me anymore."

"Well, that's a relief." Amanda laughed. "Not much chance of that anyway, is there? Can you see me stealing a bird from the county fair? Not likely."

"How did you find out about that?"

"I saw you put the bird in your pocket."

"Why didn't you say anything then?"

"I don't know. Maybe I felt embarrassed. Honestly, Mom, I wanted to rescue the little thing myself, but didn't have the guts. I'm glad you took it."

"You are?"

"Yes, and I need to tell you that I'm proud of you, too. Blue, and the butterfly garden and your helping Jessica . . ."

"Really? You don't mind that Jessica comes over so often?"

"Well, I hope Jessica and I can spend more time with each other this summer when I'm not teaching and you're gone, but no, I don't mind. I barely knew my grandmothers. Jessica has you, and if I can find a way, she'll have me, too."

"As long as I'm not in the way."

"No, you've been a big help. You and Dad. Not only that." Amanda stopped on the path and turned to Catherine. "Mom, I'm a little scared by all the changes in your life. But I'm excited about them, too. I don't know what will happen, but I'm ready to see."

"Amanda . . ." They stopped on the path. Amanda was taller than Catherine and leaned her head on her mother's soft silver hair. Catherine breathed in the good clean scent of her daughter and cried softly. After a few moments they walked on, silent while the woods around grew noisier with the coming storm.

Catherine heard a crack of thunder in the distance.

"We'd better walk faster. We're farther than halfway. If we hurry we won't get drenched."

They quickened their pace and came out of the woods as the first fat drops splashed into the gray dust of the path. A quick hug, banging doors and they were off, Amanda to drive the short distance home, Catherine back to town.

* * *

Most days, Phil found himself busy from morning until night. There was almost no time to sit on the porch and contemplate the status of the compartments of his brain. He was much too busy to worry about overflow and certain death.

He and Benny went fishing at least twice a week. Benny had become an expert at rowing the boat, at playing a fish and bringing it in. Fishing with Benny greased the track, and Phil found his truck heading to the lake nearly every morning.

He wanted to spend time with Catherine, too. He found, much to his amazement, that he liked helping around the house. In fact he felt about as peaceful washing up after supper as he did sitting in his chair on the porch watching the world go by.

As the May days lengthened, Phil's time was given more and more to planning for their trip. The first Sunday after Jack's letter came, Phil went to the store for the *Des Moines Register*. He and Catherine spread the classifieds out on the table and marked the used campers that sounded like the home on wheels they wanted. By ten o'clock they had made several calls and set out for the drive to Des Moines. By evening, they were on their way home, Phil driving their new camper and Catherine following in the car.

They pulled both vehicles into the driveway and stood looking at the camper. Catherine said, "We bought that camper so fast my head is spinning."

"Are you having second thoughts?"

Catherine emphatically said, "No."

The camper was self-contained. They could move from the cab of the truck right back to their little home. Phil spent the next week adding shelves with railings to keep things from falling off while they drove. Catherine recovered cushions and made curtains. While Phil was working on the shelves another project came to mind. When he finished it, he asked Catherine to come out and look.

When she saw what he had put together she was perplexed. "What in heaven's name is that?"

"See if you can guess." Phil stood back and folded his arms.

"I don't know. A place to stuff our pillows when we're not using them?"

"No, try again." Phil was having fun.

"I need a hint."

"Ok. A holder for something precious to you."

"To me? Oh, I know: A place to hang Blue's cage! Can we take him? Will he be safe?"

"Safe as at home. See? These louvered windows can be left open a little so he'll always have fresh air. This rocker arm will keep his cage level even if we're going up a mountain. The basket around the outside will keep him from being jostled if we have to stop fast." He demonstrated how his contraption worked. "He'll love it."

"Well, I love you. That's the most perfect thing."

* * *

They sat at the kitchen table to plan their trip, a notebook and pencil in front of Phil.

"Hank asked me if I knew about that Good Sams Club. I think the members help each other on the road. Let's find out about that and join, what do you say?" Phil asked.

"Sounds like a good idea. Good thing we're members of Triple A. I'll go over to the office in Burlington for maps and tour books for the Eastern States. I know we can use GPS, and we may have to sometimes, but I like maps."

"I agree. I want to see where I am in the big picture. Why don't you pick up a US map while you're there?" Phil opened the notebook, numbered down the page and filled the first two lines.

"Let's drive on the back roads as much as possible. I'm not much for freeways, you know," Catherine said.

"'You can take the girl out of the country, but you can't take the country out of the girl,' is that it? Well, I'm with you. I want to see the country, not have it fly by at sixty-five miles an hour."

"I suspect the camper wouldn't like going sixty-five even if we wanted it to."

"No, probably not. Say, I've always wanted to visit the National Parks."

"You have? I never knew that . . . ."

"There's probably a great deal we don't know about each other. Now we have time to find out."

"Thank goodness."

"I read an article in one of my fishing magazines about fishing spots in the National Parks. I want to visit all of them. Hank told me if you buy a Golden Eagle Pass you pay once, and you can use it at any park or monument for a year. Let's order one of those."

"Can we visit the Smoky Mountains? One of my favorite books from childhood was set there and it sounded like a magical place."

"I don't see why not. We can go anywhere we can think of, imagine that. I guess we'd better wait for the maps before we make definite plans. When do you think we should visit Jack? Right away, halfway through, or near the end? I still feel pretty nervous about that."

"That's understandable. I have a good feeling about it though. Let's wait and figure it out once we have the maps. And I worry about leaving Jessica and Benny for so long. Amanda will be on vacation, too, but the kids are used to being with us now, and here we are leaving."

"I know, but I suspect Benny will spend most of his time up in the new treehouse and barely miss fishing. We'll build it this weekend when Tom can be there to help us. Benny's friend, Joey, will help, too."

"Jessica will have her garden, our vegetable garden to look after with Jaz, and the butterfly garden with Alice. Plus both kids are working on their projects for the fair."

"She showed me her wildflower journal and some flowers she pressed," Phil said. "Looked good to me."

"She's been pressing flowers since the first ones bloomed. She also signed up for the pottery class Jaz is teaching next month. I think she'll be fine."

"The other day when I picked Benny up for fishing, Amanda told me she's looking forward to having time with them when school's out. They'll have fun, and we can send them postcards from everywhere we go."

"Good idea. How about this? Let's keep a scrapbook of our trip. We can paste photos in and other things we find along the way and write about what we see to show the kids when we're home again."

"Photos, eh? You can be in charge of that. You've seen the pictures I take. Some of them you can look at from every side and still not know what you're looking at."

Laughing, Catherine pulled a flyer from the stack of things that had come in the mail that she didn't know what to do with but wasn't ready to throw away yet. "Hey, wait 'til you see this. 'Photography for You, A Step by Step Approach to Better Pictures.' It's a six week class but we could go to the first couple."

"I'm afraid I'm hopeless in that department," Phil said.

"You can do it. Anyway, it'll be fun," Catherine said. "I wonder if our camera is good enough."

"The pictures from Benny's party turned out fine," Phil said, "but we've had it a long time."

"Didn't we buy it when Jack was in high school?" Catherine asked.

"That sounds about right," Phil said. "That was before digital cameras though."

"Maybe we should buy two cameras, one for each of us." Catherine's eyes had taken on a dreamy look.

Phil saw that look and found himself unexpectedly saying, "Good idea. Let's go to Iowa City and look."

"Ok, but you're building quite a list there." Catherine took the notebook and read: "Good Sams, maps, park pass, scrapbook, photo class, cameras . . . ."

"Enough to keep us busy until we go."

"True enough. Do you ever look back at what our life was like last year at this time?" Catherine asked. "I'd rather be busy than go back there again."

"Me, too."

* * *

Every time she walked in the park, Catherine watched over the bank where she had planted the wildflower seeds. Finally, there were tiny pink blossoms nodding in the sunshine. Crouching down she lifted the delicate bells to see inside. Golden stamen streamed from a tiny white star in each flower.

Kneeling among the flowers Catherine thought, "Here I am, planting flowers, dancing, spending time with Jessica and Amanda, too, traveling, painting as I always wanted to. I like the pictures I paint." The truth was that Phil liked them, too. Maybe next fall she would join the Art Society. Maybe she would frame her pictures and hang them.

And Phil. By giving up trying to get something from him and instead giving what she needed to herself . . . she didn't know how it happened, but Phil had come back to her. When she was with him she felt like a girl again. She found herself smiling at nothing, laughing for no reason and waking each morning looking forward to the day ahead.

Back on the path, she walked to the middle of the bridge and leaned over the railing, looking down into the stream. It was no longer rushing toward the Mississippi as it had earlier in the spring; now it meandered between sandy banks going where it was headed nonetheless. Catherine suddenly realized something else—that there was no hurry and that she no longer had to make things happen. All she had to do was watch to see how her life turned out because, for the first time since she was a girl, she knew it would turn out well.

* * *

Friday night, Phil packed a big lunch in the cooler. Hank liked to start before dawn, and Phil wanted to be on time. He stowed his gear and the cooler in the back of the truck so all he had to do in the morning was throw on some clothes and drive away.

When he arrived at the lake, mist was rising off the water. Phil carried his gear down to the boat, setting it down quietly so the noise wouldn't disturb the magic of the dawn. When Hank arrived, he spoke to Phil in low tones. They pushed the boat out into the lake and Phil rowed them way out along the far side, away from the cove where he usually fished.

They settled in. Phil was relieved that Hank, though talkative on land, seemed content to sit quiet in the boat, casting and watching, reeling in, fish or no fish, and casting again. Phil liked the shared silence as much as with Benny. Phil changed flies as the day came up to full light.

The fish bucket was nearly full. They'd caught some nice bass, and Phil was beginning to feel hot in his flannel shirt. As the sun climbed higher, his stomach felt emptier.

"There's a cove across the way where we could have an early lunch. What do you say?" Phil asked.

"Sounds good to me. All this work makes a guy hungry."

"Absolutely."

Phil rowed a leisurely course to the willow cove. Why he hadn't taken Hank there from the beginning was only now coming to him. If Hank was going to talk the whole time, Phil didn't want him in the place where he went to counsel with himself. Happily, Hank turned out to be as respectfully silent as Phil felt the cove deserved. As the little skiff pushed into the cove, a mallard and his mate swam around the bend on the far side, their family of ducklings swimming fast behind.

"I don't think I've seen this place before," Hank said. "That willow must be two hundred years old."

"Most days I come here. I do my best thinking in this cove."

"Is that so? I have the impression you think more than most of us."

"Always have. It's my nature, I guess. 'Philip is quiet and thoughtful'—that's what my teachers wrote on my report cards."

"My teachers wrote: 'Henry is impulsive and is often in trouble.' Wish I could be more like you instead of jumping without thinking."

"Well, there's probably a middle ground. Thinking, I've found out recently, can land you in as much trouble as jumping in. I've lived mostly in my head, traveling round and round and round."

"That's not the way I see it. You were an asset to the company, you raised two kids and sent them both to college, and you are hands down the best fisherman in the League."

"Well, thanks for the accolades, but I didn't send both kids to college. That was my intention, but I stopped paying Jack's way halfway through his first year. I sent him back to school without a dime. He finished on his own."

"I didn't know that, but that's a long time ago. Look at you now. Traveling with your wife, and you'll see your boy, too. At least you have a family. I blew mine out of the water by insisting that if I worked five days a week to put food on the table, I owed it to myself to spend the rest of my time any way I wanted. So I went fishing, out with the guys, whatever I felt like. You see the result. I'm alone."

"I never thought of it like that. Looks like we're more alike than I realized—at least we came to the same result. I didn't let anybody in—not Catherine, the kids or anybody. Pretty much I was my only friend. Most of my life I lived like that, and if you think that's not lonely . . . . I could be in a room full of people—Christmas, birthdays, you name it—and be totally alone."

"I hear you. I was barely there for Christmas. I ran off to the club as soon as I could or out to my shop if there was too much snow to back my car out of the driveway. I'll tell you, coming home these days, house is empty, nobody's there, and there's nobody coming soon either."

"Things can always change. Look at me. I did my best to pretend Catherine didn't exist all these years—and me married to the woman—and then suddenly I started seeing her like she was when we first met. Next thing you know, I'm falling in love with her all over again. I'm starting to think age doesn't have much to do with it."

"What happened?"

"Quite a few things, I guess. When Benny nearly died, one of those phrases I'd heard and filed jumped into my mind and wouldn't leave me alone."

"What was that?"

"'This is the only time we have. Better make the most of it.' I've heard that said different ways, but there was Benny barely escaping death, and it woke me up. I figured maybe it wasn't too late, and I'd better start moving. I just started seeing things differently."

"Like your wife?"

"Yep. One night she was standing in the doorway with the porch light shining on her face. I mean, you've seen her, she's an old gal, but I swear she looked just like I remembered her when I first saw her. That was it."

"But didn't you always love her, really?"

"To tell you the truth, I don't think I was capable of loving anybody. All I did was live in my head, either on the front porch or out in the boat. There wasn't much room for loving somebody."

"And now there is?"

"I suppose so. She hurt my pride when we were kids, and I never would let go of that. All these years I held on. Then Benny nearly died, and something in me let go in spite of myself."

"Reminds me of something I heard. 'True freedom means no longer having a choice.' I never understood it."

"Maybe that's it. Something in me that's smarter than I am decided it was time for me to change. I don't understand it, but that doesn't matter."

"No, I guess not. You have what you want."

"My wife back? Yeah, that's amazing. And now we're going on this road trip. The camper's nearly ready."

"When do you leave?"

"Early June. We don't know the exact day. It depends on when we're ready to take off."

"What about your son?"

"We're going there in the middle of the trip. First headed to the Smokies, then up to Baltimore to see him."

"Still feeling nervous about it?"

"Not so much anymore. I wrote and thanked him for inviting us, told him we might stay in a hotel. To tell the truth,

I'm so excited about seeing him I can barely wait."

"Feel like you've come around just in time?"

"Just barely in time. What about you? You going to go on by yourself like this?"

"I don't know. When I listen to you, I wonder . . . ."

"If you still have a chance with your family?"

"Yeah, I guess so. Stella's over in New London, by herself, I know. Maybe I should give her a call."

"Can't hurt to try. Besides, you're a great guy. She's probably thinking about you, too."

"I've been thinking it was too late."

"For you? No way, buddy. You're younger than I am, and here I go on the adventure of my life. And Catherine and I have more ideas. We might even build that house in the country we dreamed about. Why not?"

"Indeed."

"What's it all about, anyway? I figure if I have a chance to love somebody and let her love me, what more can I want?"

"Nothing I can think of."

* * *

One morning as Catherine came in from the garden, Phil was packing the cooler, sure sign of a day on the lake. Her dad had taken Catherine fishing when she was seven or eight. She remembered stringing a wiggly worm on her hook, dropping it in the water and letting it sink to the bottom. The catfish she caught was so ugly that she lost interest in fishing right then.

Catfishing was popular with her brothers, and, as the oldest girl, she did her share of cleaning and frying them. Even thinking about fishing gave her the willies and, though Phil had never invited her to join him, he had never said she couldn't come, either. Since trying new things was what she was all about these days, she might as well try fishing.

"Mind if I come along today?"

"What? You want to come fishing?" Phil raised his eyebrows.

"Well, I thought I might give it a try. Never know, I might like it."

"It's mostly sitting. Not much happens out there."

Catherine shrugged. "Might be nice."

"Come on then. We'd better make some more sandwiches."
Phil took out the bread and bologna and cheese.

Pretty basic sandwiches, Catherine thought.

Phil went downstairs to find a fishing rod for Catherine,
testing the sensitivity of several before choosing the one he
thought she would do best with.

When they arrived at the lake, Phil saw the usual familiar
cars in the parking lot, but nobody was around. There was a
boat on the far end of the lake.

After stowing the gear and pushing the boat into the water,
Phil rowed them out. Catherine's attention went from Phil to
the horizon and back. She hadn't realized there were so many
cottages tucked back among the trees, but one whole side of the
lake was wild with trees growing down to the water's edge.

"Can I row for a while?"

Phil shipped the oars. They gingerly moved past each other
as they switched positions. Bracing her feet on the bottom of the
boat, Catherine began rowing.

"Do you have a special place you usually go? If not, I want
to go over there." She dipped her head in the direction of the
wild shore.

"There's a cove back in the corner there. We can fish the
shore and have lunch in the cove, if you'd like."

"Yes, I would like." Catherine turned the boat and rowed
evenly and steadily toward shore.

When they were near enough, Phil showed Catherine how to
tie a fly on her line, then how to cast with a flick of the wrist.
She watched him demonstrate. She could watch him do it, but
how she would do it herself she had no idea.

She slowly took her rod back and, flick, the line swept out
over the water and her fly landed. "Not bad," she thought.

"Whoa, wild woman." Apparently Phil had a different view
of her cast. "Good thing we're not closer to shore, you'd have
your line tangled in a tree right now."

Catherine tried again.

"Smoother, better."

Catherine was on her own. She liked the feel of the solid thwart under her. She liked the feel of the rod in her hand. She liked the swish of the line and the tiny plop as the fly landed in the water. Catching fish was secondary. She barely thought about it.

Phil watched her while he pretended to be interested only in his own rod. He liked the way she brought the rod up, some little flourish, some finesse he never saw anyone have before. He was so taken with watching her that he missed the telltale signs of an immanent strike on his own line. The jerk of the strike and the line being taken sent a shock through his arm, and he nearly lost his rod. His attention snapped to bringing in the fish. He didn't notice how closely Catherine was now watching him.

"My Phil," she thought. Catherine admired the skill with which he played the fish and brought it in.

It was a good-sized bass, maybe three and a half pounds. Catherine slid to the far side of the thwart, away from the flopping fish. Phil slid the gray-green fish into the bucket. By midday, another bass had joined the first.

"Good thing I didn't care about catching anything since I didn't." Catherine had spent the morning fishing and loving the feel of the water under and around the boat, the play of light on water, trees and sky, the lilting bird call and response that echoed over the water.

Phil rowed them to the cove and tied up under the willow tree.

"Well, how do you like fishing?"

"I like it," Catherine answered. "Very peaceful."

CHAPTER

15

Together they had gone to Iowa City for two new cameras. Even for Catherine, it was time to enter the digital age. At the last minute, Phil took the photography class by himself. Catherine was just too busy. The class gave him exactly what he needed—enough information for him to take recognizable pictures but not enough to confuse him. On one of her trips for supplies, Catherine found a wonderful scrapbook with rough paper pages. She packed her painting supplies but decided rather than bringing paper, she would paint only in the scrapbook.

Catherine stowed sheets, pillowcases and towels in the wooden cabinets along one wall of the camper. She went through her check list—dishes, pots and pans, clothes, bathroom stuff, books, games, cards, painting supplies. She was elated. Nearly time to take off.

Phil was in the shop putting together a portable workbench so he could repair the camper and tie flies along the way as needed. He had brought the boat from the lake and lashed it to the top of the camper.

They met in the kitchen between trips to the camper.

Catherine pushed a stray curl off her forehead. "Whew, it's a good thing the camper's air-conditioned. This heat!"

"I'll bet we won't use it all that much. That sweet country air blowing in the windows while we drive along. It'll be like the old days." Phil winked at her.

"I swear, I can't believe we've been living in the same house all these years. Sometimes when I catch sight of myself in the mirror, I'm amazed I don't see a seventeen year old looking back at me."

Phil danced her around the kitchen table.

"Hey, I thought you didn't dance," Catherine protested.

"Well, never in public. You just had to catch me in the right mood."

Catherine leaned in to kiss his cheek. "I'd better go back to work or I won't be ready for Jessica and Benny this afternoon."

"How's your list coming? I'm about half done with mine."

Catherine took the list from her pocket. "Not half done, but close."

"If you're stuck, I'll help you finish."

"Thanks, I'll see how it goes."

Catherine stopped to talk to Blue for a few minutes. "You're going with us, you know."

Blue gazed at her steadily from his perch.

"Well, I'm back to work." As she closed the screen door behind her, Blue launched into a long trill of song.

When Phil came in after stowing the last of the tools and fishing gear, it was lunch time. He found Catherine sitting at the kitchen table.

"Well, hello, what's this? You look completely bushed," Phil said.

"I am, but I don't know quite why. All I've done is put things away out there, but I'm exhausted."

"So many things to think about, maybe—what to take, what to leave . . . . Say, I have an idea. Let's go out to lunch."

"I'll make something. We have plenty in the fridge."

"That's ok, we can bring it along. Let's go out. We could both use the break."

"Ok, but let's work on our itinerary." She gathered the pile of maps from the kitchen table.

They found a well-lit table in the back corner of the Grill. The US map nearly covered the tabletop. When she brought their burgers and fries, the waitress put their plates right down on the map.

Catherine put a finger on the Smokies and another on Route 34 where Mount Pleasant would be. "We can take our time. Jack knows we're coming sometime toward the end of the month."

They laid the state maps out to plan a tentative route.

"Let's take the smallest roads we can find," Catherine said.

"Yes, and look for water along the way," Phil said.

"The more fishing the better, huh?"

"That's right."

* * *

Catherine made banana bread, and Phil squeezed lemons for lemonade. He had more patience than she did, as the years of sitting in the boat and on the porch attested.

That afternoon Benny arrived from school before Jessica. Phil and Catherine had been talking one evening and were surprised to discover that all these months of having Jessica or Benny come home from school, they had never had them both at the same time. They had family meals together, of course, and they had all been together at Benny's birthday party in April, but they had never had the two of them without their mom and dad.

"Hi, Grandma." Benny swung his backpack onto a chair and went to Catherine for a hug. "Are you ready to go?"

"Not quite, but almost. How was school?"

"Pretty good. I'd rather go fishing."

"Now where've I heard that before? Grandpa's down in the shop if you want to go find him."

Catherine put the warm bread and a sharp knife on a cutting board, put ice in four glasses, and poured the lemonade. June first and already steaming. Immediately water started to condense on the sides of the glasses and, by the time Jessica arrived a few minutes later, they were dripping wet.

The four of them sat around the kitchen table, and Phil thought of the hundreds of meals with Jack and Amanda when they were growing up. Sadness washed over him, and he found himself watching Catherine and Benny and Jessica from a great distance.

"Now," he reminded himself. "Now is the only time there is." He looked around the table. None of them had noticed that he had been gone. Catherine was telling Benny about the day she had gone fishing and hadn't caught a thing but had a grand time anyway. Jessica was listening.

What he had said to Hank that day in the boat was wrong. He had always loved them all. More deeply than he ever said or acknowledged to himself. The love he felt connected him to these children and this woman, his wife. And to Amanda and Jack. And even, he realized, to Tom. And Jaz. And perhaps one day, he found himself thinking, he supposed he would feel connected to Jeff, Jack's partner. That thought was the most unexpected of all.

He would live differently from now on. Now he would say he loved them. He would notice them, watch them, and see who he was looking at. He had come to the end of being in the middle of his family and being stark raving alone.

"Jessica, are there still new flowers blooming in your wildflower garden, or are they done for this year?" Phil asked. "I haven't been out there to look lately."

"There're still new ones coming. Not as many as at first, but there'll be new flowers for a while yet. Plus, quite a few will keep blooming the rest of the summer."

"We can see them when we come home. How's your 4-H project coming along?" Phil asked.

"Good. I press at least three of each flower, and I'm keeping my journal. It will be pretty full by fair time."

"Will you be back for the fair?" Benny asked. Phil saw a furrow creep up his brow.

"Don't worry, Benny," he said. "We're coming back especially for the fair."

"Tell us about your project, Benny," Catherine said.

"I have a board with the different flies Grandpa showed me how to tie and my fishing rod will be in it and I have a journal to keep track of the fish I catch."

"How many do you have so far?" Jessica asked.

"One hundred seventy-two," Benny said.

Catherine was amazed. "How did you manage that?"

"Me and Grandpa go out to the lake all the time. And every time, I catch fish. Easy as that." Benny snapped his fingers, a skill Phil had recently taught him.

"And your mom's been cooking all those fish?" Catherine asked.

"Yep."

"And we've been eating all those fish," Jessica said. "If I had to choose one or the other, I'd rather have pizza three times a week than fish."

"Who wouldn't," Benny said, "but who ever heard of catching pizza? Mom would never go for it anyway."

"That's true." Jessica took a sip of lemonade. "This is good."

"Grandpa made it. Squeezed the lemons by hand."

When they were done, Phil said, "Let's go outside where the light is good and try out my new camera."

In the perfect light of late afternoon, Phil took pictures of Jessica and Benny. He took one of Jessica kneeling by her wildflower garden and one of Benny standing on the low branch where Jack used to sit and read. He took shots of the two of them perched on top of the camper next to the boat.

Just as the light began to fade, Tom arrived to pick the kids up.

"We'll see you tomorrow night. Amanda says we're having a family picnic at East Lake to wish you bon voyage," he said.

"That's right. We're leaving Wednesday morning early," Phil said.

"But Gram, I'll see you tomorrow afternoon, right?" Jessica asked.

"Thanks for reminding me, Jessica. I'll make a list for you before you come."

* * *

Early the next morning Catherine was on her knees weeding the garden.

She looked up to see Jaz squeeze through the gap in the hedge.

"I came to see about the garden. I'll put these blueberry muffins on the porch and you can take them in later."

"Thank you. I've been so busy it's an effort to remember to eat, let alone cook."

"Yet you're out here weeding like any other morning. You must have heaps of things to do besides this." Jaz squatted down and started pulling the tiny weeds between the broccoli plants.

"I needed to give myself a chance to rest—in my head I mean. I'll miss the garden on the road."

"Don't worry, I'll keep on top of the weeds."

"Thanks, and thanks for taking the extra vegetables to the food bank."

"I'll set some aside for Amanda first."

"Sounds good. Jessica can take them home when she comes to tend the wildflower garden."

* * *

Jessica came over after school to see about the mail and the plants. Then she and Catherine met Alice at the butterfly garden.

Catherine introduced them, and Alice said, "Thanks for helping with our plot while your grandma's gone."

"I'm ready to thin my wildflower garden at Gram's. We could plant some of the seedlings over here."

"That would be great."

Alice turned to Catherine. "Marvin brought home a plaque he painted at day care. I hung it in the living room where he can see it from his chair."

"It sounds like he likes going," Catherine said.

"I think he does, but wait until you hear this." Alice paused for emphasis. "Your Whitney called and asked wouldn't I like to be his partner for the competitions this summer."

"What did you tell him?"

"I said I'd think about it. I'm inclined to tell him yes."

Catherine couldn't help asking, "Just curious, did he mention me?"

"Did he ever. He was pretty steamed up because you were going away. I just let him talk and ignored him. He's a good dancer, but he takes himself too seriously, if you ask me."

Catherine laughed. "He's a good guy though."

Catherine went to sit on the bench under the sycamore while Alice showed Jessica how to bring the hose to water the little garden without dragging it over any of the other plots.

Catherine gazed out over the field. Many of the plots were in full bloom and she spotted butterflies here and there. It was working. She closed her eyes and listened to the happy hum of the field at work growing a garden.

* * *

Earlier in the day Phil and Catherine had taken the loaded camper for a test drive. Phil was at the garage now having a suspicious noise checked out by the mechanic before they started out on the road. He came in as Jessica chopped celery, onion, and olives for the potato salad for the family picnic that evening.

"Any problem?" Catherine had been afraid the noise might signify a portent of breakdowns which might very well occur far from any town.

"The mechanic said it was just the new fan belt settling in," Phil assured her. "Nothing to worry about."

* * *

When they pulled into East Lake Park, Catherine was surprised to see the parking lot full. "Must be a ball game or something, but why would they park way over here?"

"I don't know. Maybe somebody's having a birthday party," Jessica said. "Let's go find Mom and Dad. I'll carry the potato salad."

Jessica snaked through the cars in the lot, holding the bowl of potato salad in front of her. Catherine and Phil followed out across the grassy field and up to the picnic shelter at the top of the knoll.

"What're all those people doing here?" Catherine asked.

Phil and Catherine started recognizing people, but neither

could figure out why they were there.

Amanda spotted them across the shelter. "Hey, everybody, they're here."

Conversations broke off in mid-sentence and everyone turned in Phil and Catherine's direction. "Surprise!"

Phil and Catherine looked at each other helplessly, realizing that Amanda had organized a going-away party for them.

"My goodness, look at them all," Catherine said. "There's Alice and Marvin and Jaz, half the garden club and half the dance class. And there's Mr. Moore. How did she find them all?"

Phil was as bewildered as Catherine. He spotted several old friends from work he hadn't talked to since he retired, and there was a knot of guys from the Walton League. Hank broke off from the group and walked toward him.

"Hi, Hank, where'd all these guys come from? You'd think it was my wake rather than a simple goodbye for a few weeks."

"Well, Phil, you may recall that you refused to have a retirement party no matter how Ruth Ann pressed you, so this is making up for it."

"Is Ruth Ann here?"

"Right over there." Hank pointed.

Ruth Ann had been Phil's assistant and now had his old job. He vaguely remembered her telling him he owed it to all of them to let her organize a retirement party for him. The fact that he had been at the company longer than anyone who had ever worked there—forty-five years—hadn't persuaded him to say yes to a party.

Now, looking at all these friends gathered around, he realized it might not be so bad to say goodbye to folks after all. The table was full of dishes. Jessica had to move some around to make room for the potato salad. Balloons and crepe paper hung from the shelter ceiling, and all those people standing around seemed to be waiting for something. He didn't know what they were waiting for but suspected something would be expected from him. Hopefully not a speech, but, if so, maybe he could persuade Catherine to give it.

When Benny heard 'Surprise!' ring out across the field, he ran over from the playground. "Hey, you're here. I've been waiting for you." He grabbed Phil and hugged him fiercely.

"Hey, buddy. How are you doing?"

"Hungry, that's how. Can we eat now?"

"Why not?" Phil called over to Amanda who was arranging paper plates and cups. "Time to eat?"

"I thought you might say something first. You know, a few words, nothing much."

"Well . . . ok." He looked vaguely for Catherine and saw her talking to Alice. Marvin sat a little aside in his own chair which Alice had brought along.

He cleared his throat, moved his feet a little further apart to give himself a firm stance, and stretched out his arms to their friends.

"Hey, everybody, you know I'm not much for speeches, but Catherine and I are glad you came to see us off. You fellas leave some of those fish in the lake for me. Remember, I'll be back. And now, let's eat."

Phil found himself with a full plate in the middle of a group of his old fishing cronies.

"So you're going to do it? Leave us and go off on your own," Walt said.

"Do you really want to miss the Montana trip?" Greg asked.

"Are you kidding? I tied the boat to the top of the camper, all my fishing gear is stowed, and we've planned the trip from fishing hole to fishing hole. Far as I can see, nothing could be better than this."

"Fishing your way across the country, huh?" Art asked. "Sounds pretty good. You have room for a stow-away?"

"Nope, just Catherine and me with six weeks ahead of us and no schedule, no place to be, just land wherever we land," Phil said.

"Why, you old dog, how'd you manage that?" Art asked.

"Woke up one day and realized I'd better start moving if I wanted to have some fun before it's too late," Phil said.

"Good for you, buddy," Art said. "I applaud you."

"Sometimes I still feel like it's a dream," Phil said, "and I'll wake up and it won't be happening after all."

"Guess you'll see about that tomorrow morning when you hit the road," Hank said.

Greg took a card from his wallet and handed it to Phil. "Here's the Walton Club address. Send us a postcard once in a while, will you?"

"Ok. You fellas have fun in Montana and take some pictures to back up your fishing stories," Phil said. "I'll do the same and we can compare them when we come home."

* * *

After dinner, Catherine and Amanda left the party and walked over the knoll and sat on a bench overlooking the river.

"Gosh, Mom, I'm going to miss you."

"I'll miss you, too, Amanda. I'll have plenty of time to write, though, so you'll be hearing from me."

"Wish I could write you, too."

"You can always send a letter to Jack's. We'll wind up there eventually."

"I'll do that. I don't think I've thanked you enough for all you've done for us this winter. Jessica's so much happier, I can't tell you. And, Mom, she's been showing me things she's made at the pottery studio and talking to me like I'm a human being. Things are finally starting to change between us."

"I know how much you wanted that, and it looks like Jessica wanted it as much as you."

"All I know is that things are better," Amanda said. "I'm what they call 'cautiously optimistic.'"

* * *

Phil and Catherine planned to leave at dawn partly because neither one of them much liked goodbyes. They were relieved that the night before had taken care of all of them at once.

They both woke before first light. Too excited to go back to sleep, they lay whispering to each other in the dark. With the first bird song, Catherine remembered a saying she had heard in girlhood and never forgotten: "Faith is the bird who feels the dawn and sings while the night is yet dark."

Feeling the dawn, she hopped out of bed. Phil joined her, and together they made the bed.

The camper was packed. The little refrigerator was stocked and running. There was no morning paper to make Phil linger over breakfast, so they were ready to go by five fifteen, dressed and breakfasted. Phil carried Blue's cage, still draped in the yellow tablecloth, to the camper.

Coming back in for a final check, he noticed a basket on the back steps. Luckily, he hadn't tripped over it.

"Hey, Catherine, come look at this." He turned the porch light on so they could see.

They sat on the top step with the basket between them.

A bouquet of wildflowers in a green vase and a little package tied with string sat on top of a bright blue and white checked napkin tucked around the top of the basket. A ribbon tied a white envelope to the handle.

Catherine took a card from the envelope. "'From all of us. Wishing you a wonderful trip and a speedy return. We'll miss you. Love, Amanda and Tom, Jessica, Benny and Goldie.' When do you suppose they had time to put this together?"

"Must have been late last night. Nobody would be out so early this morning."

Phil held up the little vase. A tag taped to it read 'Gram' in Jessica's handwriting.

He pulled a note labeled 'Grandpa' from under the string on the package. "'I made you some extra flies in case you run out. Goldie and me will see you when you come home. Love, Benny.'"

Phil untied the string and pulled the paper off a little box lined with cotton. Hooks securely anchored in the cotton, five of the most unusual flies he'd ever seen looked back at Phil. Apparently Benny was working on his wish—to invent a fly that would be named the 'Benny.'

"I'm a lucky Grandpa," Phil said so quietly Catherine barely heard him. For the first time, Phil knew what the word 'humble' meant.

They looked under the napkin and found a tin of cookies, a jar of Greek olives, a package of crackers, and a foil-wrapped container of soft cheese.

Tears pricked behind Catherine's eyelids. "It's wonderful to know we'll be missed."

One more house check, then Phil locked the back door and put the key under the mat for Jessica. Catherine wedged the vase of flowers into a niche on the dash. As Phil was backing the camper out of the driveway, Jaz appeared on the other side of the hedge.

"Just a minute," Catherine said. "There's Jaz."

Jaz ran to greet them, breathless. "I almost missed you. You're starting earlier than I expected."

Jaz shoved a lumpy paper sack through the window. "Don't look until you're at least into the next state. I love you guys, bye." Jaz ran back through the yard, stopping to wave from the gap in the hedge.

Phil backed the camper into the street and drove toward the butterfly garden. Catherine wanted to say her last 'goodbye' to the field which had given her courage all these months. As they left the outskirts of town and drove east on Route 34 into the early dawn, Catherine looked back at the Mount Pleasant sign. They were on their way.

* * *

Half an hour later they looked down on the Mississippi as they crossed the bridge from Burlington into Illinois. The sky had grown pink and mauve with the rising sun, and the bridge stood out in dark outline against it. When the kids were growing up they had taken a couple of vacations—one to a cottage on Spirit Lake and one to a family camp in the Ozarks. They had never driven East together.

Catherine rolled her window down so she could see down river to the green islands and banks overhung with trees as far south as the gentle turning of the Mississippi would allow.

Blue Canary

When they passed into Illinois, Catherine pointed to the left of the road. "Look at the bayous. Fish galore, I'll bet. Look at those fat egrets."

Phil sat behind the wheel, his arm resting on the window ledge, wind ruffling the sleeve of his short-sleeved shirt. Lazily he looked where Catherine pointed.

"Ah, yes, life is fine," he thought.

He noticed that he was wearing his wristwatch and, taking it off, opened the glovebox and dropped it in. "Never mind the time," he said. "Don't need to worry about that anymore."

"No, indeed." Catherine never wore a watch herself, a fact that had aggravated Phil in the past because she could never be counted on to be where he wanted her when he wanted her there.

They smiled at each other and adjusted to the feel of being in a camper. The wind whistled under and around the little boat tied to its top. It was a blue sky, gusty day. The camper was a house on wheels, mostly empty living space. For a vehicle on such a big journey, it was very light. When the wind blew, the camper swayed on the road reminding Phil of the sailboat they had rented the summer they were at Lake of the Ozarks.

Phil didn't know much about sailing but he had loved the feel of the wind pushing into the sails and the tug of the tiller in his hand as he steered a course which kept the boat moving and the sails full. Now, with one hand lightly playing the steering wheel, he felt the camper in the wind sailing down the road. The gentlest move of his hand guided them through the countryside.

They charted their course with what they hoped would be interesting stops every two or three hundred miles. A few hours' driving, then, stop and play. If they liked where they landed, they would stay overnight. Otherwise, they would drive on.

* * *

A few days into their trip postcards began to show up in Mount Pleasant. The first was addressed to Jessica and Benny from Falls of Rough, Kentucky.

Hi Jessica and Benny,

Here we are on the Rough River. There's a tumble-down house, an old store and a mill right next to the falls (see the picture on the front). We rented a canoe and explored upriver. Grandpa caught a fish, of course.

Wish you were here with us. You'd love it. You won't believe how many pictures we've already taken to show you when we come home.

Love,

Grandma and Grandpa

Jaz received a postcard a day later from Mammoth Cave.

Hey Jaz,

Can you believe the size of this cave? It's the longest one ever mapped.

Cool as all get out, cold, even, but it felt good after driving all day. Kentucky is beautiful. More navigable rivers than any other state. Phil went fishing this morning. I sat on a rock by the river barefoot and painted the water bubbling over my feet. This is the best I ever felt in my life.

We opened the lovely bowl you made for us. The river here reminds me of the glaze you put on it, all swirly, brown and green. We've already used it twice.

Thank you. Hope the garden's growing well.

Love,

Catherine (and Phil, too)

A couple of days later, Walt Jamison picked up the mail for the Walton Club and found a postcard from Reelfoot Lake, Tennessee.

Hi guys,

Now you're not going to believe this, but this lake is the most beautiful place I've ever seen. Bald eagles nest in trees growing right up out of the water, and every minute you see fish jumping or you miss them and see the splash where one just landed.

We were out in the boat all day yesterday, exploring and fishing. Nothing so good as a couple of large mouth bass grilled over an open fire. Life is good. Wish you were all here. See you soon.

Best regards,

Phil

PS Taking plenty of pictures. Reminder to the Montana bunch: I won't believe any fishing tales that don't have a picture to back them up!

A week later, Fern brought a postcard to the garden club meeting.

"This came in the mail yesterday. Sounds like Catherine is having a great time. Listen to this."

Hello all,

All my life I've wanted to go to the Smoky Mountains and here I am. I do believe it's the most beautiful spot on Earth.

We stopped the camper on the side of the road and immediately heard the sound of rushing water. Walked down a little path to a creek crashing over huge boulders with sunlight streaming through green leaves. Wildflowers everywhere. I couldn't design a garden as lovely as this.

Say hello to our butterfly garden. Thinking of you all.

Love,

Catherine

A few days later a postcard arrived in Baltimore. Jack picked up the scattered mail from the rug under the slot in the heavy oak front door. He leafed through the pile on his way into the kitchen for a Spritzer.

Dear Jack,

We'll be there in a few days. I'm really excited to see you. Your dad has looked at the map several times so we'll know how to find your house when we get to Baltimore. He's figured out when we'll arrive, too. Look for us late Saturday afternoon.

I'll call if anything changes. See you soon.

Love,

Mom

Early in the third week of June, with Phil driving and Catherine navigating, they drove south on US Highway 441 from Smoky Mountain National Park through Cherokee in western North Carolina. From Cherokee they headed east on US Highway 19 through Maggie Valley, then drove back roads to a remote campground on Lake Powhatan. They filled the picnic basket and laid their old woven picnic blanket over the top. Carrying the basket between them, they left the trail along the lake shore and climbed to the top of a deserted knoll. Spreading the blanket in the grass, they shared a simple lunch under the arching sky.

Jack's story is "under construction"
and will be available soon.

We'll announce its availability
at virginiastclaire.com.

Please visit as often as you wish.

Gratitude

I am grateful to the many people who helped make this novel possible. Any errors are my own. My editor, Virginia McGuire, provided unflagging support and honesty. Candace Freeland inspired me by playing the marimba and vibraphone while I wrote.

Keith Rhodes told me about Mennonite life. Tom Hoskins shared his rural Quaker childhood. Kelly Strassheim sent me a packet of information from the Mount Pleasant, Iowa Chamber of Commerce, and Carmen Heaton welcomed me to the Iris Restaurant in Mount Pleasant. Rich Craddick and Ralph Zorn told me about quality control at Kent Feeds in Davenport. Jim Wilson gave me invaluable information on fly fishing. Kathy Wilson and especially Jason Brunner from St. Croix in Park Falls, Wisconsin, makers of starter rods for children, told me about rod building. Mike Thorson gave me expert information on warm water fly fishing in Iowa. Laurie Phelps and Dan Walderbach, EMT, Mount Pleasant explained emergency procedures and air lift to Iowa City. Pat Jennings of the Mount Pleasant Public Library helped me trace the history of rural Quakers in the area,. Ronda West of Garden Florist and Greenhouse gave me information on flowers which attract butterflies.

Finally, special thanks to early readers Deidre Grano, Lisa Gifford, and Nancy Leahy.

Made in the USA
Columbia, SC
17 November 2019